# SHE SMILED SWEETLY

MARY-ANN TIRONE SMITH

# She Smiled Sweetly

· *A Poppy Rice Mystery* ·

HENRY HOLT AND COMPANY / NEW YORK

This is a work of fiction. All characters and events
portrayed in this novel either are products of the author's
imagination or are used fictitiously.

Henry Holt and Company, LLC
*Publishers since 1866*
115 West 18th Street
New York, New York 10011

Henry Holt® is a registered trademark
of Henry Holt and Company, LLC.

Library of Congress Cataloging-in-Publication Data
Smith, Mary-Ann Tirone, date.
    She smiled sweetly : a Poppy Rice mystery / Mary-Ann Tirone Smith.—1st ed.
    p.   cm.
    ISBN 0-8050-7224-1
    1. Rice, Poppy (Fictitious character)—Fiction.   2. Women detectives—
Massachusetts—Boston—Fiction.   3. Government investigators—Fiction.
4. Drowning victims—Fiction.   5. Irish Americans—Fiction.
6. Boston (Mass.)—Fiction.   7. Politicians—Fiction.   I. Title.

PS3569.M537736S535   2004
813'.54—dc22                                          20030557577

Henry Holt books are available for special promotions
and premiums. For details contact: Director, Special Markets.

First Edition 2004

Designed by Victoria Hartman

Printed in the United States of America
1   3   5   7   9   10   8   6   4   2

I would like to dedicate this book
to the bright and lively students
and their devoted staff
at Saint Enda's Secondary School,
Inishmore, the Aran Isles.

# SHE SMILED SWEETLY

# 1

Hancock Beach on the northern fringe of Boston Harbor is not a place where people come with their towels and coolers. It's a beach where you have to step around detritus, where you smell jet fuel instead of salt air, where the water is thick and sluggish. There is more marsh grass than sand—the swamp behind the beach willfully encroaches. Today, gulls with tar-spotted feathers were strung out in a line along the water's edge, pecking at a summer's bounty of over-turned horseshoe crabs. A substantial percentage of this species fails to survive a penchant for mating at the tide's high-water mark, where the large, lumbering arthropods are frequently capsized by receding waves and left stranded on their backs. Because of their bulk and sex-saturated faculties, their fate demands ensuing waves to be generous enough to roll them over again before the outgoing tide deserts them. Waves in contained harbors such as Boston's tend to be, at best, too puny to make the assist.

I had recently returned home from what was supposed to be a vacation on Block Island, where the beaches are pristine, unlike Hancock Beach, but where treachery lurked not only for vulnerable sea life but human life as well. Block Island had this last in common with Hancock Beach.

I took it all in, scoping the sands from one end of the crescent to the other. There was nothing to see beyond shore, water, and fen. Nothing to see in the distance either. Boston has only a couple of skyscrapers, and I could just make out the top floors of the Prudential Building above the marsh behind us. Except for the view of its roofline, I might as well have been in Newfoundland.

The Boston homicide detective first grade walking with me was named Patel. *Rocky* Patel. An immigrant from the Gujarat state of India who had acquired an American nickname.

He was saying to me, "We are now standing on the exact spot where I examined the body."

"And your report stated people digging for clams found her."

"Yes. But actually the clammers weren't the absolute first to spot her. Several passengers on a flight from Paris saw her through their windows just before the plane's wheels touched down. In the arrivals pen, the Immigration Service was unable to calm them and could not figure out why they were so worked up. Naturally, airport security detained them—herded them into an isolated room, which only served to panic them further. When we were called, Immigration advised us to bring a translator, their own being overwhelmed."

He had a slight sarcastic edge to his tone. Didn't like the idea of Immigration personnel so incompetent as not to understand the language they're supposed to be translating. Cops get that way. The progression is from actively pissed to whining and complaining and then to acceptance. But not without still feeling pissed.

"Were you among the first officers on the scene here at this beach?"

"About."

"Why about?"

"Because it was necessary for me to first see that the airport was not in the hands of some radical Islamic sect from the Seventh Arrondissement."

Oh.

"Nothing was touched?"

"My people are liking their jobs."

It was one of the few times when I would be working with Rocky Patel that he'd slip into the present progressive. He'd come to this country when he was seven. Just a trace of the subcontinent was left in his speech.

"What exactly did you find?"

"It was winter. Not much damage to her, considering how long she'd been dead. The water temperature was thirty degrees. This water freezes at the perimeter of the beach because the polluted run-off from the swamp dilutes the salt content. She was fully clothed, wore a big jacket, mittens in the pockets, no hat. The bulky jacket acted as a flotation device. Her hair was short, chopped off like a little street girl's. As when a poor mother uses the only method available to her to control lice. Very dark red. She was beautiful. Beautiful in the way a child is beautiful. Adorable. Pretty rather than beautiful, to be exact."

*Adorable.* Never heard a cop refer to a corpse as *adorable* before. "Like a sweet kid, Detective. I believe that was the description you used in your letter."

He smiled. "That's right." Now he came up with the word he'd wanted, the one he'd used in the report. "Sweet, yes. Rather than adorable."

"Detective, what do—"

"Please call me Rocky."

If he'd asked me to call him Patel, it would have come more trippingly to the tongue. "Rocky. All right. So what do you mean when you say someone is sweet? What does sweet mean to you?"

Little wrinkles appeared in the smooth skin between his brows. "I would say that someone who is sweet is kindly."

"Women and children are sweet, though, not men."

"That is true."

"But men can be kindly."

"Yes."

I said, "Sweet—at least to me—has a sense of squalor. Pitiable, though, granted: winsome."

His eyes came up from the sand where the girl had lain to meet my own. The top of his head was level with my chin. He had eyelashes that were as thick as they were long. Very black, unlike his hair, which seemed faded, charcoal gray, dark but not quite black.

He said, "That is a very Hindu-like thing to say."

"Really."

"Yes. And I should know, though I am now a Catholic. A conversion is the very least of what happens when a Hindu marries a girl named McCafferty from Boston. We are making small talk then, Agent Rice?"

"Not small talk. I was just thinking about the victim aloud."

But if he wanted to make small talk, why not? There wasn't too much left to say anyway. We were strolling along the high-tide mark, scattering the feasting gulls. Strolling a beach and small talk go together, even a decrepit beach like this one.

So I said, "You're not the only one with a nickname. You can call me Poppy. Instead of Agent Rice."

He smiled again and then he laughed. His laugh was like a jingle bell, merry and clear. My name does get a laugh, now and then, but he wasn't laughing *at* my name.

He said, "I have a rough-and-tumble name but I am a reserved fellow. You have a girlie-girl name, yet your reputation is such that people know enough to move out of your way when they see you coming. I have an appreciation for that which is incongruous. And your actual name is?"

"Penelope."

"Ah. Ancient Greek. A woman of magnificent fortitude. So our real names, the ones people don't know about, suit our true nature. A nature I believe we both want to keep hidden in order to take advantage of even the smallest element of available surprise."

True, though I hadn't thought about it like that. "And Rocky, what is your . . . actual name?"

"Rakesh. I became Rocky because my family lived next door to a gym. Boxers trained there. I began to hang out at the gym when I wasn't working with my family. The trainers let me box too, one little Hindu child among all the young African-American men. At first they called me White Boy, even though my skin was far darker than theirs. And then the movie came out. They began calling me Rocky. So it's an ironic thing that my name is Rakesh. My parents were overjoyed that I could have an American nickname so close to my own name. They knew nothing of Sylvester Stallone. They were overjoyed because my older brother, Sanjay, had become known as Paul, because the boy who sat next to him in school didn't like the name Sanjay and told him he should be called Paul, which was his own name."

Sweet. But enough.

"Rocky?"

"Yes?"

"The girl was definitely drowned?"

"Definitely. Though I like to think the shock of the icy water made her dying easier. That is the Hindu in me wishing."

The shock of getting shoved into the water, perhaps, made her dying harder. There is no Hindu in me.

We walked on. I said, "How did Hindu parents feel about their child taking up boxing?"

He laughed. "There was no joy there. But they would accommodate the new culture."

～

Rocky Patel had written to the FBI eighteen months earlier asking for assistance in identifying the body of a woman found during an especially low tide by amateur clammers on Hancock Beach, a depressed suburb once dependent on Suffolk Downs, a New England racetrack now rendered impotent by the Pequot and Mohegan casinos 75 miles away. Parenthetically, the detective had mentioned that another aspect of the suburb's depression was that the clammers had all gone from voting for Democrats to voting for Republicans, but to no avail. As long as there were clammers digging for dinner with their toes, the trickle-down theory of economics remained bogus. When I read the letter I'd thought, *I hope I meet this guy some day.* A cynical sense of humor has always appealed to me. I didn't really expect I'd ever meet him, though; his letter was only one of so very many.

The detective was granted the assistance he'd requested from us, but in the end we weren't able to be of help. The body was never ID'd.

Jane Doe files haunt me, there is such a plethora of them. Maybe *taunt me* is a better way to put it. Because there are so few *John* Doe files. In a homicide investigation when a man's body is found, you look in his pocket, take out the wallet, read the name on the driver's license, and that's that. But a murdered woman? Her body is almost always stripped of its identification, including, sometimes, her hands. Even her head if the killer is particularly efficient and/or enraged.

Happily, now, what with DNA testing, such finishing touches are less macabre in the case of the more systematic killer. No more burning the body into ash and no more of the benchmark—feeding it into a rented wood chipper. If the killer is rich, he goes up in a private plane and dumps his victim into the Gulf of Mexico. If he's middle class, he gets himself a boat, heads out, and shovels her and the weights he's secured to her over the side, and she might end up just as far from shore as the victim of the rich guy in the plane. If he's poor, though, it's off to the nearest bridge, where he hefts her over the railing and hopes for the best. Money, as always, talks. It's far easier for us to finger a perpetrator with limited funds. Of course, sometimes, if the moneyed perp is in a hurry—say, he intends to be at a meeting a thousand miles away to establish or expand upon an alibi—the bridge route is often his most expedient course. Simply a matter of seeing that the trunk of his car is assiduously cleaned and vacuumed.

Rage, however, trumps efficiency. The enraged still delight in chopping a woman up. An abhorrence of women knows no economic boundaries.

Our crime lab did of course question the body via autopsy photographs and Patel's report, starting with what the detective wanted to know: *Who are you?*

We got bits and pieces of answers but really just one that held any significance: the body told us it was eighteen to twenty-five years old and three months pregnant.

We asked: *When did you die?*

Answer: In the water ten to fourteen days, a determination based on the kind of water she was in, the depth, the variety of life that inhabited the water, the weather.

*How did you die?*

No hidden agenda. She'd drowned.

*Did you drink or take drugs before you died?*

Yes to drugs, a little alcohol. Sedatives. The body told us it went into the water in a semi out-of-it condition.

*Did you jump?*

A baffling suicide note did not turn up anywhere.

*Did you fall in accidentally?*

Maybe. Sedatives affect balance.

*Did someone push you?*

Maybe. The answer depended on the Boston detective getting somewhere with the very first question.

*If someone did push you, who was it?*

The answer did not compute at that time and still hadn't when I was sent up to Boston nearly a year and a half later. The file had no updates.

Finally: *Where did you jump from, fall from, or were pushed from?*

No witness had come forward to aid in reaching a conclusion.

P.S.: *Who is your dentist?*

Her dental work matched no records. Making such a match used to take weeks. Computers now store such answers and you can get the information in seconds, but only if a central record exists. For this particular Jane Doe, it didn't.

Consequently, she remained Jane Doe.

But there was that final, final question: *What does this all mean?*

Before considering how to respond to the final-final, one must decide whether the answer—even if it is obtainable—will benefit the investigation. Usually, not. Esoteric pondering to whatever avail is best left to sociologists.

When Rocky Patel was called to the scene, he had gazed down upon her and later felt free to reveal his opinion as to her character—sweet—in his letter. And he'd addressed that letter to me: *Personal* is what he'd scribbled on the envelope. Sometimes, law enforcers will do that—find out the name of a higher-up and address the letter accordingly, adding *personal* to the bottom of the envelope. I admire the ruse. It's a little frustrating that more cops don't think of it. Creativity, even such transparent creativity, is so important in our job.

A week before my walk on the Boston beach with Rocky Patel I'd returned from the hellish vacation on Block Island, where I had nearly been killed. I'd not only said goodbye to Block Island but goodbye to Joe, too.

Joe.

Joe Barnow is my longtime friend and confidant. We are as sexually compatible as I could ever wish for. I was introduced to him the day I took my FBI tour. He happened to be there consulting. He is Chief Field Adviser with the ATF—Alcohol, Tobacco and Firearms. I really like him a lot, but on our recent deadly vacation, he proved to be more private a person than I'd ever been aware of. Too damn private for me. I needed a break from him; he knew it and did not protest, although he'd said, "I'm glad you made that decision. It's for the best, Poppy." He said it in an intonation that translated to: *I hate that you made such a decision—I need you.* I could only thank my lucky stars that over the past couple of years Joe and I had done no more than waffle about moving in together. Thanked the stars even more vigorously for his not continuing any conversation tack wherein he alluded to marriage. I was not committed to a life with only Joe, even though I'd step in front of thousand-pound gorilla to protect him.

We'd landed at Dulles after the hop from Block Island and he drove me to my apartment at the Watergate. When we pulled into the drive, he'd said, "We'll talk," which was the same thing he'd said on Block Island. He said it again because he hadn't liked my original response, which was, "Fuck off." He was hoping, now I was home, that I'd be calmer. I wasn't. This time I said, "Just don't call me, Joe. When I feel like talking I'll let you know." With each passing minute—both in the air above the Atlantic and driving home—I'd become more and more furious at the ease with which he hadn't been truthful with me.

So that night, once I'd unpacked my suitcase and put away my stuff, I'd gone directly to my office for solace. The longtime security guard at the FBI building was one of the first friends I made in Washington. When we were introduced, all Bobby had said was, "The coffee is always cookin'." I had a standing invitation from him to keep him company while he secured the building. I was happy to find him on duty tonight.

We gave each other a hug. While he poured, he said, "From what I hear—some vacation."

Yeah. But I was glad to be home where I felt most at home— within the world of the FBI—and a friendly welcome is always appreciated.

Bobby and I shmoozed awhile, and then later, in my office, I swung my chair around and took in the comfort of my four walls— two of them making up a windowed corner—and my view down Pennsylvania Avenue. Night views in DC are a spectacle, the monuments all lit up. I never cease to be in awe, so immediately I'd felt happy again, excited yet serene. All was sublime. Exactly the way things are supposed to be when you're on vacation, but it's how I feel when I'm working. I had learned my lesson. I would never take a vacation again.

I didn't have long to vegetate right then. I had to meet someone in half an hour, something my assistant had arranged just as I was leaving the island. At first, I barely registered the name: Danny O'Neill. Then she gave me a little extra nudge. "You must know who I mean. The fireman. The hunk." But as we have all come to know, every fireman is a hunk. "You met him at the seminar you held for fire marshals two years ago in Boston. Cornflower-blue eyes, I believe you said. Jet black hair. Irish, from Ireland."

Oh. *That* Danny O'Neill. I hadn't a clue that the city of Boston would shortly gather together Danny, Rocky Patel, and me.

"He told me he had to see you, so I told him I thought you'd be back sometime this afternoon. He said he would be camping outside the FBI building by seven o'clock, waiting for you."

My assistant, Delby Jones, leaves the office at the stroke of five to pick up her kids at our day-care center. I find that her walking out in the middle of things grounds us all, helps us keep our priorities in order the way she keeps hers. We're here to fight for justice, period. Delby's adherence to her schedule of putting her children first makes for our sticking to the program, recognizing self-indulgence, seeing with clarity the value of efficiency.

I would meet Danny at the bar at Kinkead's instead of my office because, one, it would be after hours, and two, it was not official. Unofficial, he'd told Delby. He'd asked her to relay a message to me. "Tell her I haven't any right to ask for her help, but I have to ask." He was not willing to tell Delby just what help he needed.

There was a third reason for meeting Danny at the bar rather than here at the office. Far more appealing to sit with him across a little round table, twirling a drink with a swizzle stick, than playing with paper clips five feet away from the man on the other side of my desk. I told Delby to get back to him, tell him to meet me at Kinkead's at seven. I'd thought, *Danny O'Neill, cornflowers and jet and a disposition of calm and utter kindliness.* Just what the doctor ordered.

I stopped staring at monuments and checked my watch again. I had fifteen minutes before I had to leave, so I spent the time bringing the Danny O'Neill file up on my virtual computer—the one in my head—where he'd lain pretty dormant, far down at the bottom of the stack.

I closed my eyes and opened the file.

When Danny O'Neill was a student at the National University of

Ireland, Galway, he traveled to Boston each summer to work painting houses, which gave him enough money for the ten months of
study back home. Every year, he had a different name on his work
visa. This is not difficult to accomplish, as we all learned by 9/12.
The man who owned the painting business had manipulated the
system so that his hard-working illegals wouldn't be hassled. When
Danny told me that, he'd excused the offense with, "Wouldn't be a
house in all Boston wearing a single coat of paint were it not for the
fraudulent sons of Erin."

And I said, "Wouldn't be any English literature were it not for
Erin's sons either. Or contemporary literature without the daughters
who weren't allowed to read, let alone write, when English literature
were abornin'."

At the time, his blue eyes warmed. We both enjoyed the art of
purposeful flirtation, and he liked finding someone he could trust—
particularly if she happened to be in charge of renovating the FBI
crime lab.

This guy who owned the painting business was also a firefighter.
Having a sideline enterprise when you're a member of the Boston
FD is as illegal as issuing your employees false work visas, but nei-
ther fall under my jurisdiction or into any moral imperative I hold.
You have room to obsess about just so many injustices.

Danny said he'd never intended to emigrate to the United
States—to stay—but he liked the way of life: "For starters, sunshine
fifty percent of the time instead of ten. Just the right mix. Florida?
Well, it's got the reverse of Galway, and I wouldn't be wanting that. I
found the relentless Florida sunshine to be just as depressing as the
relentless Irish drizzle."

He came to hold his boss in such high esteem that during his
third summer, drinking beers at a saloon, listening to his stories,
smelling his sooty smell, Danny began to sense the allure of fighting
fires, saving people's lives, becoming part of a brotherhood. He told

me, "When a fellow wants a job with the fire department, it helps to know someone. And it helps far more if you have the Celtic connections."

Danny became a citizen, got a job doing all the things his boss had described, and then found that his main interest lay in wringing the necks of arsonists. "I speak metaphorically, Poppy," he'd said. Danny had risen to fire marshal.

He and I arrived at Kinkead's door at the same time. I wondered who the older woman was, standing behind him, watching as we exchanged smiles, pecks on cheeks, and how are you's. He turned to her, then back to me. "Poppy Rice, this is my mum, Nuala O'Neill."

And she said, "The pleasure would be entirely mine."

It certainly would be entirely hers.

Into Kinkead's we went.

# 2

They'd both have whiskey, a little water, no ice. I find if you drink what the fellow is in the mood for, you get past intrusive thoughts like *What sort of person would drink that?* Drink it yourself and maybe there'll be a clue. But then it's imperative that you knock yours down before he's finished picking up his glass. Power play. Danny's mother beat me to it. She met my gaze, same blue eyes as her son's only merrier, because a fire marshal's eyes lose most of the twinkle that might have once been there after a very short time on the job. There was an edge to her merry eyes, though.

Nuala O'Neill said to me, "And I'll be bettin' you're glad we didn't want some tropical fling."

Read me like a book. "I am. I gag on pineapple pulp."

She was probably sixty but she looked a lot younger. Her unlined, smooth skin boasted the benefits of Irish rain, mist, and cold drizzle. She was wearing a sleek black pants suit just like me. She had on a blouse, though; I didn't. When I go out after five, I remove the blouse, add two carats to my earlobes, put on strappy high-heeled shoes—and my two closest pals, Smith and Wesson, go from holster to purse.

It took Danny awhile to get around to explaining her presence, but then he's Irish so I kept patient. "About a week ago, my mum gave me a call. She was calling from Logan Airport, where she'd just landed after leaving her home, Inishmore. My mum was born on Inishmore, one of the Aran Islands in Galway Bay. A bay it is not, if you're thinking the Chesapeake. The waters are as fierce as the rest of the North Atlantic."

Mum's turn now, which fortunately ended further color commentary as to Galway Bay. "When he told me of yourself—a solution to our problem—I asked Danny why it was you were owin' him such a large favor. He said to me, 'She owes me no favor at all. I will be relyin' on professional courtesy.' We know of no such thing in my home, but I trusted him to be tellin' the truth and not just raisin' my hopes."

Danny could still smile despite his job. "In Ireland, my mum relies on bullying, what with the lack of professional courtesy."

I said, "Sometimes, so do I."

We ordered a second round.

I was curious not only as to the motivation for the requested courtesy but also, naturally, what it was exactly they'd come to ask me, so I didn't hurry this whiskey, left it sitting a little to show I was all ears. They took my cue and the three of us sipped, they talking and I listening.

Danny said, "You know, Poppy, in Boston people hear my voice and guess what I am—Irish and therefore a fireman—and then they guess further accordingly. They imagine I'm the ninth of twelve children, that my father back in Ireland is a drunk who never comes home except to beat his children and beget yet another, and that my mother is a charwoman. Though I can't be bothered setting them straight, I will set things straight for you, as it is a part of our need for help. I was actually the first of who knows how many children that might have been. My dad died banding puffins one month before I was to be born."

I wasn't the least bit surprised to hear a parable in prelude to what he'd come to say. Ah, the Irish.

His mother would tell that tale. "The isles once had a huge population of puffins. And a good thing it was; otherwise the English would have succeeded in starvin' us islanders—every last one—out of existence. But thirty-some years ago, the puffins began to disappear in large numbers. My husband decided to learn why and took to bandin' them, down at the base of the cliff below Dún Aonghasa. But one especially windy mornin', a rogue wave came and washed my husband away and his birds with him. One month later to the day, our Danny was born. To the hour, if you're wantin' the exact truth of it. I have been alone since. There never was another man for me after."

I thought, At least she found the one.

Danny said, "There was no one who cared about things like the dwindling puffin population as much as my dad, Poppy. Or who wouldn't think of leaving the job what with the rising of the wind, a wind that could blow you off the rocks in a second. Not if the guns were to arrive that morning."

He looked to his mother. I believe she was about to come up with a parable of her own. I now decided the skill of listening was secondary to jumping in, so I did, careful not to abandon the tone or ruin the moment. I wanted them to be sure they could trust me. Trust—always so important. I said, "Maybe I could have been the first of nine children, myself."

Danny's gaze flickered, his mother's too.

"My own father died before I was born. There was an accident. He and my mother were very young, only nineteen, and my mother did marry again, to a man who was much older. I came to learn he married my mother because he was alone and I was alone, and he was the only one available to take responsibility for me. He was my mother's cousin. He wasn't interested in children other than me.

Also, it wouldn't have made much sense for my mother to have more children. One can't bring up children too effectively from a psychiatric hospital."

Nuala said, "Ah, a choice. In Galway, if you're in a psychiatric hospital you will still go on to have nine children because you have a duty to your husband and you'd be wise not to speak up about it."

Danny said, "Times have changed."

She said, "Of course they haven't, I'll tell you that. Not enough to count, at least." Then she said to me, "I'm sorry for your troubles."

"Thank you. I'm not looking for sympathy."

Maybe I was. I love the bar at Kinkead's; it evokes the comfort of my stepfather's den, where he taught me, as a very young child, to appreciate edgy sixties rock 'n' roll, among other things. My refuge—not so much the den itself, where vinyls were treated like maps from the fourteenth century—but him, my stepfather. He'd died a few years back. I missed him.

I said, "My stepfather and I were a good match. I just thought the coincidence was interesting. But never mind. Nuala, since I'm an American, I will act with the boorishness I'm entitled to. My curiosity is officially and sufficiently piqued. Please tell me: Why are you here?"

She said, "Danny?"

She had asked him for a favor, so now it was his turn to ask the next guy down the line. He looked from his mother to me, took one more sip of whiskey, and said, "My mum has held a secret for a long time. Since 1972, the year a body came ashore by Carraig Ghiolla, where the road from Oatquarter ends at the sea. The body of a woman. I was five years old. I don't remember the body, but I remember Padraic Logain's dog. He came racing into Kilronan barking like there was no tomorrow. It was in his genes to bark when trouble arrived.

"My mum had me by the hand. I remember that clear as glass.

We were in town to buy our groceries. It was only mothers and small children about. The men were off in their boats. And I remember following Pad's dog with the rest, but that's all. I remember nothing else of that day."

Nuala said, "That was because we put the children behind the wall when we saw it was a body the dog was leadin' us to. Not a sight for the young ones, as so often a shark takes the head. Or Pad's dog could well have done such a thing, I have to admit. We had to tie the dog up, he was so wild over it. Understand, we would get the bodies of sailors soon after news that a boat had disappeared, but never a woman, and so we soon recognized the reason for the dog actin' so wild. One of us saw to keepin' him, along with the children, behind the wall.

"But the dead woman . . . no more than a girl, really . . . her head was intact, and long dark-red hair flowed from it in all directions like an open fan. Hair the color of iodine. We could see she was pregnant. We pulled her above the tide line and covered her with three shawls and weighted the shawls down with rocks all around the edge. Then we went for the priest."

At that point, the report I'd glanced at a year and a half ago, from one Rocky Patel who'd also told of a young drowned pregnant woman, didn't cause any flashes of recognition. Not yet.

Nuala folded her hands together, not in prayer but in a reflection of the frustration she'd felt back then, a frustration that returned to her now. I could see it in her grip.

Danny said, "This was a mistake, going for the priest. The year was 1972, which was a significant year, and the priest . . . he was an old, old man."

Then he gave me some filler on that particular year, 1972.

"It was the year of Bloody Sunday, when thirteen Irish civilians were killed by British troops and the decision to find peace in parliament rather than in the streets of Belfast was abandoned. Also in

1972, married women were allowed to work outside their homes for the first time in Irish history."

And Nuala said, "Too, it was the year the Rule of Thumb law was abolished."

My ears perked right up. I didn't know that the rule of thumb was an actual law, I thought it was an adage. "What was the rule of thumb law?"

Nuala smiled at me, sardonic smile. "The rule allowed that a man was allowed to beat his wife only so long as the weapon he used wasn't bigger round than his thumb."

Oh.

Then Nuala said, "When we heard it—that the rule had been abolished—we thought it meant revision, not abolishment. That now the husband could use a fence post if he liked." The twinkle in her eye had returned.

Danny said, "My mum has a sense of humor."

She said, "Black humor it is, Danny, Irish humor. But now I believe your friend here would like us to get to the crux of the matter."

Crux. A truer word has never been spoken.

"All right then. This priest on Aran saw there wasn't a wedding ring on the hand of the body, so he determined she was living in sin at the time of her death and the child was a bastard."

Nuala said, "It did us women no good to argue that the ring surely could have slid off into the sea."

"In the end," Danny went on, "since the body was found in our priest's parish, it was left to him to determine the course of action. He decided that after she was examined she would have a grace period of thirty days, thirty days for someone to claim her, for a priest to verify he had either married her or she'd confessed to her sin and was in a state of grace. If that didn't happen, she would not be buried in consecrated ground but, instead, tossed in the potter's field. First, though, the fetus would be removed, and he would be buried in a killeen."

"Or she," Nuala slipped in.

"Or she."

I slipped something in myself. "Excuse me. What was that last part? About the fetus?"

"Yet another law to be abolished in the same year, 1972. But not passed in time to change the priest's decision. That law did not go into effect until October, and this was February."

"But what was that word you used? The fetus would be buried where?"

"Understand," Nuala said, "the Church once had special burial grounds for infants born dead. For fetuses, too—for any baby who died before the rite of Baptism could be accomplished. Killeens, they're called. Reserved for the unbaptized, who are carried to Limbo by the angels."

"Refresh me. Limbo is?"

"A second paradise. No different from Heaven, except those who are there will not be seein' God. Never see God."

Danny said, "All bullshit."

Nuala told him to mind his manners. Then she said, "That year, the pope said Limbo was a myth. That the babes go to Heaven after all. It only *had* been bullshit, Dan."

Danny lifted his glass and before he had another swallow, he said, "It was another way to prevent abortion. If you aborted your child, the child would never see God. Wonderful."

I asked, "And there are no more . . . ?" but I'd forgotten the word. I wanted to say *colleens,* but that wasn't it.

"Killeens," Nuala said. "No."

Danny said, "The most notorious killeen in Ireland is on the twelfth fairway at the Galway Country Club."

Wonderful.

Nuala said, "It's my belief the black humor arises from the impotence to right an obvious wrong. Black humor releases the frustration and anger."

Danny apologized for venting his frustration and anger. Then he said, "The killeen at the golf course was discovered a few years ago when the club expanded. Members liked the idea of the fairway leading right to the edge of the sea. The little hillocks along the perimeter of the strand were to be leveled. It turned out they were graves, small graves, each bump bearing the remains of an unbaptized infant or fetus interred there probably several centuries earlier."

We were now moving far afield, and much as I adore parables, myths, and legends, I said, "You know, I think we should go directly to the professional courtesy."

Danny said, "We are there, in fact."

Nuala said, "Here is what happened on Inishmore that day over thirty years ago. After a brief conference, we women protested to the priest his decision; went right to the rectory door, our group did. Because if the dead girl was a member of the IRA, there would have been no official identification if she'd died while in custody. She'd maybe been drowned in the manner my husband had surely drowned.

"The priest did not invite us inside. He told us the gardai had already been dispatched from Galway, along with someone from the coroner's office. The gardai would take care of the body. Our husbands, he said, when they came off the water, would take care of us women. He shook his finger at us when he said that. And then he pointed his finger at me. He said, 'As for you, Nuala O'Neill, you should be devotin' yourself to helpin' these women with their young ones since you have but the one small boy. Instead, you encourage them to fight the will of our Blessed Lord. And by doin' so, you expose your boy to the nonsense that lies within your own cold heart.' Then he slammed the door and locked it, so as not to hear any further argument from us.

"We dispersed, all but the three of us who had continued in my husband's mission, who kept it alive. Their own husbands, though out on the sea, had spent some years in jail in Dublin. The ostensible bandin' of the puffins. The priest condemned all of it, not the jailin' but the mission.

"We traveled back to Oatquarter, down to Carraig Ghiolla, and we wrapped the body in our shawls and carried her behind the stone wall, a mile or so up from Carraig Ghiolla to Cora Phort Chorruch, where the land was higher, to the very spot where the first primroses bloom in February. It is a mighty headland and all but inaccessible, except across flats of cockles at low tide. It was a struggle to carry her, but the dog seemed to take heed of our zeal and he shepherded the children along behind us." Her voice had cracked just a little bit. She felt the crack and she lifted her chin. "Why should she have been separated from the child she carried? Separated against her will. Why should she have been?"

Yes, I had to wonder that too. Nuala's cheeks were getting pinker. She was not an accepting soul; she felt it right to allow her fury to rise. My great virtue as well, though not seen as such by most. It tended to scare Joe, admiring of me as he might be. She took a deep breath, had a swallow of whiskey. She said, "I know I'm talkin' about the will of a dead girl, dead since 1972. All the same. . . ."

"No need to make an excuse to me, Nuala, but I am wondering about the leap from then to now."

She didn't answer. She was thinking—thinking of an answer that would explain this leap rationally. Danny tried to buy her some time. "I didn't know she was coming until she called me from Logan Airport."

Nuala sighed. "I had not the time to try to convince my son of the dilemma. There had to be the fullest drama so that any action he might decide upon would be the result of takin' me seriously. I had to be sure he would." Her eyes met mine again. "You see, the truth of it is—we were found out."

"Found out?"

"Yes. The leap from then to now? We women have recently been betrayed. And we don't know who to credit for the wretched betrayal."

"I'm sorry. I'm missing something. Betrayed as to what?"

"Why, as to our hidin' the body. The gardai suspected it had been stolen and hidden, though we swore the tide must surely have washed the body back out again. But someone must have seen us. Perhaps one of the children there that day remembered. And that someone, or that child now grown, has gone and told them about the body, and they came to know where she lay. After all these years."

"But betrayed why?"

She smiled. "You are an investigator. If I knew why, I wouldn't be askin' Danny to help me. But that is another kettle and it doesn't matter. They'll not do a thing to us for a crime we committed over thirty years ago. Someone wishes us to be exposed. But our cause has become moot, has it not? No more gunrunnin' from Aran these days. No more hidin' those that needed hidin'. The puffins are gone, never returned, just as my husband has never returned.

"And just so she was exhumed, the girl was, and given a decent funeral. The woman and her child are now buried in our island cemetery, a proper burial on consecrated ground, but with no one from her family present at the service, as nobody knew of her family. No name on the headstone. No name. But she will not be restin' in peace. She will not until . . ." The cheeks were growing pink again.

Danny signaled for the bartender and ordered a third round. *Did we want to move into the restaurant?* the bartender asked us. We had been polishing off his bowls of peanuts as soon as he put them in front of us. No, we didn't. Danny had not let his mother finish what she was about to say. The favor itself, the personal courtesy, was finally rearing its head. Danny apparently felt I should ask, not be told, in case I didn't care to know. So I asked.

"Nuala—again—what is it I can do for you?"

"Only one thing. The time has come to find out who she is so her family can come and pay their respects."

"But don't the police want to find out? Didn't they when you first found the body?"

"The gardai?" She all but spat it out.

"Yes."

"They didn't care to know at the time. And now they will not look into the death of a woman washed onto the shores of Inishmore so long ago."

"How do you know that? Why wouldn't they?"

Danny said, "The gardai have no compunction to explain anything to my mum. There was an autopsy on her remains just before the new burial, and it was determined she died of drowning. There would be no unusual effort to identify her. Too many years gone by. Back then they said her family would be better off knowing of just the disappearance rather than the far greater dishonor in knowing their daughter was pregnant. That she was dead would be the lesser tragedy."

I let that sink in. "There is a more rational reason why they didn't investigate, isn't there, Danny?"

He placed his glass in front of him, a half-inch of whiskey still left, and talked to it rather than to me. "I can only guess. I would imagine the gardai themselves wanted the identity of the woman kept secret, and maybe still want it kept secret, but they cannot stop the proof of the DNA, which might tell us who she is. They refused to do the DNA testing, though, and that is why I have come to you."

Nuala placed her hand on my wrist. It was ice cold. "I have not a knowledge of how far professional courtesy extends, but know this—there is but the one thing we can do for the wretched girl: See she's claimed." She looked at her hand, still on my wrist, and then up at me. "In order to answer the questions we wanted answered, the same questions you ask now, we requested the gardai take tissue samples from the body before the new burial took place and test its DNA. Because what is left of the body wouldn't be but bones and hair. She was only wrapped in our shawls. An autopsy would not have helped to identify her. And we already knew how she died." She looked into my eyes. "Even though it's true we do not know what lies behind her death. We looked upon the body carefully when we found her. There were no bullet holes, and her neck wasn't broken. She drowned. She went into the water alive."

"How can you know that?"

"By the signs."

"Which signs?"

"The signs of her struggle to breathe."

I guess I just looked at her.

Danny said, "Many bodies have come ashore at Inishmore. Sailors. The islanders begin to search as soon as they hear of a fishing boat going down. Not local boats; we haven't lost a local boat in a generation. Trawlers from Spain, from France. Depending on the time gone by, islanders know what to expect as to the condition of the bodies. And if the time is not too long, faces of the drowned reveal their suffering. Or their lack of suffering, if they've smashed their head on the rigging before going in."

Nuala said, "Each village policed itself. The authorities were not to be trusted, since we were an occupied land."

Oh.

"We were prepared for the gardai's first line of resistance. Influenced by the Church they are, as are all Irish institutions. There is a distaste for the takin' of samples from bodies for DNA tests, as our bodies are considered the temples of Christ. We cannot desecrate our bodies, and that includes the bodies of the dead."

"How is taking a tissue sample for DNA testing any more desecrating than an autopsy?"

Nuala said, "No different. The Church needed five hundred years to give the nod to the autopsy."

She took a Baggie from her purse. Inside was a spiral of hair. The hair was indeed the color of iodine. "This lock came from her. We expected to get the DNA material from her hair. The gardai asked us, *What will you compare the DNA with?* even though they already knew the answer. They made us give the answer so they could laugh at us."

Danny said to me, "I promised my mother you wouldn't laugh."

Now that Nuala felt assured what he'd promised was true, she told me what she'd told the gardai. "We will go into records. Find out ourselves what young woman went missin' during the months before and after our poor girl washed up. The body was in the water no more than a week. Possibly five or six days. The currents were strong. The fish do not run in the strong spring currents. She was all but untouched.

"Every mother in Ireland saves a lock of her child's hair. We will go to the families of the women gone missin' and ask them to part with a few strands from the lock. It is the miracle of DNA that finally allows us to find out what we never could before."

Every mother in Ireland. How true might that statement be? I wondered. I sympathized with the strength in her voice, however. It's the determination I would have shown if I were Nuala. Say something strongly enough, and most people won't question the words themselves.

"And once we Inishmore women have collected our strands of

hair from any poor family who lost a girl in that time, we will send them to you to make the comparison. That is what we are here to ask you."

Danny said, "I know such a request will consume some of your valuable time. I know that. Still, I ask."

Nuala's face reflected her dire need for me to say yes. To grant a professional courtesy. She tried one last card. "If we identify her, then the gardai will have no choice but to investigate how she came to drown. Or be drowned."

"Be drowned?"

"Yes."

Danny looked up from the glass.

I said, "There's a lot more to it, isn't there?"

Danny said yes, while at the same time his mother said no.

I said, "I need all the facts before I can agree to the one thing."

Danny said, "I told you, Mum. This is a good woman. Go ahead, then. Tell her. We owe her what she asks if she's to do us this favor."

Nuala's lips were pressed together.

"It does not come easy to drown accidentally when you're raised near the sea," Danny said. "My father's body was never recovered. It was stolen to deprive the people of a martyr's burial. The Church will not celebrate a Funeral Mass unless the body is present. So this is all come to be very important to me. I intend to approach the gardai myself in that regard one day, one day when I have as much knowledge as I can acquire about his death. If we could set a precedent here. . . . There *will* be a precedent if I have an American connection that trumps their proclamations. The call from my mum—her wanting the girl known now that she is buried in a public place—it stirs my own interests."

Aha.

Nuala began to dig into her purse. She came up with another

Baggie. "Perhaps this would help you too. The girl had an American friend or relative send her clothes. Or, more likely, she had visited America." She handed me the bag. "I believe it was the latter."

Danny said, "The women cut the labels from the clothes she wore before they buried her."

Nuala qualified. "No, Danny. It was your godmother, Peggy Ann, who did that. She always had the foresight. And now our wait is over."

Judging by the condition of the labels, the body hadn't been in the water long. Nuala was right about that. The brand names, the sizes, the fabric content were still readable.

Danny said, "The name on the dress label was an actual store in Greenwich Village. In business from 1964 and into the seventies. The designer herself is still designing clothes."

He separated out that label and gave it to me. The letters were not only still readable, they were still colorful: BETSEY JOHNSON FOR PARAPHERNALIA.

The bartender brought us another round, this time without our having to ask.

Nuala said, "She bought the clothes while visiting America and then she returned to Ireland."

"How can you be so sure she wasn't an American?"

"I am trustin' my instincts."

"How do you know she bought the clothes in America herself?"

"Because when we get gifts of clothing from America, the items are practical, not whimsical as was the dress she wore."

"So what you know of the woman, besides the fact that she was pregnant and hadn't been shot or strangled—based on the experience you've had with dead bodies on your shore—is that she was Irish and she'd visited the United States between 1964 and her death in 1972. And that is based on instinct."

"Correct."

So sure of herself. So resolute. Self-assurance and resolution can lead you down the wrong road; sometimes you create such a strong scenario you come to believe it rather than question it. Manipulating a jury so that they remain loyal to a story rather than the facts is the forte of a great lawyer—able to convince a jury to believe the story with their collective heart and soul even though it's made up. Such a road parallels one that I took myself a year ago and which, I hope, I'll never travel again: seeing innocence where none exists.

Danny watched me. He said, "My mother comes a far way to ask you for help. Her friends chipped in to pay her airfare."

I lined up all the little labels from the Baggie on the table. One wasn't readable, actually: A white square with a satiny feel.

Nuala said, "From her panty hose. Probably had been rinsed several times."

I read the second label: VANITY FAIR, 34B.

Nuala said, "The bra was a little padded."

The next: LOLLIPOP, size 5.

I thought: a slim woman, height unknown, conservative juvenile underpants, comfortable unfancy bra, and a dress bought from the hottest boutique in New York at a time when the rest of the country didn't yet know what the word *boutique* meant.

I said, "You'd like me to do more than get her DNA tested."

"Yes. Insurance. In case my mum doesn't come up with that matching lock of hair." Danny was trying to make a case for reality. "That is the real reason for the apology I made to you. Asking you to consume your precious time. I am asking for more time than I have the right to."

He knew that making a DNA sample from a lock of hair would consume only the time it would take me to ask my director's permission to have the lab complete the testing required. He also knew his mother's plan to search out locks of hair was perhaps far-fetched.

"Danny, I don't know when I'll be able to get to the labels. That *will* consume time—they're not laundry tags. It's something I'd have to squeeze in somewhere."

"I know. But you are a genius, after all."

He raised his glass. So did Nuala. I had to smile. I raised my glass too. I'm not modest. We clinked and they had my assent. Danny's toast was in Irish. If we ever discover life on Jupiter and the life there has a spoken language, it will not sound as alien as Irish.

"What's the toast in English, Danny?"

*"To beg the saints is more useful than prayer."*

Then Danny looked at his watch and said he had to be back at the firehouse at eleven. He and his mother should leave for the airport. They stood and so did I, disappointed, actually, to see them go.

Before we parted, I said to Nuala, "How is it you're so sure she was Irish?"

"By the look of her face. The girl, I could tell, was a sweet one."

She said that and I squinted. Squinted in order to see past the flash to where I'd heard that line before. Either she or Danny must have asked me something and I hadn't answered, because I felt Danny's fingertips on my arm.

"Are you all right?"

"I am. I just thought of something. It's nothing, really."

Danny took my hand, kissed my cheek, and said, "Nothing. All right then." And he said goodbye.

I smiled at both of them as my mind raced, raced because I recognized the flash, had followed it back to the letter I'd received from Rocky Patel. I saw the line he'd written, a line eerily similar to the one Nuala had just used: *She was a sweet kid.* In reference to another drowned pregnant girl, no less.

I scrolled my memory during the taxi ride home. Then I went to my computer—the real one. I opened up the file. There was more coincidental information in Rocky Patel's Jane Doe file than simply the cause of death and the sweetness of her face, or even the pregnancy. The woman also had red hair.

A couple of interesting coincidences, Poppy, is what I told myself. The stuff of TV crime shows, nothing more. Still, I felt like conferring with Joe.

But I got into my bed alone. Instead of a calm and relaxed bedtime conference with Mr. Soul Mate, I had to content myself with tossing and turning until I finally fell into a restless sleep—dreaming of two redheaded girls and their sweet faces and how they died: their desperate but futile struggle to get air into their lungs.

I would come to know them both.

# 3

When I went to my director, I didn't mention the bizarre coincidences between two drowned young women. I simply passed along Danny's request.

"Do you know how many pregnant Irish girls commit suicide each year?" is what my director asked me.

"No, sir."

"Neither do I. But I heard a statistic once—figures per various populations—and those figures shocked us all. I remember the agent at the meeting, the one who gave us the statistic, calling the number heartbreaking. What was more heartbreaking, of course, was the number of female members of the IRA held in jails who had supposedly committed suicide. Supposedly. Because they were pregnant."

He was clearly having a problem with the professional courtesy I'd asked permission to offer Danny and Nuala O'Neill. He'd been figuring we were on some sort of hypothetical level, locks of hair and all. But ordering DNA testing without consultation with the Irish connections? He was waffling. So then I told him about the labels, how I'd like to try to put a pattern together. On my own time. And that's when he knew for sure I wasn't hypothesizing at all.

He said, "On your own time?"

"Yes."

"You mean right away, don't you? That's what this is about."

"Yes, sir. I have another week of vacation left."

He had to smile. "True."

A month ago, when I'd debated whether or not to take my vacation, he told me he would refuse to allow me to come back to work for a few weeks even if I decided, in the end, not to go to Block Island. "You need to heal, Poppy," he'd argued. He meant physically, but I knew he'd meant emotionally too. So at the time, all things considered, I figured, What the hell? I'll go.

Now he said, "I take it you're just letting me know what you'll be up to and where you'll be in case an emergency arises. That you would have used your free time to check on the labels without my permission."

Also true. "Yes, but I wanted your opinion, sir. I'd like to take Delby to New York with me. Seeing as how she has expertise in the matter."

"Her expertise is wide."

Delby Jones. The FBI is her number-two job. Number one is as mother of three little girls. Number three, she's a singer. Number three, she says, is a hobby. Jazz bands come through, they want to pick up a girl singer, they call Delby. I go listen to her when I can. When I'm there, she'll ask the band to squeeze in a nouveau cool-jazz arrangement of some sixties song because she knows I'm such an oldies nut. Name a song; my stepfather could give you the group without having to think. Sometimes, Delby tests me. Sticks her head in the office and says, "'Riders on the Storm,'" And I say, "Jim Morrison," and she says, "Gotcha! It was The Doors!" So I explain how I'm still right. She doesn't know how easy that one is.

Delby tells me the bands she sings with don't have contracts with record companies. Only sexy, pretty, very young women with a range of three notes, and musicians who hold their guitars upside down, have recording contracts. The music business is not what it used to be, she says—her way of assuring me she's not going to run off with one of those bands and leave me high and dry.

I said to my director, "What if Danny O'Neill's dead woman turns out to have been an American, perhaps naturalized? Then Delby will be able to hold down the fort while I investigate further, since she'll be up on things."

"She could hold down ten forts, whether she's up or not."

He looked across the vast expanse of his desk. It was stacked with folders, littered with reports. "Poppy, I am influenced by the gentleman who asked for the favor. Danny O'Neill is a dedicated fellow. We have relied on him on the several occasions we've needed a voice of reason when it comes to arson. Arson is unconscionable, isn't it?"

"Yes, it is."

"So you've got what you want. I'll ask for tissue samples from the dead woman. The gardai will ask for a favor in return—down the line. Actually, I believe they owe us, but never mind. Take Delby with you. But we'll need to discuss a couple of cases while you finish up your vacation time. If that's all right with you." He smirked first, and then he became serious again. "One is pressing. I think it's going to be yours."

"Can we discuss it now?"

"I knew you'd say that. Thank you. Suddenly, I need to discuss it with someone, but not anyone. You. The case doesn't meet the criteria for rising to the top of the agenda. So much attention to what must come first these days. I will never clean this place up with such a mind-set—babbling debate that goes nowhere. Where did that mind-set come from?"

"It all started with the necessity to invent reasons for going after Vietnam war protesters while organized crime was purchasing New Jersey."

"You were born after Vietnam, Poppy."

"Thanks, but not quite. I studied the government before I took the job. Actually, I've studied the agency itself since high school. This is where I have always wanted to be, sir."

A shrink friend of mine has offered to help me find out why. Why? Who *cares* why? Who's got time?

"Poppy, you rid our lab of that mind-set, the only department in the entire FBI that now operates with straightforward efficiency."

"That's because their work is the most straightforward. The lab solves crimes already committed. Suddenly, the rest of the FBI has to anticipate crimes to come, anticipate who the hell's going to commit them. It's different."

"I'm interviewing anyone who knows the difference between the Arabic language of academia and the Arabic spoken in a souk."

"I know you are, sir. And about that case you mentioned?"

He smiled again. "Thanks for listening to me vent."

"Sure."

I understood the need to vent. Fifty years ago there were fewer than twenty federal offenses, most to do with treason, the rest revenue fraud. Now there were three thousand, covering the entire gamut of crime, crimes against the security of the homeland being the most pressing.

He said, "Okay then. I checked to see if you were at the staff meeting I called where we took up prostitutes who went missing from railroad stations. You were. Then I remembered you referring to them as *disappeared*."

"I remember." The meeting took place around the time he was ordered to shift focus and manpower away from crimes against children and go find a guy mailing anthrax spores to the Senate Office Building. Several of the disappeared prostitutes were under eighteen. One was twelve. He would not follow the orders. He told Congress to get him a bigger budget. The case would not go to the bottom of the agenda.

"We're still in the preliminaries. But all of a sudden a lot of diplomacy is required. While you were away I got a call. Mike Turner—you know him?"

Junior senator from Kentucky. "Yes." Pleasant-enough fellow.

"His oldest kid, grown daughter, mid to late twenties, kind of a Bohemian, got into the family business: Thoroughbreds. Trouble is, she didn't want just to own Thoroughbreds like the ladies of the family, she wanted to breed them like the boys. She moved to a farm she bought in New York. In business three years now, several of her foals looking good, selling as two-year-olds for a lot of money. She's been missing a week."

"Tell me she's not a prostitute on the side."

"Not that we can tell. But naturally, a missing twenty-something woman doesn't set off alarms. Unless her father is a senator. The big problem is that she was last seen in Manhattan, at Grand Central, heading upstate from a big party. New York Racing Association party. Apparently, she was dressed in a very sexy dress and had too much to drink—she couldn't find a bag with sweats and sneakers she'd brought along to wear back home on the train. Her friends said one heel of her shoe had broken off and she thought walking with one foot on tiptoe was funny. Worked hard but when there was time to play, she played hard. The last two prostitutes have gone missing from Grand Central. I'm meeting Senator Turner in an hour. I have to tell him that there's a terrible possibility out there."

"I'm sorry. Very tough, sir."

"Very tough. But if there's a possibility that whoever is killing prostitutes killed her, the case will become very public. It will give us the opportunity to point out that prostitutes are often children. I want you to be part of this because you're the one I can count on. Politics come last with you, and Senator Turner will need to understand that."

He meant internal politics. I'd seen to it that the head of the crime lab was no longer a political appointee. I was the last appointee to that position, in fact. The new man hired by the new director is a

master chemist. He made the choice between heading up our lab
and taking a chemistry chair at an especially fine university. His son,
a college kid, was on the plane that was sent down in Lockerbie. He
told me the opportunity the FBI offered him brought new tears to
his eyes. He also asked me if Delby could stay with him.

I wished I could have given him a straight-out yes but I couldn't.
"A decision best left to Delby."

She wished she could have given him a straight-out yes, too, but
she wanted to stay with me in my new job as independent investigator, choosing my crimes myself 90 percent of the time. She told the
chemist she'd be at his beck and call until he was happy with an assistant. And she was, shuttling between the two of us. A man who has
lost his child fit in completely with Delby's priority, her girls. If you
want to have lunch with Delby, meet her at the day-care center from
noon to one and make sure you like fish sticks and oatmeal cookies.

As I walked down the corridor I pondered the parallels. Nuala
O'Neill wanted to find a mother who saved a lock of her child's hair
with the understanding that she might have to verify that mother's
worst fear—the disappeared child is dead. And in this case, an unborn
grandchild as well. The poor mother. And poor Senator Turner with
a disappeared child of his own. I looked forward to getting to that
when the time came.

But that other one, in Boston. I thought maybe I'd call, find out
if the detective who'd sent the letter had come across anything new.
When I had a chance.

Law enforcement is both exhilarating and wrenching. You can't
have one without getting hammered by the other.

～～～

I knew Delby would be pleased to accompany me to New York. If I
tell her she has to go to California with me, she moans. She says, *My*

*body doesn't like to go backward in time.* All trips, however, hinge on her mother's being able to drop everything and fly up from Macon to watch the three little daughters. The money for the flight comes from my slush fund. Delby's mother has almost always managed to make the drop-of-a-hat trip.

Delby loves clothes but she can't afford the clothes she loves. So she cuts out pictures of dresses and mails them to her mother in Florida, and her mother sews replicas. Delby splurges on shoes but does without bras. Tells me models don't wear bras either. Delby, like a model, is built like a willow branch.

Besides dresses, Delby wears blouses and skirts or pants to work, all made by her mother, plus she has five black jackets, each different except for their perfection. I wear suits. Expensive designer suits, mainly Armani, sometimes Versace. Trust the geniuses is my feeling.

After the meeting with the director, I stopped by my office one floor down from his. "Delby, I need you to find a number for me, make a call, and try to set up an appointment for tomorrow. New York. If Mom gives you the high sign, go home and pack. We'll go tonight." She grabbed a pen. I said, "Betsey Johnson. Try for morning. Insist."

She looked up. "Betsey Johnson? Not the designer?"

"Yes. The designer."

"Oh, boy."

First the call to Mom, who said *For sure*; and then Delby called our New York office and gave them the job of setting up the appointment, which they did.

I don't know who ran out faster to splurge on a new pair of shoes, me or Delby.

◂◂◂

Betsey Johnson's reception area had a Japanese reflecting pool with lily pads and carp. Beyond that, any hint of Japanese simplicity and minimalism of space was absent. We were surrounded by contemporary art of the vivid variety. Besides paintings, there was a mattress on the wall with the stuffing hanging out, a sculpture. Staffwise, commotion reigned. But someone beautiful and British appeared and asked us to follow her.

Betsey's office was not full of commotion. The Delfonics were playing on a sound system, music to be soothed and inspired by. The desk looked not unlike my director's—long and wide, his litter of papers and evidence bags and photographs taking up all the space between the neat high stacks of folders. Betsey Johnson's litter, amid her high stacks of folders, included sketches, piles of fabric pieces, tissue paper, buttons, beads, zippers, and spools of thread. She was coming around the desk to greet us as we were led through her office door. She had on a black-and-white hound's-tooth miniskirt—the hound's-tooth pattern enlarged about a hundred times the size you see in a man's jacket—knee-high boots, and a long tight ribbed silk sweater. Clothes to match the era of the music.

She was not built like a willow branch—she was barely five feet tall—but hadn't let her personal biology affect the clothes she liked to design and, obviously, wear. Her hair was orange with stripes I'd have to call metallic, randomly sprouting from her head in various-length ponytails. The frames of her huge glasses were pearly blue plastic. As she approached, she looked us both up and down and said, "I hate skinny girls. I hate tall girls. I hate both of you. But tall skinny girls are my bread and butter, so what the hell can I say?"

To the willowy British girl who had brought us in, she said, "Bunny here yet?"

"Any minute, likely. Rang from a taxi."

Betsey Johnson sighed. "Never on time. Never. And I warned her we'd be entertaining the Feds." Then she smiled. "So let's take a load off, girls, shall we?"

She shook both our hands and had us sit down in a corner fitted with Italian chairs and a coffee table made of something black. She saw me take notice. I said, "Not marble, is it?"

"No. Polished, poured concrete. Dyed black before it was poured."

Concrete shimmery as glass, black as anthracite.

She said, "Go ahead, feel it. Everyone does."

I did. I said, "It feels liquid. Like mercury, maybe." I may have seen to a mop-up at the FBI crime lab, but I'm no chemist.

"Mercury! That's what I've been wanting to say since I got it. First three months we kept wiping it down. Thought water had spilled on it. Thought there was a leak in the ceiling. *Mercury.* I love it."

Coffee service was laid out on the table, each piece reflected wetly in its surface. She aimed the pot at the cup in front of me and poured. She moved on to Delby's cup but Delby declined.

"You having a mammogram or something?"

Delby smiled. "No."

Betsey said, "Don't you love it that caffeine is supposed to make your breasts especially sensitive to the pain of being pressed into a pancake? I mean, crushed is crushed, no?"

I enjoy people who repeat their rigorous thought patterns aloud. Makes life more interesting.

"Tea?" she asked Delby.

Delby said, "I'd like a glass of water."

"With that skin you've got, why didn't I guess you'd want water. You know, in Italy, no one drinks water. They tell you water is for washing the floor. Drink *wine,* they tell you. 'Course they have skin like lizards."

But water was fetched and Bunny arrived at the same time. We stood up without having to think about it because she was around eighty years old and might have been the queen of somewhere. She had on a beret. She walked with a cane. The head of the cane was made of amber with a large number of trilobites suspended within. When she leaned it against Betsey's desk, I saw that the soft glow of the shaft wasn't brass, just like I could see the coffee table wasn't marble—brass would be too heavy for a cane anyway. I think it was gold leaf on wood, coated the way an eagle might be, perched over the entry to a New England town hall.

Betsey said, "This is Bunny Metz, the first manager of the debut Paraphernalia store, my chief adviser and best friend since the day I started out. Give me your coat and cane, Bun, and plop yourself down." Bunny slipped out of the coat, which Betsey passed off to the British woman in charge of the escort and water-bearing duties.

Betsey watched the coat go. "Nothing like a summer coat. Silk gabardine that weighs maybe as much as a sparrow feather. Keeps the heat of the sun away from you." The coat was coral and had big buttons. "They don't make coats like that anymore."

Bunny said, "Not since Jackie, anyway."

As the coat left the room over the arm of the British girl, Betsey was still looking at it wistfully, I'd have to say. And so was Delby.

Bunny turned to us. "How lovely to be with you ladies today."

Betsey made formal introductions, first our names and then "of the Federal Bureau of Investigation, Bunny. *Whew.* How cool is that?"

Bunny chose not to say how cool.

We all sat down and Bunny took a cup of coffee. Then Betsey wanted to know right away if we had the actual labels on us.

Delby had faxed them photographs before we left so they would have a good idea of what they were about to see. I told them we had indeed brought them.

Betsey said, "This is so exciting, isn't it, Bun? I love puzzles."

Bun seemed a little unsure. A partnership requires that at least one of the pair be of calm demeanor. Two Betsey Johnsons would be bedlam.

I took out Nuala's little bag with the labels in it and handed it to Betsey. She put it down, went and got a box from her desk, and dumped it out onto the coffee table. She had a hundred labels of her own, which she spread across the surface of the table with her fingers. Betsey had also brought over a large magnifying glass with a battery-operated light that she wielded with authority. She and Bunny nestled together, carefully took out the contents of Nuala's bag—as opposed to just dumping it—and examined the four labels. While they turned them over and over, feeling them between thumb and forefinger, they talked about the graphics on the labels and the colors of the graphics—the ink—and they looked at the codes on their own labels, almost as faded as ours, which annoyed them, the annoyance mild since they were able to read them and knew how important legibility would be. They discussed samples and trunk shows, shows that were the real thing, and then which models wore which clothes when and where.

Betsey became misty-eyed. "Will we ever come back from Penelope Tree, Bun?"

"No. But never mind. We have another Penelope here, an FBI agent on a mission. It was that damned sailor dress, wasn't it, Betsey?"

Betsey put her hand to her face, a gesture of resolve. "I'm afraid it was. My summer folly of which you so disapproved."

"I knew it was bad luck, what with the navy lobbing bombs into Cambodia. I couldn't talk you out of it."

"Henry Kissinger was doing the lobbing, not me." She turned my way. "I wasn't inspired by the U.S. Navy. I was inspired by a royal wedding. In British weddings, there are these little boys instead of bridesmaids, and they wear replicas of vintage navy uniforms—their navy, not ours."

Betsey buzzed her secretary. She said into her intercom, "It's what we thought from the beginning, Monica. Bring in the sailor dress."

The British woman, Monica, glided back in, carrying a four-foot-long box that she laid on the black table. The box was sealed. Betsey gestured, and Monica cut the seal with a little knife and lifted the cover. Inside was another box with a heavy cellophane viewing window the length of the dress within. We all peered through. The dress was laid out, stuffed. Stuffed with some sort of packing. Not unlike looking at a clothed headless body. Delby shrank back.

Betsey said, "I keep samples of everything in these boxes. I try not to refer to them as coffins, but it's hard not to since they're all stacked up in what is essentially a mausoleum in my temperature-controlled basement. I don't think I've ever opened one of them. We'll see how good my undertaking service is. The inside space is supposed to be airtight."

She lifted the windowed cover up from the box and sniffed the air. "Good. No mildew at all, Bun."

Bunny sniffed too and agreed.

"We'll just compare the labels, even though Bunny is never wrong and I'm only wrong once in a blue moon."

Bunny said, "Summer line, 'sixty-nine. And no one bought it."

Betsey said, "No, Bunny. Someone bought it. And she drowned in it." Then she looked back up at Delby and me. "And that's why these two jazzy ladies are here—to find out who she was. But if the two of you plan on asking me if we have records of sales going back that far, no, we don't. This was pre-computers."

I certainly was going to ask her that. Too bad.

Bunny leaned over and put both arms under the dress and lifted it up. Betsey moved the box out of the way and her old-time partner laid the dress on the table. The beginnings of a fashion autopsy. It was very dark navy and I might have thought it black, except that it was laid out on a jet table so the contrast was clear. The dress had gold buttons with embossed anchors down the front and a sailor collar with white braid and two embroidered stars. Plus a long wide burgundy tie, styled in a perfect knot.

Delby's eyes were following the path mine were taking exactly. She said, "Windsor knot."

Bunny said, "As if the customers could ever hope to duplicate it. We had some duke friend of Betsey's tie it."

Betsey said, "You know, I still love this little dress. Low V-neck meant to show one inch of cleavage and an A-line skirt meant to start that same inch below your crotch. Symmetry has its place."

Delby said, "What's that sheen to it?"

Betsey and Bunny exchanged glances. They both smirked. Betsey explained the sheen to us. "The very finest grade polyester. Wad this dress up into a ball, put it out in the road, let three cement mixers drive over it, and you won't find a single wrinkle."

"There was good polyester and there was shoddy," Bun said.

"I love it that fashion depends so strongly on topflight chemists." Betsy leaned back into the sofa. "How the hell could we live without our polymers?"

I said, "Somehow, we'd manage. And, hopefully, we've got the chemists, not you."

"Who's we?"

"The FBI."

"Oh, yeah. I forgot who you were for a minute."

She passed the magnifying glass around. The labels were an identical match.

Betsey said, "So here's your next port of call, ladies. The summer those dresses were sold"—she turned to Bunny—"very few of them as opposed to *none,* we had a fabulous, smart girl selling in the shop. We hired her just out of college while she was job-hunting for a more serious fashion position. Tragic how they all come hunting year after year and never make it past floor sales. But not her, right, Bun?"

"Not her. And the girl had *no* credentials whatsoever. She said she graduated from some design program in the Midwest. I'd certainly never heard of it."

Betsey said, "I'd never heard of the Midwest till she came along."

"But she had style. Grand style."

"Yes. Innate."

"And class."

Betsey said, "She told us her grandmother was a White Russian who had three rubies and an old yellow diamond sewn under her skin, because if she was going to be spirited out of Russia she did not intend to arrive on unknown shores penniless. She'd rather die in the gulag."

"The girl didn't let a day go by without saying she learned everything she needed to know about fashion from her White Russian grandmother and everything she needed to know about selling fashion from her summer on the floor at Paraphernalia. She still says it."

"She said she learned the latter from you, Bunny."

"The truth is she learned it all from nosing around you."

Their mutual admiration was lovely, but it was time to redirect. I said, "Of what significance would she be to us?"

They redirected back to me. Betsey said, "Well, let me tell you this, that girl knew how to treat a customer. Which meant she knew how to *sell* a dress. She remembered every one of them second time they came in, greeted them like old friends, and they just kept coming back. Spread the word about us too." We waited. "She's the one who sold the sailor dresses that summer."

Delby has less patience than I. "Who is she and where's she at?"

Bunny said, "Oh, dear."

Betsey gave a little gasp of surprise. "Omigod, Bun! We forgot about that part, didn't we?"

Betsy reached out and patted my knee. "I have to apologize. Silly me. People in the business would have known who we were talking about without our needing to say. Only so many White Russians around these days. We have to get out more, Bun."

Bunny chuckled to herself. "When I talked to her this morning, she said, 'I'd love to dress a female FBI agent.'"

Betsey hooted. "As soon as the two of you leave, I'm going to call her again and tell her the FBI agent has already been dressed by Georgiana Donatella and that her assistant is in a top-notch Dolce and Gabbana copy." Then she said to Delby, "Who did it, if you don't mind my asking?"

Delby said, "My mother. She was influenced by her grandmother too. Her grandmother wasn't a White Russian, she was a black share-cropper who learned how to sew so she could get out of the fields."

Bunny sucked in her breath. "Sew indeed. I do love it when, yet again, someone shows that fashion is a clever, wonderful craft as well as an art. But never mind. Our darling shopgirl from that summer so many years ago never had any White Russian grandmother of any sort, and there was no such school in the Midwest with the name she gave us. She was from Brooklyn and went to Cooper Union just like everybody else. Her talent, as Betsey has pointed out, was innate."

Betsey said, "Many talents, matter of fact. After she left us, off she went to London to reinvent herself yet again. Now she has the most influence in the industry of anyone."

I said, "And this woman's name is?"

The two women looked at each other and then at Delby, who obviously had figured out who the former shopgirl was because she said, "Man, oh, man."

Betsey said, "We're talking about the editor of *Vogue*."

Oh.

"Agent Rice of the FBI, I am happy to brag that we organized ourselves before you got here. Bun and I had the same conversation we've just had with you, only on the phone. First conversation was hypothetical, but I called our girl anyway. She said she would be glad to see you"—Betsey looked down at her see-through milled-Lucite watch, vintage, the fifties—"in half an hour. That cutting it too close?"

"No, that would be perfect."

Betsey gave us the address.

As we were leaving, qualmless Delby asked for the best place to buy three yards of lightweight black silk brocade.

Betsey said, "Damascus. But don't worry, I'll get it for you. Give Monica outside your mom's address."

Somehow I got Delby—who had become rooted—out of there and off to the editorial offices of *Vogue* as soon as she had managed to scribble her mother's address down on a piece of paper. Monica took the paper, looked down at it, and said, "I haven't been to Georgia. Is it nice?"

Delby just shook her head.

∿

The building housing *Vogue* magazine reminded me a lot of the FBI building. No fish ponds. All business. The editor's office was spare and white, the windows at perfect distances between the works of art on the walls. Unlike Betsey's, the sculptures on the various pedestals were not inspired by mattresses.

She was more than happy to tell everything she knew. We sat while she paraded about, gesturing dramatically, posing perfectly, wrinkling her wrinkleless brow.

"I clearly remember selling two of those little sailor dresses. The criticism was actually that they were infantile. It was only Bun who was still a hawk at that point and deemed them anti-military. But I saw them as costume and both girls who bought them were really interested in them as such."

She sashayed to the window. Pose.

I didn't know what she was talking about. But I could tell Delby did. That's why I wanted to bring Delby. I wore clothes that made me look the way I wanted to look, my only criterion. Delby knew from costumes.

The editor turned from the window, where she'd been gazing at one of the hood ornaments sticking out of the top of the Chrysler Building. Again, dramatically. "One of the two girls bought an entire wardrobe in one day, all there in our store. She said she'd just returned from the Peace Corps in some equatorial place, and her clothes were riddled with cockroach holes. She looked forward to buying sneakers, too, because those little plastic things at the end of shoelaces were a cockroach's favorite treat. She said she couldn't lace anything within a week of the start of her service. What she wanted to buy—even before replacing the sneakers—was the world's shortest dress. She'd been out of the country for the miniskirt revolution and needed to make up for lost time. I told her the sailor would be perfect, what with the long sleeves. If you want to look like you're wearing the world's shortest dress, cover your arms. Then you're nothing but legs."

She put a finger to her cheek, now gazing skyward through the ceiling. "The other girl"—she faced us again—"well, it was a sentimental purchase. Her brother was in the navy. She was here visiting him. He'd just become an American citizen and was, of course, immediately drafted. He had joined the navy because he was familiar with the sea, is what she said. The next day, he had to report for duty. Ship out. The sixties weren't all charm, believe me. After that, she was going home. I remember her because her eyes kept filling up and I had to keep passing her one Kleenex after another. She and her brother would be having dinner that night and who knew when they'd see each other again. I thought it would be great fun for her to be in a funky little sailor dress while her brother was in civvies for the last time.

"She put it on. She was very lovely, and I told her she'd turn heads—which she would have done wearing a burlap sack. The girl from the Peace Corps, on the other hand, was a little bit chunky for the dress but she couldn't have cared less. That's the main thing though, isn't it?"

Delby nodded.

I said, "Do you remember what country she was going home to?"

"Well, I knew as soon as she opened her mouth. No, I knew before that. Her hair was thick and long and the color of Secretariat. Soon after, when he took all our hearts away, I was actually reminded of the girl who bought the sailor dress. They only make that color in two places—on particular stud farms in Kentucky and in Ireland." Delby shivered, but the *Vogue* editor didn't notice. "You certainly can't make it in a salon. Any salon. Not here, not in Paris, not in Rome, anywhere. Heaven knows, many have tried."

I said, "You've come very close, though."

She tucked a wisp behind her ear. "Thank you."

"Would the dress have hidden a pregnancy?"

"She wasn't the least bit pregnant that I could see."

"A future pregnancy?"

"Yes. The dress had no waist—an A-line of course, it being the sixties—and it flared a bit. Some women . . . well, it could have hidden my pregnancies through four months."

Delby said, "Mine through five."

Again, I was glad to have Delby to clarify things.

Now the editor of *Vogue* came and sat with us, leaning forward from the suede chair opposite the sofa. "Can you tell me what this is about? I mean, a little bit at least?"

I told her she was offering us a huge amount of help and therefore she was entitled to know. "If the girl you remember is who we believe she could be, she died a few years after she bought the dress. In 1972. Drowned. She was wearing the dress when her body was discovered. We are trying to identify her."

And like the Irish girl she'd spoken of, her own eyes filled. "But she was such a pretty girl. Though a sad girl. Very sweet."

Sweet. Yet again.

"How did she drown?"

"We're hoping to know that. But first we have to find out who she was. Do you think you can estimate which part of the summer you sold the dress to the Irish girl?"

She thought. "The Peace Corps girl early on. She didn't care how much anything cost, didn't look at the sale racks. Apparently the Peace Corps gives you a readjustment allowance when you come home so you don't starve. That's what she called it—her readjustment allowance. And she was going to spend every dime. The Irish girl looked at the dress only when I told her it was on sale. So, end of July. By August, we had to get rid of everything for the fall lines."

I told her how much that information would help us. We shook her hand. The *Vogue* editor could only be described as ethereal, but she had the handshake of a truck driver.

Afterward, out on Fifth Avenue, Delby asked me who Secretariat was.

"A famous racehorse. He won the triple crown in 1973. Year after our Irish girl died. He was called a chestnut, but his coat shone like a flame. His nickname was Big Red."

Delby was looking into the Saks windows.

Delby and I were both pleased with ourselves. Sometimes the least promising trail leads to something substantial: in this case, a naturalized American citizen—our Irish girl's brother—who joined the U.S. Navy, midsummer 1968. The Department of the Navy would give me a list. We'd learn her name.

Delby said, "Considering the condition of the label, she hadn't worn that dress a lot, had she?"

"I'd say no."

"Either that or she never threw it into the Kenmore. Washed it by hand, maybe."

"She wore it the day she bought it and the day she died. Maybe she never wore it any other time. It was costume, after all. Unless, Delby, she wanted people back in Ireland to notice her. I don't think so. The Irish girl just wanted to see that she and her brother would relax and enjoy themselves, be happy on their last day together. Maybe someone put the sailor dress on her, after she was killed but before she went into the water. So that if the body was found, the gardai would think she was an American."

Delby didn't respond. I hadn't expected her to. She cannot speak of murder with any ease. Her silence reminded me that crime was my job, not hers. Hers was to keep my feet on the ground.

# 4

Once I was home again, I called Danny O'Neill and told him what I'd learned, what I'd guessed at, too. And that I hoped we'd soon know who the dead girl's brother might be.

He reverted to his mother's turn of phrase. "Would that we come to wonder at such a miracle, Poppy."

"Would that we do."

"Even though we don't believe in miracles."

"Even though, Danny."

Sometimes, tracking down information, then finding what we'd only been dreaming of finding, does seem miraculous. He asked when I might expect to be in Boston again. I told him Boston was not on my calendar, alas. He would pass on my information to his mother, and we would keep in touch; anything new I learned, I'd call him.

Then, the next morning, my director told me I'd be going to Boston.

My first thought was the missing prostitutes. Some were missing from the train station there. That's what he first began talking about. "The technicians are still putting a few things together. A little more evidence, some proofs. And when we have what we need to officially step into this investigation, your job will be to sit with Senator Turner.

You'll give him all we've gathered and at the same time question him about his daughter's habits. Right now, he's reluctant to consider that she might be part of any of this. The reluctance is always telling, isn't it?"

Yes, it is.

"And then you can find her. Or figure out what happened to her. We'll see if she crossed paths with the prostitutes. The disappeared prostitutes. But meanwhile, Poppy, there's this thing in Boston. Another kettle of fish. You're not going to believe what I have to tell you."

"What's that, sir?"

"We've recently identified a body discovered at the edge of Boston Harbor around eighteen months ago. You might remember because you refused to close the case when we couldn't ID her."

I felt myself blink. To see if I was awake and not in my bed dreaming. I was awake. "If you're talking about the body of a young pregnant girl, sir, you're right. I won't believe you. This whole Irish business triggered a memory of that case the other night, after I'd spoken to Danny O'Neill. But—"

"The very case, Poppy. It hasn't made the papers yet. There was an autopsy before she was buried. She's been ID'd via DNA material. Auerbach remembered the case too. Had them send some tissue samples to him, extra ones, needed to verify something. Trust Auerbach: my mantra, thanks to you. But you'll be glad to know she didn't wash in from Ireland, though her great-grandparents were Irish immigrants over a century ago. The family owns the biggest shipyard in New England, the biggest one in Newport News, the biggest shipyards all around the globe. This is high profile."

"I'm missing a step in the sequence, sir. How was the connection made to this shipping family?"

He shrugged. "Step was so simple I forgot to say. The ubiquitous phone tip to Boston PD."

"Do we know who made the call?"

"Not yet. What we know is that this girl had been taking off from home ever since she was eleven. The family handled it themselves, didn't go to the police. They'd find her, try to sober her up, try to ignore people who told them she bought drugs from the money she made selling drugs. That and making porn movies. They ended up cutting her off, cut her out of their lives. But the father reported her missing when he hadn't heard from her in over a period of many months. Guilt. Too late."

"But they must have sent someone to view the body when it came ashore. To see if—"

"They *were* contacted and they did, in fact, send a family member to view the body. Apparently, one of the girl's uncles."

"And?"

"Said it wasn't her. Happens."

It does. For all sorts of reasons, some that make sense, some that are suspicious.

"Presumably, it was a matter of denial, Poppy, rather than a lie. Or maybe mortification. The girl's uncle saw the need to protect the family's emotional health and, I'd have to guess, the health of their business."

"We haven't questioned the uncle?"

He smiled. He has an especially shrewd smile he lets loose now and again. "Thought we'd wait and sic you on him."

What that meant, really, was he wanted us to sneak up on the uncle. The FBI's presence should not inadvertently warn him off. We have to do that when the perp is rich.

I thought back on the report from the Boston detective. Turned out he was wrong about her being a sweet kid. Apparently she wasn't. Whereas it seemed the Irish girl in the mischievous sailor dress may well have been.

My director said, "The homicide detective who is on this case—

an especially thorough man—called the crime lab two days ago. Asked them to search out a dental match again, now that we had an ID. Asked them because he couldn't find a dental record. Neither could we. He visited the dead woman's childhood dentist, the family dentist. And guess what? The dentist couldn't understand how her record came to be missing. Missing? Someone *disappeared* it. Another reason I want you to take care of this."

I had to smile.

"Delby will be here to put in order all the information we're gathering on the disappeared prostitutes for when you get back. In the meantime, enjoy Boston. Take in a Red Sox game."

He smiled. Benevolently. There would be no enjoying Boston.

⌁

I went back to the file on the missing Boston girl who now had a name: Kathleen Sullivan. Back to the file with the letter from the homicide detective, Rocky Patel. No wonder I hadn't recalled the name. I got him on the phone, introduced myself, told him the FBI had an interest in the case. Told him I'd like to talk to him right away, that I wanted to meet him at the place where the body of Kathleen Sullivan had come ashore. I needed to get a feel for his case. Then we'd talk. He said, "This is a huge surprise. Your assistance would be perfect with me. When would be best?" That's when I first noticed he had an accent of sorts. More a precision of pronunciation.

"I'm coming up tomorrow. My plane gets in at eight-thirty in the morning."

"Tomorrow? The FBI certainly *does* have an interest then. I'll pick you up. Your flight information?"

I asked Delby to call him with the flight information.

Delby said, "Okey-doke," and then told me she had Auerbach on the line. My man Auerbach at the crime lab peruses information in his computer for fun. He gets his assigned work finished, and then he peruses just the way I peruse the material in my brain. Like me, sometimes he peruses all night. His skin is dead white. Auerbach doesn't take in the light of day for weeks at a time. Delby suspects Auerbach is a vampire. A celibate one.

Auerbach's theory is that it is possible to find a needle in a haystack, and you should be shot if you're afraid to tackle a haystack. "It's what they pay us for," he tells the skeptics.

He's not only willing to put in the time required to find a needle in a haystack, he's even more dedicated than that because what Auerbach figures he's paid for is to *roll* in haystacks till he feels a stab somewhere in his body. He is actually the one who taught me the value of listening and observing, in addition to the more aggressive tactics I might use, and to follow up on details that appear awry, no matter how innocuous they might seem. My list of the awry is alphabetical; he's programmed his computer to code his own list in some way no one will ever crack unless they torture him. Even then.

Now Delby said, "I would have put him off, boss, at least till I knew what he wanted, but I'm detecting a slight choking in his voice. If he's just gagging on his potato chips, I apologize for my poor intuition."

Auerbach lives on junk food. Now, however, when I said hello, there was no sound of munching, no telltale crinkle of a cellophane bag; he was gagging on his excitement. He told me I had to squeeze in a class he was giving for certain new lab employees. The subject matter would have a bearing on the Boston body situation.

I asked, "How?"

"What I've got here is big, Poppy. It's very big, and you'll want to see it unfold."

I never second-guess Auerbach. When I'd first arrived at the crime lab, newer lab employees were friends or relatives of old lab employees. The new and the old had two things in common—patronage connections and no credentials. I replaced all of them. The very first new hire was the enthusiastic Auerbach, who I stole from IBM research, where he'd already been stolen from academe, a practice IBM continues to deny, I don't know why. He is my chief puzzle man. Give him puzzle pieces, and even if ninety percent of the puzzle is missing, he puts together what's left and re-creates what's not there. I find him to be one extraordinary magician, and I congratulate myself almost every day for the powers of persuasion demonstrated in enticing him to sign on. Actually, it was easy.

I told him I'd give him whatever he asked for. Also, as it turned out, his father is a cop. His grandfather was a cop. His uncles are cops. His brother's a cop. He'd recently gotten word that his sister decided against graduate school—she would not follow in his scholarly footsteps; she wanted to be a cop too. He said to me, "I realized I had the same nagging need she described to me. I want to enforce the law. But I wouldn't make a good cop. I like to hunker down in caves. So I talked to them—my family—about your offer. Vote was unanimous."

I asked him, by the way, what his mother did.

He smiled.

She's a cop.

His unbridled enthusiasm—and whoever stuck the word *unbridled* in front of *enthusiasm* must have known Auerbach—arose from the lack of fulfillment he experienced his entire life until he became a federal agent, and he's making up for it. But it sometimes gets the best of him, and then I have to rein him in. He'll go outside the puzzle and bring in extra stuff, which sometimes obfuscates the issue at hand. Once, early on, I had to say, "It's not about your enjoyment that you're doing this. Personal satisfaction is secondary." He was genuinely contrite.

Lately, he's been doing exercises to calm himself, to keep his vision directed rather than overreaching. I was in the lab recently, and he was on the floor in some convoluted Yoga position breathing with his abdominal muscles. I had to talk to his feet.

Now, on the phone, his voice seemed to be caught entirely in his throat. "Poppy, I was intending to show this to you alone, but there are so many lessons to be learned. You know how you overlook the individual trees because you're sizing up the forest? I want to show the new recruits how looking at each and every tree is far more important than what the forest has to say. Fuck the forest."

His enthusiasm just overflows. Still, I almost said no to his invitation because I'd assumed I'd hear a forensic discourse showing the number of days the Boston girl had been in the water and, I hoped, how she died—that beyond the fact that she'd drowned, the autopsy revealed how she'd come to drown. Auerbach knew I wanted that very carefully verified. He knew I'd be interested in the verification itself. That's what he was wanting to show me. I decided I simply had to trust his reasons for showing rather than telling. Besides that, I enjoy going to the projection room once in a while.

*Projection room* is an old name for a new theater with wide, comfortable chairs. We now project computer images instead of those grainy, barely discernible black-and-white transparencies via an overhead projector. Also, an overhead projector never allowed the technician to zoom in, to enhance, to turn scrambled eggs back into raw eggs in their unbroken shells. I love the shows Auerbach puts on. I had an hour to spare, so I told him okay, I'd be there. Once I'd agreed, I got back to Delby. I said, "It wasn't potato chips. He was choking on excitement."

"That should have been my vote. Anyhoo, what special stuff do you want me doing while you're in Boston?"

"Haunt the director a little bit. Anything on the prostitution business—find out if there's anything you're not getting. Stay on top of it and make sure I know it all as it's happening. Call me as often as necessary."

"You know I'll be doing that anyway, right, boss?"

"Yes, Delby, I know. Want to sit in on Auerbach?"

"I do, I do."

〰

Auerbach had invited our director too, who'd sent his chief administrator—James—a man who happens to be his closest associate, someone he brought up with him when he took the job. The director had also heard the catch in Auerbach's voice, which was why he'd sent his top dog, the eyes and ears of the FBI, a finger always on its pulse. Delby has said James *is* the pulse. She's right.

Until our new director and his James came along, the FBI had no pulse. It had tics.

"Hey, Poppy," he called out.

"Hey, James."

"And how are you, Delby?"

"Fine, sir. You?"

"I'll be fine if the chemistry show is a good one. The Boston shipping family is breathing down our necks. They want this taken care of . . . cleanly. Meaning no ruffling of their feathers. I told them our best independent agent had been placed in charge of the case. I'm glad you're going to be there, Poppy. What I didn't tell them is that you don't do anything cleanly. Screw them. They need to be ruffled up."

From what I've found, in the days of J. Edgar, this particular shipping family's involvement would no doubt have meant the girl's body evaporating into thin air; forget ever finding it in a potter's field, which is what the Boston PD had managed to do. And the police reports would have vaporized as well.

Then James asked, "So what's this business about some woman dying in Ireland three decades ago?"

I said, "Just a private interest of mine, James."

"Then why do I know about it?"

"Because you know everything."

Auerbach was hunkered down in the back of the projection room behind his equipment; in front of the equipment were twenty rows of seats, a dozen across, all filled with recruits who would be dispersed around the world. Auerbach reminded me a lot of Captain Kirk and his *Enterprise,* except Auerbach had on jeans and a T-shirt with a couple of faded words on it. I squinted. J. GEILS BAND. The oldies stations he listens to aren't old enough for me.

James, Delby, and I stood around Auerbach, peering down over his shoulder at his monitor. We like to watch what he does with his hands as well as the stuff that comes up on the big screen. We'll watch his monitor, then glance up to where he has his dancing arrow doing the James Brown. Also, with us right behind him, he could whisper stuff to us that might muddle his recruits. He meant to simply dazzle them, not confuse them.

The opening half-minute was filled with the usual preliminaries of welcome and then what was known: The victim had drowned and the alcohol she'd drunk had been spiked with Xanax. Not the big show quite yet, since so many people love their Xanax these days; just the beginning of the path into the haystack. But then he went on to tell his assembled crew-to-be the story of Danny O'Neill's Irish girl, of all things. He told them nothing had been known of the facts of her death but that recently her body had been exhumed and he came to be in possession of tissue samples of his choice. So our director had obviously seen to the gardai. Now Auerbach wanted the recruits to hear the anecdotal information he had via my conversation with Nuala O'Neill. He mentioned that the Irish girl and the Boston girl were both pregnant.

James whispered to me, "Where's he going with this?"

"I wish I knew." No wonder he wanted me there: Something was about to break.

Auerbach was a closet cinematographer. He began with a trailer, a Disney fantasia, an artistic interpretation of the human DNA, the screen filled with the neon strings of the double helix, with bright bouncing balls of spiraling molecules of DNA, their many thousands of genes hugging each other at points along the stretch of the helix—neatly packaged chromosomes.

Auerbach showed chromosome sequences that inform a human being to develop arms rather than wings, feet instead of hooves, two nipples rather than two rows of four pairs. Then, different sequences along the chain that varied only slightly. His little white arrow did its dance across the screen as he spoke. He clicked to a particular sequence: "This variation means blue eyes"—*click*—"this, brown." He asked if we could see how the arrangements differed, though subtly. Yes.

"These divergences are what make us exclusive of each other, each of us distinct."

The differences in arrangements were to me like musical arrangements. The Beatles singing "Fool on the Hill" compared with Brasil '66 giving the song the sex of the samba.

"So we take the DNA from biological evidence and match it against corresponding samples from, say, hair in a brush or a cheek swab from a relative. If a probed set of four or five matches are the same in each, we've got the same person. The more probes, the stronger the odds of being absolutely sure."

*Click.*

Up came the picture of a tooth.

"The most optimal place to extract DNA, the inner pulp of teeth. Alas, X-ray exposure destroys DNA. Besides that concern, we have to pulverize a tooth. But because of a tooth's diagnostic value—teeth being as distinctive as DNA markers—we don't like to do that.

"DNA from a living person makes our job simple. A cheek swab is all that's required. Someday, all babies will have cheek swabs taken directly after birth, right there in the delivery room, and the result will be registered and stored for when law enforcement might call for it. Naturally, we'll have to figure out how to hide such information from the health insurance industry. And big brother." A glance to the politician, James.

Titters arising.

*Click.*

A picture of two white shards.

"Take a look at these two samples. This picture I'm showing you are bone samples from the two women, both drowned, one in Ireland in 1972 and one in the United States—Boston—a year and a half ago."

He compared the probes he'd arranged. His arrow kept zipping back and forth between the packages of chromosomes. "As you can see, not even close. Clearly two unrelated people."

Clearly.

*Click.*

A picture of two white dots—pinheads.

"These are the earliest beginnings of human teeth. Fetal teeth, undamaged by X rays, from the fetuses of the two women. If either mother had visited a dentist during the months their fetuses were developing, they'd have been protected by the lead apron."

I saw James glance at his watch just as I was glancing at mine, both of us losing patience. Maybe James had a plane to catch this morning too. What possible point was Auerbach going to make that would have any real value? Delby, however, was mesmerized, so relieved she wasn't having to look at photographs of a drowned corpse or, worse, autopsy shots. Once she said to me, "Any Tom, Dick, or Harry can look at these pictures. Don't dead people have rights?"

None, though not according to the Catholic Church, as Nuala O'Neill had informed me.

*Click.*

Dancing colored balls. "These are sets of markers, five sets, placed side by side. After pulverizing the tiny bits of developing teeth I just showed you, powdering them via a centrifuge, incubating them, buffering by extractive material and leaving them to rest in order to absorb a silicon medium, the silicon then vacuum dried, we eluted the DNA that you're looking at here.

"You have seen the difference between the DNA markers of the mothers. Here are the dozen DNA markers I have specifically separated out from the fetal teeth: on the left those from the Irish fetus, and on the right those from the Boston fetus."

Auerbach's little white arrow drifted off the screen. There was no longer any need for it. These particular DNA markers from the two fetuses were identical.

Auerbach hit a switch and the bright overhead lights flashed on. The recruits all swung around to peer at him, the expressions on their faces as identical as the patterns we'd just seen. They were utterly flabbergasted and so was I. Who would have checked for matches between the two fetuses, one of them conceived thirty-odd years ago? No one. Just Auerbach.

Delby was the first to speak. "The women were sisters?"

Delby is no featherhead. But she's lay. The insidiousness of totally unanticipated drama is foreign to her. As soon as she spoke the words, she squinted at the big screen dimmed by the overhead lights and announced to all of us that she was an idiot.

Auerbach said, "Actually, even though what you instinctively conjectured is invalid, your words contain irony, Delby. It's the fetuses who were sisters. Half sisters, obviously."

A waxing glow on the faces of the recruits reflected the pleasure that was rising in them, knowing they would work under a man whose creative mind would take them beyond the depths of their own powers of imagination. They gave in to the need to stand up and applaud their new boss more vigorously. James, Delby, and I joined in the ovation. Auerbach put his hand up. "Just another slant on your basic paternity test. Hundreds of labs do the same thing every day of the week."

But that wasn't what we were applauding, and he knew it. No one, anywhere, ever, would have taken the extra time to compare the DNA of the two fetuses. We seldom had time to do things to no purpose. But Auerbach needed no purpose. During the ovation, James leaned his head toward mine and whispered, "Jesus H. Fucking Christ."

My feeling exactly. James was anticipating the hell that was about to break loose—and was as shamelessly overjoyed as I was. Not only did we have a little extra biological help in solving a crime, the discovery that a crime probably existed where there had been no concrete suspicion of a crime in the first place was a thrill.

Like a good RN who wants a wheelchair-bound patient to know she's listening to him, I squatted down next to Auerbach's chair so that my face was level with his. I would not hover above him while he was closing down his computer, getting things in order so he could move on. I wouldn't let him move on quite yet.

"Anything you've been apprehensive about asking for?"

"Yes."

"What?"

His eyes met mine. "Poppy, we can copy stretches of DNA to produce a ton of usable quantities. We can do it pretty fast. But our DNA database is the tip of the iceberg. DNA chip technology is about ready to explode. Thousands of DNA sequences can be embedded in a single chip that will allow for rapid analysis via hundreds of probes. We'll be able to—"

"Please get to whatever the hell it is you're talking about. I've got to catch a plane."

"The technology is *about* ready. But it's possible that I can get my hands on—"

"Do it, Auerbach. Be first in line. Under the auspices of my division."

Independent agencies never order anything outside of manpower. Our budget was in the black. Auerbach's was so far beyond red, the budget committee was wanting his head, damn fools.

James was squatting too. He said to Auerbach, "You'll have my stamp."

Then James was up. "Till we meet again, Poppy." A nod and smile to Delby, and he was off.

***

On the way back to my office, Delby said, "Who'd have dreamed such a thing?"

"Auerbach."

"Boss?" She stopped walking. We had been scurrying down a corridor. I put on the brakes.

"What?"

"I'm sorry if I embarrassed you."

Damn.

"Delby, you voiced what probably ran through several people's heads before your ensuing thinking meant it was too late to censor yourself. You don't censor what's coming across your brain; out it comes. Maybe these chemists learned to examine their thoughts when they were in graduate school at MIT while you were a teenager having babies. Who knows? What I do know is, I need you *because* you skipped the class that teaches censoring yourself. Someone down the line is going to suggest what you said, I have no doubt. I'll be prepared."

Her agony melted away. "*Prepared* means you won't call the person an idiot? Like I called myself before anyone else had a chance?"

She's too hard on herself. I said, "Depends on who might suggest the women were sisters. If it's someone I need to take down—someone who actually *is* an idiot—I might. Whatever works."

She looked at me. She laughed first, and then so did I. We gave each other a hug. We continued on down the corridor arm-in-arm, still laughing. We have a very professional relationship. Professional chums.

~~~

I called Detective Patel from Dulles.

"You're headed elsewhere, after all. Am I right?"

"No. I just wanted you to know we'll be meeting up with a Boston fire marshal right after you show me where the body washed up."

"Are we? Which fire marshal?"

"Danny O'Neill."

"I see. This should be very good. Earlier, when you called me, I sat holding my phone in wonder: How did I come to be at the receiving end of the attention of someone of your stature? I knew your position with the FBI because, a year and a half ago, I researched personally who I should send my letter to. And now of course I realize the stature of our newly identified drowned girl; it is nothing to sneeze at. But Danny O'Neill? I suspected this case might be more complex than meets the eye. So where does the fire marshal's interest lie? I don't believe the drowning victim was a fire starter."

"Long story, Detective. Can you wait on it till the three of us meet?"

"Well, why not?"

"Where is a good place to tell him to find us?"

"My office will do. I'll see that I'm—"

I can't stand police precincts. "Someplace without commotion."

"All right, then. There's a bar at the end of Hancock Beach, a bar that caters to fishermen. The fishermen will have left for the day. The owner will get us some breakfast."

"A bar that serves breakfast?"

"It's open twenty-four hours. The bartender lives in the bar. And do I understand Marshal O'Neill will join us on our beach walk prior to breakfast?"

"No, he won't. He's not official. He just has an interest."

"Then tell him John's at Hancock Beach. Tell him around ten o'clock. I look forward to our meeting."

"So do I. See you at the airport. Thanks, Detective."

"You're welcome, Agent."

I called Danny. He'd heard about the recent ID on the harbor drowning victim. I said, "I need to see you, to talk to you about this girl, Kathleen Sullivan. I'm coming to Boston tomorrow."

He said, "My mum isn't interested in every body that washes ashore, Poppy."

"She'll be interested in this one, and so will you."

"I know there are coincidences. I know about studying parallel cases. But I don't really—"

"Danny."

First there was a pause and then he said, "All right. Sure. What the hell is my problem? Poppy Rice is coming to Boston and I'll get to see her."

I told him where and when.

"Okay, then."

And I wanted to see him too. Without his mum taking up the rear.

# 5

Rocky and I were silent for a while, walking Hancock Beach together amid the dead horseshoe crabs after he'd finished telling me all he knew. He wore loafers, stepped carefully. Bits of seaweed stuck to them. I was wishing I had on rubber boots, what with the disposable diapers, hypodermic needles, and smattering of used condoms. An especially humid morning, so unlike the cold day the Boston girl's body had come ashore. Even though we now had a name for her, I was still thinking of her that way—the Boston girl—so as to differentiate her from Nuala's Irish girl.

August in the Northeast is almost as hot and sticky as Houston. I didn't want to think what it would be like at noon. A humid wind blew the detective's bone-straight charcoal hair back off his face and turned mine to frizzy, long spirals. The detective and I swatted at mosquitoes, horseflies, and gnats, and we'd been forced to pause in our conversation every few minutes while we waited for a jet to miss us. We'd watch until it had flown the hundred yards between where we stood and the runway where its wheels touched down. The detective never batted an eyelash, whereas the whole time we were on the beach I very much looked forward to when we'd take shelter and end the risk of being clipped.

"So Rocky, who made the call to the police? I mean, someone went to the trouble of taking her chart from her dentist's office. She obviously wasn't supposed to be ID'd."

"The call came from a public phone in Cambridge. The youngest of Kathleen Sullivan's family is a first-year student at Harvard. A very bright boy without doubt, but still only eighteen. Probably he was the caller, suspected something, felt guilty about not coming forward sooner."

"Maybe didn't feel guilty. Maybe didn't like his uncle. Wanted to shake things up."

"Maybe. But I have been ordered not to make such an accusation since it would not be based on concrete fact. The ramification of such an accusation will prove too great a distraction to the investigation."

Yeah. "I hate when money deflects the cause of justice."

He was quiet. He decided not to go there. Instead, he said, "Since there is no verb *to hate* in my first language, I have determined that feelings of hatred should be supplanted."

"You have? You can hate the Ku Klux Klan, can't you? I mean, it's normal."

"If by normal you mean instinctive, no, it is not. It is a learned emotion."

"According to who?"

"Vishnu."

Oh.

"Rocky?"

"Yes?"

I pointed. "Is that the bar?"

There was a decrepit little building at the end of the beach. The remains of a couple of other buildings beyond the bar were in various stages of decay. A car was pulling onto the sandy lot. Danny got out.

"Yes, that's John's. Then we are through here, Agent? Oh. Excuse me. Poppy."

"Yes."

"Then on to the Boston Irish temperament."

"I take it you don't relish the idea."

"But I do. In fact, I love it. Remember, I have married it."

Inside the bar, Danny was sitting at a table under an open window, a fan nearby blowing on him. He'd been watching us while we walked. He stood, shook my hand, said hello to the detective, and shook his. They were two people who had made an acquaintance at some point but who didn't know each other well.

We sat down and John called out from behind the bar, "Coffee?"

We said yes.

"Breakfast?"

We said yes. He didn't bring menus, just started cracking eggs.

"Rocky, here's why Danny is with us. Because I have some pretty astonishing news to add to your investigation, and to a personal investigation Danny's family has taken on, too. In Ireland. So before I tell you my story, Danny has to tell one of his own."

Rocky said, "Excuse me. This family story is connected to the girl who came to shore out there?" He looked out the window across the expanse of dirty beach. "To Kathy Sullivan?"

Kathy, not Kathleen.

"Yes."

Danny looked out the window, too, as if she were still lying there. Then he said, "Listen, Poppy, I didn't want to involve anyone else. I don't think Detective Patel needs to be—"

"Danny, would I have arranged all this without good reason?"

John brought the coffee, a jug of it plus three mugs. We helped ourselves. Danny said, "I'm willing to hear the reason. But do I have to—?"

"Yes."

"All right, then."

Rocky looked at his watch. "How long should I plan on?"

I said, "The man's Irish. He has a certain temperament. Let's hope he can finish sometime this month."

Danny said, "I love getting picked on."

John, the barman, was bringing over three platters of food: fried eggs, pancakes—each one an inch thick—bacon and sausage, potatoes, stewed tomatoes. He left and came back with a stack of toast.

I said, "Go ahead, Danny," and Danny went ahead as soon as Rocky stuck his fork into the middle of an egg yolk. The yellow poured forth. We all dug in, presently offering each other trades once it became apparent that Rocky had vegetarian leanings—some of our potatoes for Rocky's bacon and sausage, which he'd pushed aside, our end of the deal the far better one.

Danny said, "I'll keep it to a nutshell." And he did. Coconut shell. The same story that he and Nuala O'Neill told me minus the puffin banding. All our plates were three-quarters empty when he'd finished.

The detective said, "This was over thirty years ago, correct?"

"Yes."

"And, Poppy, you're here with a connection between the two deaths? Exactly what? The manner of death? Something that will give us, both of us, Danny and me, a clearer path?"

He was trying to establish order, so, yes, a clearer path was exactly what I wanted to give both of them.

I said, "The manner of death was simple in both cases. Someone killed them, or they committed suicide, or they had an accident. Only one's a crime. We need to find out which it was."

Rocky said, "Suicide is what I believe. We've just found out the Sullivan girl had everything to die for. Your body in Ireland had but a pregnancy. However, an unmarried pregnant woman in Ireland? Very difficult for her."

Danny put down his fork and knife. "We don't know if she was unmarried. We don't know yet who she was. We don't know anything about her beyond her pregnancy."

The detective was using two pieces of toast to wipe up the last of the yolk from four eggs. He sluiced it all down with a slug of coffee, wiped his chin with a paper napkin, and said, "Both the fire marshal and I know very little, Poppy. So now it is time to hear of the connection in order that I may, hopefully, feel some optimism."

I put my fork down. There was one piece of toast left. I'm always one for dessert, even a quasi-dessert after breakfast. I took the last of the toast, opened a little packet of grape jelly, spread it on, took a bite. They waited, watching, focused on me and my toast.

"I want to spring this on both of you the way it was sprung on me. I want us all at the starting line together. And I want us to stay together until we reach the finish without anyone trying to beat the other guys out. I don't just believe that two heads are better than one, I believe the more heads the merrier. I'm about to become involved with a case in Washington where there will be a lot of people trying to keep secrets. Same problem here—secrecy has reigned. Reigned to the point where there has been no justice in thirty years' time for a young Irishwoman, and none in a year and a half for Kathleen Sullivan. Some of the victims in this next case I'll be taking up are children. Here, we have no children. But we have fetal tissue." I ate the final corner of toast and jelly. They watched me chew, trying to dope out what the hell I was talking about.

"I need you both with me. I don't want any vigilantes screwing me up."

That they understood. Danny said, "She means me."

And Rocky. "I know she doesn't mean me."

"And I don't want a wishful spin getting in the way." I said that because I was thinking *sweet kid,* and the detective had just referred to Kathleen Sullivan as Kathy.

Rocky raised an eyebrow. "Now she means me. You have ruled out accident and suicide, haven't you?"

"Pretty much."

"Why? And what's it to do with fetal tissue? Tell us."

"We found a match between the paternal DNA markers of the two fetuses."

There was no Delby on hand to break the long ensuing silence. It was Rocky who finally checked in. He said what James had whispered in my ear, the exact same unholy epithet, only Rocky pronounced each syllable as though he were a poet reading a line of his work whereas James had belted it out.

Danny let the revelation sink in a little longer than the detective had, controlled any words of shock, and once he'd suppressed those, let it sink in longer yet. He looked to me, to the detective, and to me again, and then he spoke. Forcefully, loud enough for the barman to startle. Danny said, "This revolts me."

Revulsion is usually unexpressed in those of us who work the mines of justice. Simply feeling revulsion and not putting it into words allows us to keep going back down into those dark, miserable tunnels. I figure when I'm no longer revolted I won't be any good in the mines. But I'd never jinx myself by saying what Danny had said aloud. There was such a sadness in his voice too, calling whatever he was feeling *revulsion*.

Then he said, "Two very young women were killed, and someone is protecting the killer."

Rocky asked what he meant by that.

But Danny was staring into the table, thinking. So I asked what he meant by that too.

He looked up at me. "Poppy, my mum revealed something more to me when she came for her visit, after we'd seen you. She couldn't tell me from Ireland. She had to tell me in person, or otherwise I'd have been on the next flight to Limerick, where I wouldn't have been restrained by any gardai. And she didn't want you to know because one favor was more than she dreamed of."

He knocked down what was left in his glass.

"When my mother was returning from Galway to Inishmore on the ferry, the day she'd seen the gardai, she was pushed from the deck into the sea."

The deep blue of his eyes became deeper still.

"Pushed?"

"Yes." For a moment he was back in Ireland, again with the rhythm of his mother's speech in his words. "And 'tis a rough sea. A killer sea, truth be told." And then he became American again. "She tried to calm me before my shock could turn to lack of restraint. She reminded me how all the children of Aran learn what to do when washed into the sea, as we can be washed from a rock collecting cockles just as surely as my father was washed away banding the puffins."

Instead of wondering aloud as to Nuala's belief that her husband had been pushed into the sea, or whether Nuala herself had actually been pushed from the ferry and thereby insulting Danny and ending this entirely intriguing episode, I asked innocently, "What exactly are the children taught to do?"

Rocky almost jumped in—to brush me aside—but he caught my glance and contained his impatience. Danny said, "Tread water while we pull off our shoes and clothes and then float until saved, praying all the while a boat saves us rather than a band of angels."

"Or the fairies, who you will owe plenty to."

He couldn't help but smile; he relaxed just a little bit.

I'd spent twelve hours with Danny once, the kind of progressively drunken hours where lonely people feel free to reveal truths about themselves. I hadn't paid too close attention to his blathering but now I remembered some of it—the more romantic details. He'd told me that, in Ireland, people believed, when God banished Lucifer from Heaven and Lucifer fell to what is Hell, not all his angel side-kicks who fell along with him plunged to the depths. Some were caught on a breeze and landed on earth, where they came to be called fairies. The Brothers Grimm and Walt Disney knew all fairies weren't good.

I said, thinking of the devil fairies, "Who does your mother think pushed her?"

He didn't hesitate. "Someone who knew the identity of the pregnant girl or knew who killed her. Someone tipped off by the gardai. But my mum didn't ask you to find out who pushed her. She will find that out for herself. It's the girl's name she wants."

Rocky said, "I can only say I'm relieved your mother wasn't pushed from a ferry in Boston Harbor."

I asked Danny, "What about Nuala's welfare when you go back home?"

"I've taken care of that. No one's to go within a hundred feet of my mother's shadow without our men knowing about it."

He wasn't talking about his Boston firefighters.

"Danny, does the gardai know yet?"

"They received a report from my office." Then he said to Rocky, "You've had cause to work with the gardai then?"

"We're in Boston, are we not?"

"It isn't easy."

"They do things differently."

Danny said, "And I would like to drink to that. A breakfast Guinness all around?"

Rocky said, "I abstain."

Too early for me.

Danny called for more coffee.

Then I got down to business. "We know who the Boston girl is. We don't know who the Irish girl is. Not yet. The key is that this information my lab has turned up must be kept secret, no matter that I just spoke ill of secrets. It is a trump card that we'll need when we've got our hands on the man who impregnated the two women."

I wasn't sure if Rocky knew how serious I was about that. Danny did, which is why he said nothing. So I said *detective,* this time, not *Rocky.* "Detective, you have no compunction about keeping this information from your superiors?"

"I'll file my report late. I have no compunction, Agent. You do what you have to do; so will I. We're on the same side."

Danny was looking down into his cup.

"Danny?"

He took his time looking up again. "Poppy, you made a decision to include me in what you've learned. I will respect anything and everything you ask."

"As for the gardai . . . well, we'll cross that bridge when it rears its head."

Danny said, "If the protector is in Ireland, is Irish, the gardai will have their faces in ours, and if they determine they've got a security issue, they'll continue to protect the protector. They'll—"

Rocky interrupted him. "Security, Danny? You suspect another agenda in all this, I can see. But it's not my agenda. Kathy Sullivan is my agenda, just so you know."

So I said, "Rocky, Kathleen Sullivan might not have died if the gardai had done their job thirty-odd years ago. The attempt on Danny's mother's life may well connect his agenda to ours."

Danny's voice became a few decibels lower. "I'll feel free to say it again, Detective Patel. The protector is real, and he's still trying to kill people."

"Or another person is connected more indirectly, someone simply trying to scare people off. If your mother weaves together the death of Kathleen Sullivan with the Irishwoman, the gardai will be more likely to—"

My turn. Everything had to be sorted out and stay sorted out.

"Listen, we have to do this incrementally. We start with what's sitting on top of this haystack before we burrow in looking for needles. Listen, Danny. Rocky and I have people who can sift the hay for us. You are on your own. We have the evidence that the same man fathered the babies of the two women. So somewhere out there is a man who, when he was, say, twenty, got a girl pregnant and then she either committed suicide or he—or maybe even someone else, a protector—killed her. And yes, maybe she accidentally *fell* into the ocean. But meanwhile, that same man left Ireland, came to the States, and got another girl pregnant the winter of last year. She also fell, jumped, or was pushed into the sea. The first idea—the accident— we can rule out, based on how ludicrous such a coincidence is. And suicide is just a little too Victorian for me; these women weren't fourteen years old, they were adults—"

Danny interrupted. "They were Irish."

"One was Irish."

"The American's last name is Sullivan? She was Irish."

"Still, I would like our starting point to be the assumption that whoever impregnated them killed them and then dumped their bodies into the water. So now we've got this guy; let's say he's in his fifties. That at least narrows down our search to some extent. We'll assume a middle-aged lothario killer. We have found, therefore, the first needle in our haystack.

"Now let me give you the few details I haven't had the chance to get to yet. It's time to fill Rocky in entirely so he knows everything I know. I've found that the dead Irish girl came to the United States for a short time in 1968. Her brother was an American citizen who enlisted in the navy that same year. We'll find out who she is because a fax will soon come from the Pentagon with an ID on the brother. The navy will give my office whatever information they have, and then my fact-checkers will search her out from there. Slightly easier than rummaging through haystacks."

Patel said, "And can you tell me something about *my* girl that I don't know yet?"

"No. We learned yesterday what you learned: who she is. I'm going to speak to her family as soon as I can see them."

"I've done that."

"But you spoke to her father."

"How did you know that?"

"Guessed. A guess based on the ongoing tradition of chauvinism."

He smiled. "I can vouch for the universality of that tradition. The assumption that the father will be stronger than the mother."

"What did the dead girl's father tell you?"

"He said they hadn't seen or heard from her in two years."

"Two years up till now?"

"Yes."

"That means six months before her death. And the uncle who didn't tell the police the body was hers. Which side of the family?"

"The mother's brother. I talked to him too."

"And what did he say?"

His gaze drifted for just a second and then came back.

"What?"

"He knew it was Kathleen when he viewed the body. But he told the police her hair was always long, fell below her shoulders. The corpse had short, cropped hair so he told them no, it wasn't her. And he told the family the remains were so mutilated he didn't realize it was her. To me, he claimed the lie to the police and the lie to the family were to avoid destroying his family further than the girl had already done while alive. He apologized. Then he asked me if we could let Kathleen Sullivan finally rest in peace."

"Is this guy in his fifties?"

"Yes."

"Then I guess we check to see if he spent some time in Ireland as a young man."

"I doubt we have an international serial killer, Poppy, one who impregnated and killed his own niece, though I am not fool enough ever to eliminate the unlikely. But here's what we do have—something you obviously don't know—and it is a large problem."

"What?"

"This uncle is the circuit court judge for the fifth district. A federal judge. His name is Sean Scanlon. A fairly recent appointment."

Danny sucked in his breath. "*That* Sullivan family?"

And I sucked in mine. "My director never told me that."

"Well"—Rocky gave a little sigh—"all the information just hadn't filtered up to your director yet."

No? Then a head would roll or was maybe rolling already. But the end wouldn't have been any different. I was here.

"But, Danny, I'm afraid it's so. *That* Sullivan family. He is Rosemary Sullivan's brother."

Danny said, "Shit."

I asked him, "Who's Rosemary Sullivan?"

"The dead girl's mother. Scanlon's sister. She and her husband raise large funds for certain political candidates, not just local politicians—though that's the claim they make—but politicians throughout the country. Republican candidates who have a shot at dislodging Democrats holding office; that's their specialty. And so the family got a gift, a federal appointment. When it comes to appointing judges, political connections are paramount. The way it is. Forget skill, forget independence, forget honesty."

Okay. "So what has this family got against Democrats, Danny? I mean . . . Scanlon? They're Boston Irish."

"The grandfather—Rosemary and Sean's grandfather—grew up with Joe Kennedy. Grew up to become his business partner. They built shipyards together. Mightily successful. Then Joe decided he liked bright lights, so he went to Hollywood. This was in the thirties. He invested in RKO and cut Scanlon out. Joe Kennedy didn't have lineage, but once he added glamour to his life it was the ticket he needed to get into national politics. Scanlon found himself left high and dry, a nobody. Rich, but still a nobody. The vestige of an old feud is what the Scanlons have against Democrats."

He was quiet. He seemed to be thinking about what he'd said and banged his fist on the table. The bartender's eyes flickered toward us and away again. Then Danny addressed Rocky Patel specifically.

"Listen to me, Patel, you either blow the miserable fucking whistle on this guy—this *judge*—or watch me do it. Find out where he really is in all this."

The detective finally stopped eating. "Don't insult me, Marshal. I've blown the whistle. Loudly. I confronted Scanlon immediately, and when I finished letting him shed his crocodile tears, I told him that the body had not been disfigured; her face was preserved by the coldness of the water and the dearth of marine life in the harbor. So that's when he changed his story, admitted what he did and why he did it, and showed remorse for a foolish decision. He is presenting his case to the media as we speak. A press conference. I've got two officers there, under cover, keeping their ears open, watching Sean Scanlon's sister and brother-in-law, how they might be protecting him, ready to spin if there's a slip of the tongue. The plan is for him to make a public apology to them. And then they're all three going to thank the police for finding Kathleen, for all the work we did in our attempts to identify her.

"So the actions he took most likely speak to his true motives—he simply didn't want a dead body to interfere with his federal appointment. In the end, Sean Scanlon will be guilty of a misdemeanor: misidentification. And no doubt he will be convincing in showing the misidentification was certainly not some deliberate malfeasance. The sort of mea culpa that has been planned will go a long way. He'll be the recipient of much sympathy, though his dead niece will receive little or none. Kathleen Sullivan was an addict, a dealer, a hooker. He will not be so much as censured." Rocky picked up his napkin, wiped his face, folded the napkin, and laid it on his plate. "I have work to do."

His gesture actually had a lot in common with Danny slamming down his fist. I said, "We all have work to do, so what? It won't help for you to get agitated, Detective."

He leaned back into his chair. "As much as I detest money impugning the quest for justice, I dislike it far more when politics impugns."

He used the words *detest* and *dislike,* but he was thinking *hate.*

I said, "But in this case, the impugning brought the Boston girl to my director's attention. So let's stick with what's immediately at hand. Our job right now is to determine the circumstances behind the deaths of two young women attracted to the same man, who got them both pregnant. Beyond the sweetness of their faces. Besides the red hair."

Danny said, "Half the women in Boston have red hair. And they're all sweet, I'll vouch for that."

"Then let's hope we find more coincidences. The Pentagon will have information that could lead to the identity of the Irishwoman. But you, Rocky, must track the Sullivan girl's steps from the final time the family saw her through to the last person who saw her before her death. Second to last, assuming a killer who will naturally be elusive. And you'll keep me posted."

"And so I will. Here is my first posting. Kathleen Sullivan's hair was cut off at the time she died."

"How do you know that?"

"Those clammers who were standing around her body when the police arrived. A couple of them contacted our office a few days afterward, once they'd had time to settle down and think. Long clumps of human hair washed up in the week before her body was found. Red hair. So in some sort of irrational last-ditch attempt to confuse an identity in case she was found, whoever lured her to the sea cut her hair off before he got rid of her.

"In the last few days I have tried to envision that beach the day I investigated the crime scene. I recalled the debris of the place, not too different from what you see now." He gestured out the window. "Today, Poppy, we saw bits of net tangled with seaweed. But that day, I saw rope. So now I am forgetting the word *suicide.* The word *accident.* I am thinking she was probably weighted down with something tied to a rope. The rope came loose. Killers are often in a hurry. This killer was not in so big a hurry to be inefficient; he took the time to cut off her hair. He was just no good at tying knots in heavy rope. Suicides who mean business, who mean to drown themselves, don't tie themselves to weights. They think about the deed incessantly, but they actually do the deed on impulse. They fill their clothes with rocks.

"I will go back to my forensics team. See if the autopsy noted some bruises that might have been rope marks. I will look at the photos of the body carefully. Perhaps I will see rope marks myself."

I told Rocky that if there was anything I could do, he should feel free to ask me.

He said, "I will."

"I hope to cross your path many times, Rocky."

He smiled. "And I yours. Since you picked up the tab." I'd plunked a twenty-dollar bill on top of the check the barman had tossed on the table.

"Detective, I need you to know I'm going to see the girl's immediate family right away, before I head back to Washington."

He remained smiling. "Good. The commissioner told me to lay off; he didn't see a need to bother them at this time. The wake is tomorrow, the body to be released to the mortician in the morning. A few days ago, the commissioner told me I should contact only the father. And I agreed, due to the universality of chauvinism. He doesn't know I saw Judge Scanlon when I did. He doesn't know because the judge never complained. Therefore I believe the judge hides something. Whether that would be an involvement in the death of his niece or information he may be withholding remains to be seen. As yet, we have nothing. I am unable to imagine I could ask the judge for a hair of his head to test his DNA—to see if he fathered Kathleen Sullivan's fetus. Certainly not at this time."

I smiled too. So did Danny, with the image of such an unlikely scene. I suddenly had a change of heart. This detective was too good to let go. "Rocky, I'm going to let you know when I have a time set up to meet with the Sullivans. I'll be trying for tonight. I would guess they'll be together working out the funeral arrangements. I want your path to cross mine sooner rather than later. I want you there with me. I want your presence as a signal to the family that the police aren't going quietly into the night just because the FBI has stepped in. After we've met with them, just tell your commissioner I'd needed you at the meeting. Come up with a reason for not having told him before the fact."

"I'll tell him there was no answer when I called to ask his permission."

If he followed that particular plan through, it meant Rocky Patel was the kind of fellow who let the chips fall where they might. I was really liking this guy more and more—as much as I'd liked him on paper.

Danny said, "And what are you seeing for me, Poppy?"

"Frankly, I think you should go to Ireland. Friendly visit with the gardai. Fellow peace officer tipping them off rather than our dealing with their shock when they hear officially what I've told you. Then they'll owe you, Danny."

"There will be no need to go to Ireland yourself?" Danny was feeling undone. When the personal and the professional get mixed together, you lose your footing. He'd get it back. Danny would handle the gardai properly.

"Listen, if you think the FBI is needed in an official capacity, I'll surely consider doing that."

"Well then, if it turns out you do, you'll have to know how to drink a Guinness properly."

The detective stood. "I have no reason to know how to drink a Guinness properly. Don't get up, either of you." He took a card out of his pocket and handed it to me. "Use my cell phone to call me, Poppy. I'll be on the road all day. Once you have a time set up, I'll try to reach the commissioner. I shouldn't be completely reckless. I will save complete recklessness for a more crucial time. I'll tell some aide I can't let you go to the meeting without a representative from Boston PD. The aide will be the one unable to reach him." Rocky's black eyes twinkled. "Several people already owe me." He looked to Danny. "Just as the gardai will owe the marshal."

Then he was looking at that watch of his again. He headed for the door. John the bartender called out to him as he left, "See ya, coppah." Rocky waved.

Danny returned to the more pleasant business he'd touted. "There isn't anything better than a Guinness to wash down breakfast, Poppy."

Well, why not? I would humor the marshal, a man who no longer had to work the second or third shift as he did when he was a fireman. Yet he maintains an office in his old station house in addition to the one at department headquarters. At the conference where we'd met, he told me he worked extra shifts when he could fit them in, though he wasn't in any rotation. If he was at the station and the bell rang, he went out with the men. "And the woman," he'd said. "We have one." Then: "Poppy, I have no wife, no family whatever here in this country. If I keep my firefighting skills up to par while

I'm looking for arsonists or fire starters, those skills will keep me alert to the other."

I'd asked him about the differentiation, fire starter and arsonist.

He said, "To me, a fire starter is sick—fire holds a thrill for him—a pyromaniac as we used to say. But arsonists are dirty bastards. They set fires to kill, to maim, to gain."

"Gain money, you mean."

"Yes."

That conference had come to a close just prior to our having the conversation. We chatted together. While he helped me get my stuff back into boxes, the room cleared. I hadn't needed any help and we both knew it. We'd ended up going to dinner at the restaurant in the hotel adjacent to the conference center. We closed the restaurant. And then Danny asked if I'd like to see his apartment, and I asked if it was nearby. Not too far, but it was January and therefore the wind-chill outside was about two hundred degrees below zero because, after all, we were in Boston. So I asked if he'd like to see my hotel suite instead, only a few floors over our heads. Six floors. He would. The elevator didn't stop at six but we didn't notice. We didn't notice it go up to the penthouse, or the pause it made there, or the trip back down to the lobby. The doors opened; we leaped apart and walked out. Once we'd caught our breath, standing there in the dead of night in the empty lobby, we laughed like fools. On the second ride up, I remembered to press six.

Now I found myself liking the idea of another elevator ride. There is a difference between a one-night stand and a fling. A fling happens when there is more to a meeting than smiting an especially intense moment of loneliness. You move on to a fling when there is more to the fellow than meets the eye—combined with convenient logistics. Mainly, that you will not be collaborating on cheating on a wife.

Danny called out to John to bring us two stouts. Then he thought for a second and said to me, "Come to the bar, Poppy. Come watch John. The man's roots run deep. He's an expert. You should watch, so you can appreciate the skill of filling a pint and then it will taste even better."

We left our table and bellied up.

"The lady requires an appreciation of your grand bartending skills, John."

John shrugged. He put a glass under the tap. He opened the tap all the way and filled it three-quarters up. Then he walked away and washed down his counter, ignoring the Guinness altogether. He returned when the beer had gone black. Then he filled the glass the rest of the way until a head was just cresting the rim without a bit of it flowing over. He picked up the glass, held it an inch under the spout, touched the tap gently with one finger, and the narrowest stream of Guinness ran down. He swirled the glass and the outline of a shamrock crowned the stout's head. He put it in front of me. He repeated the whole process and pushed Danny's glass to him. No coasters.

Danny said, "It is important to understand, Poppy, that the head of the stout is bitter. You'll want to avoid tasting it, touching your tongue to it. The goal is to keep the shamrock intact."

I looked down at the two inches of creamy caramel foam. Enticing, if you were fond of root beer as a kid, which I had been, but I knew what he meant by *bitter*. Unpleasantly so, which is why I'd only had a Guinness stout once. But I couldn't imagine you drank a Guinness with a straw. I awaited Danny's instructions. I do enjoy a state of curiosity fulfilled, even inane curiosity.

He said, "Now first, you dip your top lip down into the glass, beneath and past the head, until you sense the stout itself. You'll feel the difference; the beer is wet, not poufy." Poufy. I loved to hear this man talk, the shadow of Ireland rising up every so often. "Then you move the foam out of the way with your top lip and tilt the glass up."

He demonstrated. I watched as a quarter of his stout disappeared. He put the glass down, the head with its shamrock still unscathed.

"See, Poppy? That is how to get the stout and none of the head, though some of the foam will attach itself to your lip." He smiled at me with his poufy new mustache. "So you wipe the foam off your mouth with your sleeve. Well . . . no. You, being a lady, you'd use the back of your hand."

He wiped his mouth on his sleeve. Before he did, I controlled the urge to lick it off him myself, bitter flavor be damned. He'd read my mind. Or probably my eyes, which were glued to his mouth. But being a gentleman with an appreciation of subtlety, he said, "So, Poppy, you'll be tempted to lick the foam from your lip with your tongue but you must maintain control, as that would defeat the purpose. You must use your hand. Now give it a try."

I followed suit, even down to emptying my glass of a quarter of the beer in one swallow. That was easy; the Guinness was delicious.

Danny glanced toward John, whose back was to us, leaned in toward me, and licked the foam from my top lip. Then he said, "Have you got time for the tour you passed up? Way back? Would you like to see the place I call home?"

I certainly would.

We finished our stouts, slid off our stools, leaving the heads of the Guinness lying neatly at the bottom of our glasses, the shamrocks only a little wobbly, and he gave me one last instruction. "Remember, in Ireland you ask for a *half*-pint. You don't want to be one of the boys."

"So if I get two half-pints, do I get charged extra?"

He laughed out loud, a rarity. "I can't imagine any Irishman sitting at the same bar with you letting you pay for your two half-pints. And if you're alone, which I would doubt, the barman won't take your money."

I called Delby from his car and told her to reach the Sullivans and tell them I'd have to see them tonight. To insinuate that I was wanted back in DC so they'd be more apt to be done with me. She called back as we entered a peninsula sticking out into the Atlantic above Boston Harbor, just a few miles or so beyond Hancock Beach. She told me she'd reached our Boston office, and an agent talked to Kathleen Sullivan's father, who directed Delby to speak to his staff. Delby and staff arranged a meeting for me before the family had dinner together. Delby said, "The staff I spoke to said *take dinner.* Six o'clock is when they'll expect you."

I told her to call staff back and let it know I'd have a local officer with me in respect of Massachusetts law. Delby said, "No such law, right, boss?"

"Right."

"And the local officer will be a fairly big shot so I'll be sure not to have his name."

"Right again, Delby. Sure you don't want to take the exam?"

"Positive, but thanks."

I reached Rocky on his cell. He agreed.

Danny reached the end of the peninsula where there was a little town surrounded on three sides by water. Danny said, "As close to Inishmore as I could find. Not terribly close, but the best I could do."

He lived on the second floor of a two-family house on the top of a rise. We climbed the stairs, and at the landing there was a window with Hancock Beach and the airport across the harbor and, just past, the city of Boston neatly laid out. He said, "Kathleen Sullivan could well have washed up on my doorstep just as my mum's girl washed up on hers."

His keys jangled and he opened the door to his apartment.

Danny collected vintage posters—his favorite, an advertisement for Guinness stout lithographed in 1898. He said, "I keep it here in the prized spot, long wall of my dining room above the sideboard, a place reserved in most Irish homes for the Last Supper. My mother shipped the sideboard to me. It was in the Inishmore cottage since her great-grandfather built it. A present when I became an American citizen. She wanted her influence upon me to be represented by the biggest thing in my new home. And she wanted it to be a *real* home. She knew there wouldn't be a place for it in my rooming house, where I was living in a very few square feet of space. Mothers have a way of manipulating."

I had to admit to myself I was with Nuala. I do like a man who has a dining room. Danny's dining room, though, was meant to be the apartment's second bedroom; it required a bit of a hike from the kitchen. Besides the sideboard, a round table for four was all that would fit. He said he mostly used his dining room for poker games. Okay.

The sideboard gleamed with waxing, with no sign of smoke burns or rings from the poker players and their beer bottles.

The fire marshal was a man who made his bed as opposed to tossing a comforter over it. I like that especially.

The sheets were from Ireland, just as he was, and like Danny they felt creamy and smooth.

# 6

I didn't know if Sean Scanlon would be with Kathleen Sullivan's immediate family that evening, but I did want to get a sense of the man. My guess, he was at best a control freak who viewed his niece's body and decided, like Rocky said, to contain damages—figured it would be better if she simply stayed disappeared. And at worst? Remained to be seen.

I called his chambers, identified myself, and he took the phone. No, he wouldn't be at the family gathering this evening, but yes, he'd be more than happy to see me. After his dreadful mistake in judgment, after all. He sounded appropriately contrite. I didn't say, You're a judge—yours is not to make mistakes in judgment.

I walked into the robing room and found a man grieving, perhaps not for his niece but for his circumstances. He wore an expression of profound sadness.

"I appreciate your taking the time to see me, Judge."

He came around the desk from where he'd been standing. "And I appreciate the attention the FBI is giving my family. My sister, my brother-in-law—all our family want to eliminate any possibility of foul play so that we can move past this. And, of course, to finally have Kathleen rest in peace. Sit down, Agent Rice."

He shook my hand, waved me into a chair, and went back to his. He saw me as a stamp of approval. The police had found nothing untoward, and my agreeing with such an assessment would end an unpleasant period of their lives, end it in a concrete fashion as well, which would come with the burial of the offender, his niece Kathleen. I wasn't there to tell him that there would still be nightmares, that members of her family would still suffer, not knowing what really happened to her and why she was such a destructive person to begin with.

I asked the pertinent question. "I would like you to tell me what exactly possessed you to lie to the authorities."

He gave me a very weak smile. He was quite a big man but gone to seed, what with the paunch and the slack jaw. His gray hair had just a little copper left to it, slicked straight back to control the curl. He was not unattractive, but his pale eyelashes and eyebrows blended into his skin, too fair and too fine, and his blue eyes were watery. If he were a woman, people would say, *She's lost her looks.* In the case of Sean Scanlon, federal district justice, he'd certainly lost them—to alcohol. It wasn't just the watery eyes, it was the bogginess of his skin. *Pickled* is not simply a derogatory epithet.

"Agent Rice, my sister produced three beautiful children. And then there was the fourth child, Kathleen. The eldest, her son, runs several businesses, is highly successful. The youngest—born years after the others—is not only as handsome as his brother, he is a scholar, a good athlete, his future the sort all of us would hope for a child. The older girl, Nora, is a beauty. Stunning. Married to a winner, an upstart who made his way to the top. A fellow who will—"

"And what does Nora do?"

Slightly stronger smile. "She chose the traditional route. She sees to her husband's domestic requirements. Like her mother. Like my own wife. But getting back to Kathleen . . . I don't mean to be harsh, Agent Rice, but every litter has its runt. She was always small for her age, a dark girl, quiet and disturbed from the beginning. She was never treated as a lost cause. Her parents, her brothers and sister, all the family tried to do their best by her. But she was just one of those people who shut others out. She created a life for herself that was too terrible for any of us to imagine or understand. I doubt we ever will."

He sighed. Such a bad actor. I said, "Did it ever occur to you that if the time came when she actually was identified, the pain it would cause her family would be so much worse than if you had been honest to begin with?"

"I don't see it as dishonesty. I see it as a matter of preservation. I see it also as a terrible mistake on my part, for the reason you have just pointed out."

"A mistake in judgment is what you said initially."

He squinted. "Yes. But I can't go back and change what happened. The family will get past it. Now I can only hope for understanding and forgiveness. I have opened my coat, fallen upon my sword."

And I thought of Rocky because I really do *hate* people who say things like that: falling on their swords. Did he think he was Mel Gibson or Russell Crowe, doing battle centuries ago? This fool couldn't *change what happened.* He was not about to take responsibility in a more substantive way.

I stood. Control freak. And if he was possibly more than that, I didn't want him to know I would be investigating him.

He wished me a safe trip back to DC. Wanted me to say hello to a few friends there if I had the chance. One friend was a member of the Supreme Court. I saw his forehead was damp. Not nerves, I didn't think. The need for a swig of something.

I gave him a smile, a real friendly one. We shook hands. Still with the smile, I reached up and touched his shoulder in a gesture of sympathy for his troubles, and he smiled back, thanking me for allowing him to express how terrible he felt.

Balding men so often have a hair or two lying on their shoulders. The one I'd pinched between my thumb and forefinger would shortly be off to Auerbach.

~~~

Led by staff, I walked past the arched entrance to the Sullivan dining room and paused. It was where the dead girl ate with her family growing up, where they'd no doubt discussed her ensuing absences from the table. The sideboard was not a hundred and fifty years old, as Danny's was. The dining table, even without its leaves, had room for twelve. *The Last Supper* in a thick gilt frame held the reserved spot on the wall. Da Vinci surely could paint a skunk. I once saw Christopher Plummer play Iago, and I knew his performance was inspired by da Vinci's Judas. The actor would pose often, in that posture of Judas, whispering in Othello's ear, telling him his wife was screwing another man and insinuating exactly what a husband should be doing about it. In my job, I always watch the fellow whose mouth is to the ear of the powerful. They are the villainous ones, as Shakespeare knew, but they are never weak like Judas. Shakespeare was a far better intuiter of human nature than Matthew, Mark, Luke, or John, who never suspected Judas till his deed was accomplished.

At this point, I was fairly accosted by the dead girl's elder brother, who didn't seem to appreciate my interest in the dining room. He cleared his throat, which dismissed staff, and brought me into a small living room. I decided it wasn't the real living room, it was a place to receive guests. A parlor. Before introducing me to the assembled gathering, he whispered into my ear, "My dead sister and her ways are not a reflection of my family," basically telling me I wasn't actually needed there and he disapproved strongly. Too bad.

Rocky Patel was already in a chair. I'd wanted him there ahead of me and he'd complied. His earlier arrival was important. I needed them to think that he was the one in charge and I was only some sort of adviser who would soon be back off to DC and out of everyone's way. I knew their mind-set; the family liked the idea of a trophy investigator to keep the Boston police in line. With the influence they held they could get the most expedient service in a distasteful situation—one of the more creative insults that police forces and the FBI are used to weathering.

When I'd first arrived at the FBI crime lab a few years back, I found a good number of people there who prided themselves on their trophy status. I excised that mind-set posthaste. The new director was doing the very same thing now with the rest of the departments, doing his mightiest to clear the dresses out of J. Edgar's closets.

I was introduced to each family member and given a seat to the side of the fireplace. The patriarch occupied the chair on the other side. I would be the guest of honor. The detective had been placed at the opposite end of the room. Divide and conquer. The elder brother sat alongside Rocky in a matching chair. On one of the two sofas, the dead girl's mother sat with the second brother, the youngest of her children, who wore a dark blazer. There was a patch on his blazer pocket, a club or school emblem. A good boy, a poster child, the kind of child a parent gets to brag about. Unlike his dead sister. Across from them, the other sister in the family, the living one, with her husband sitting very close. Had to be the son-in-law, he was so physically different from the rest—big and bearlike as opposed to tall, slim, and patrician. The son-in-law and the sister were holding hands. Actually, *he* was holding one of his wife's slender hands in both of his. Comforting her. Taking care of her.

Only the father had the flaming hair of the deceased daughter. And thinking of red hair, I saw none of them had red eyes from crying. They had probably done all the crying there was to do when the deceased was sixteen. This was a family relieved that closure had occurred, *closure* in this case meaning they believed they could officially stop agonizing about the shame and misery the dead girl had brought upon them now that the episode that was her life had come to an end. But it was not at an end, it never is. Closure is only a climax, acceptance the very elusive denouement.

Big brother introduced me to them: the father, Hugh; the mother, Rosemary; the sister, Nora; the little brother, Kieran. The father made a move to speak but the mother managed to ward him off, holding her palm up in his direction.

She said, "Agent Rice, my daughter took every illegal substance a human being can procure by the time she was fourteen years old."

Fourteen, not sixteen, was when they'd thrown in the towel. The mother was bound and determined to set the pace for the meeting, with her need for me to know it wasn't her fault that her daughter went bad. It wasn't her family's fault; it was drugs. She meant to get in the justification before she allowed her husband his turn. That's all she wanted, so she pretended she was letting herself be set aside by Hugh Sullivan's deep voice.

"We did what families will do, Agent Rice, everything possible in hopes of stopping Kathleen's self-destruction. At first, we tried to accomplish that on our own. I sent her to doctors—specialists— who put her in one rehabilitation program after another. We saw to urine tests, every other day. But she'd pay our cleaning people for their urine. She'd tape a vial of urine to her stomach and manage to give samples that weren't her own even when someone was watching her. Then she'd come home and we'd soon realize she was still using drugs, so she'd run away and we would find her yet again. One of the things I did during this futile effort was to keep an inventory of what she stole from us. That is the kind of foolish man I am. In my arrogance, I intended to subtract what she owed from her inheritance. A symbolic gesture. A reprisal. I was thinking about how I'd get even with her instead of trying to block the road she was on. I was supposed to be the adult. I was not.

"In our desire to avoid the police, we reached a point where there was nothing left to do except send her to some so-called *school* to have the evil stomped out of her. The school was in Arkansas. We wanted our two sons to go to colleges near us. But we sent Kathy to *Arkansas*. Tough love. The people there told us they would create an empty space in her heart by getting rid of the evil residing in it and then refill it with goodness and light. Dear God, it was no more than incarceration, incarceration without due process. An allowed travesty when it comes to children who have no rights."

The mother had remained angry and bitter, only interested in convincing herself that she was not responsible for her daughter's destruction, but the father's anger and bitterness had turned to cynicism and defeat.

He wasn't through, either. "She was a fragile child and we treated her as though she were a piece of steel."

His wife's nostrils flared but she didn't dispute what he said. She'd do that later.

The elder brother took up his father's thread, the one left dangling before Hugh Sullivan had expressed his failure to recognize his daughter's nature. "Tough love was the only answer, is what we were told by many people . . . by the professionals we depended upon. Of course, she managed to escape from the school in Arkansas within a week. She—"

Hugh interrupted him. "It was not a school. It was a prison."

The son ignored his father. "She tricked a guard. She tricked him by having sex with him. Several times. Once she learned his sleep patterns, she just walked out. They didn't tell us for a month.

And when they finally did, their excuse was that they thought they'd find her."

I asked, "During that month, did you not try to visit her? Call her?"

The son looked up from the floor where he'd been concentrating on the pattern of the carpet. Hugh Sullivan came to his rescue in his own way. "Worse than a prison," he said. "No visitors, no calls."

The son picked up speed again. "We had many private investigators along the way. When we'd find she was . . . missing. In the end, once it appeared she was lost for good, we went slowly backward into her life, year by year, with the help of other investigators. We learned she'd been prostituting herself—among other things—probably even before she'd begun menstruating."

I said, "Children don't prostitute themselves, adults prostitute them."

He chose to ignore that. "Finally, in the end, my father did go to the police. Reported her missing. But she was an adult. The police could promise nothing. Now we are tired. It's over at long last. And I believe there is a simple explanation. She was a bad seed. That's all."

No one spoke. I waited and so did Rocky. We eyed one another. They were all surprised when Nora was the one to break the silence. She especially surprised her husband. She was as beautiful as Sean had said. *Stunning* was the word he'd used, a word that fit. She spoke in a whisper, though none of us had any trouble hearing what she had to say. All eyes were on her, and the room was still as a tomb.

"I don't believe Kathy was a bad seed. I'm only glad to know her suffering reached an end. If only she'd come to us when she learned she was pregnant. If only we had her back—her and her baby."

Nora's husband pressed her hand to his lips. He was using her hand to force his own thoughts and opinions to stay in his mouth. As the son-in-law in such a family, he knew his place, though it required great effort to stay there.

The mother's reaction to Nora's words was to roll her eyes.

Well, I've known bad people, one in particular: a woman convicted of an ax murder when she was seventeen. She was not a bad seed. There is no such thing. An infant is innocent. Murderers are taught to be bad. *You have to be taught to hate.* My stepfather liked listening to oldies from the sixties, but he'd sing songs from Broadway shows when the radio wasn't on. I would have to discuss the line from the song with Rocky. Maybe he was right. There is no innate hatred. We are taught to hate, Rocky.

Only the younger brother remained stone-faced, though he displayed surprise at his sister's proclamation in the momentary rise of his eyebrows. The youngest in a decaying family tends to stay fixed or goes off to listen to loud music via a headset, turns to his homework, plays at his computer, calls his friends. The fixed succeed and get into the best schools, where they are invited to join the best clubs. They set themselves outside the range, outside the noise of the family—into their own heads—where they'll be out of touch with the unpleasant racket abounding. At the same time, they watch very carefully while taking care to keep their own lives ordered and removed, taking care to stay above the chaos. And the family ignores the youngest because they're so grateful to have an independent child who can see to himself. When I interview these children, they always say, "I didn't know anything about it. I had a big math test coming up." Such a child has a craving for prominence; they're the ones who just might volunteer a pearl if you trip them over their own egos.

So I said to the younger brother, "Kieran, who forced your sister to have sex when she was a child?"

He never paused. If he had, his family would have snapped out of the flabbergasted state I'd provoked and attacked me before he could respond—not that they, in their wildest dreams, would have expected him to answer such a question. His gaze remained level. He would finally interact with this family he so detested.

He said, "I would say it must have been my Uncle Sean."

~~~

After all hell had broken loose, after the outcries and the shouting and the terrible wail of the sister who moments before had spoken so softly, the father ordered me out of the house, which was pretty much what I'd wanted. I meant to shake them up so I could expose something that was, I hoped, important. How satisfying to get the momentous rather than merely important.

The detective wasn't ordered out, but he hustled after me.

Out in the street, he marveled. "How could you have known?"

"It was patently likely. But I certainly didn't know *who*."

The direction of his gaze shifted from my eyes to all of my face. Reading me. "You are very much self-assured. I am so admiring of such a quality."

"Oh, Rocky, it's something we see so much."

"But you knew who to ask."

"Yes."

"Instinct."

"Study."

"Indeed. Poppy, the judge didn't identify the body. And if he did kill the girl he once abused, he took greater pains than were actually necessary to see his secret remained safe. Cut off her hair. And now such diabolical actions come around to bite him. Because of your astuteness."

"Don't give me so much credit. I only wanted to find someone who would tell the unvarnished truth. The truth is what always brings us to motivation."

"Poppy."

"What?"

"He could well have killed her, couldn't he?"

"He could have." Then I told him about the shred of hair I'd pilfered from the shoulder of Sean's jacket.

Rocky had to tilt his chin up a little to look back into my eyes again. He said, "A man must often resort to muscle—sometimes physical muscle, sometimes emotional muscle—to get what he wants. You put your superb attractiveness to work."

That's what I'd done. Attractive women distract men, render them goofy—unable to pay attention to what they're supposed to be thinking. Attractive men distract women, too, but women become instantly alert. However, I set Rocky straight. "I can drop a man who weighs twice as much as I do if need be."

He smiled. "Please be sure to know that I am proud to be working with you."

"Thank you." Enough. "Listen Rocky, one of them will be back. One of them will need to find me, talk to me. I will get a call, maybe even tonight. It will get me more of the truth. Frankly, I hate the presumption that law enforcers take their own time. All I really did in there was cut to the chase."

"A sharp cut. So, do you think it's the college boy who is going to call you?"

"No. He doesn't have strength of purpose. He is at the age when he's only just realizing the importance of positioning himself. He'll be too busy getting himself back into position."

"He's the power that will be."

"Yes, he is. He's smart enough to understand that his older brother, being less well endowed in the brains department, will get a share of the assets, but as the brains he will run the company. Or he'll be a senator from Massachusetts some day, who knows? The parents will be too busy ravaging each other to call me. I'd bet it'll be the sister. She's the one who feels guilt. The others stopped blaming themselves long ago, but not her. The mother never blamed herself, the father decided self-pity was better than blame, and the two brothers have put their sister Kathleen into a barricaded compartment."

Rocky said, "Maybe the son-in-law will have something to say."

"Maybe. But now I've got to get to my hotel so I can be there if one of them does contact me."

"Poppy?"

"Yes?"

"There were no rope burns on Kathleen Sullivan's skin. She was found with her jacket on, though her shoes were gone. Without shoes, we often think suicide. Why they remove their shoes before they leap, I don't know. But her socks were gone too. They take off their shoes but leave on their socks. I'm sure there is some symbolism. I think the shoes and socks were pulled off by the currents. No one has ever found a suicide note. I believe the jacket didn't come off because her killer had tied a rope around her waist. When the rope came loose, her body was brought ashore on the next tide. That's what I think happened. I am sure now she was murdered."

I'd been sure for a while.

I said, "Then we have to work on who would murder her. If Sean fathered the fetus, we've got a serious suspect. Do we know yet if he was in Ireland in 1972?"

"He traveled a lot during his school years. Traveled with his parents, too. We assume Ireland, but we haven't pinpointed that."

"All right, then, it's possible he killed them both, though still mind-boggling. But Kathleen Sullivan, we can't forget, lived on the streets, commingled with lowlife—we'll have to find some dealers. Pimps, too. The thing is, now you have to go back inside and tell them you believe it's doubtful that Kathleen committed suicide. Make clear she was emotionally destroyed as a child and possibly murdered just as she reached adulthood. They have to be made aware of that possibility. Then, Rocky, get your thumbscrews out and see what you can do about seeing to Uncle Sean, who is now in deep shit. Your jurisdiction, not mine. Unless I make it mine, which I will if you don't get the job done."

He didn't like that. Neither did I, but I couldn't risk him being wishy-washy. He said, "Jump ahead to another chapter of your FBI handbook, Agent. I don't require threats." The streetlight came on just over our heads. His eyes were jet, glinting. Reminded me of Betsey Johnson's table.

"I'm sorry, Rocky. That was glib. I didn't need to rely on jarring you to save time, but time-saving is all. As important to me as it is to victims. Please forgive me. I'm real glad you don't suppress your anger. That's what happens when you start burning out. I'm relieved you haven't. I need local help at full strength."

His eyes grew maybe a touch softer. "I don't suppress a goddamn thing."

Except hatred. "Good. Then go after that dirtbag, Judge Sean Scanlon, like you should have the minute you found out the identity of the Sullivan girl. The sweet kid was debauched by the very man sent to identify her body, maybe the man who killed her, maybe the man who made the decision to take out ridiculous insurance by cutting off her hair before she went into the water. We can't get him yet for what he did to her as a child; we need her little brother—the rest of the family—to do that. But you can cause trouble for what he did to her as an adult, which was, at the minimum, misidentification, at max, seeing to her death or killing her himself. Very soon we'll at least know if he'd gotten her pregnant."

His eyes lost their glint. He put his hand out and rested it on my forearm. "Sean Scanlon is a judge. That fact has defused my department's investigation. You are correct to accuse me of laxity, after all. But I will make up for it. Sean Scanlon is dead meat. I will hang him out."

Not bad for a vegetarian. And no need for me to respond. The detective wanted only one thing for the sweet kid—justice.

~~~

Nora didn't call me that evening from her parents' home or from her own. She called me from the lobby of my hotel, late. I went down to meet her. I suggested we talk at a table in the bar. She agreed. As we headed in that direction she said, "My husband thinks I'm in bed, tranquilized. We have a very sumptuous house. Even if he checks on me and sees I'm not there, he won't take on the daunting task of noting which other room I've taken myself to." She was as efficient at sarcasm as she was at lying. Once she knew she'd convinced her husband not to disturb her, she'd left. I complimented her on doing what she had to do.

She made a sound that could have been an especially tired laugh. Then she said, "It was Uncle Sean who taught me lying. And sarcasm? I suppose—" at which point she broke down, put her face into her hands, and began to sob. There were people standing nearby who turned to stare. I said to them, "She's had some very bad news," and I put my arm around her and guided her toward the bank of elevators. Inside, she buried her head into me, crying even harder. My shoulder didn't get damp, though; there were no material tears. Nothing new. I once asked my doctor if people who cry a lot reach a point where they can't manufacture tears anymore or was I imagining it. He said I wasn't.

I got her into my room, poured her a scotch, and she knocked it down.

She began to talk, a trembling babble, nothing specific I could make out. No real tears and no real words either. Not until she'd downed another two shots did she became decipherable.

"He stopped," she said. The babbling had been directed at the air in general, but she wanted me to understand those two words. She'd said *He stopped* into my face. Then she took a big breath and wiped her dry cheeks. "One day, he was just through with me."

"Your uncle."

"Yes." I didn't know words could possibly be comforting. But I had to say something. "How terrible" is what came out.

She said, "But I didn't help her." Nora took a few moments to get in more air before she made the huge effort to move on from there to what was to come. "I didn't help Kathleen because I was so glad it was someone else's turn. I could have stopped him. I didn't." She touched the back of her fingers to her lips and said through them, "I'm the one who killed her."

She put her hand back down into her lap. She wasn't speaking literally.

"How old were you when your turn ended?"

"Eleven."

"How old was your sister when you were eleven?"

Nora tried, but she couldn't answer. She doubled over, face in her hands again, failing to muffle the terrible sounds she was making into her skirt. When she lifted her head, the new sound she made, I believe, was the word *seven*.

"Seven?"

"Yes."

How I wanted to go back to Sean's chambers and strangle the man! I *would* strangle him, one way or another. "Look, Nora, a degraded, manipulated, and physically injured girl of eleven is not capable of helping anybody. Parents are the ones who are supposed to protect their seven-year-olds."

She raised her head. "How did you know I was injured?"

"It's the way it is."

"But I could have—"

"You could have done nothing. Nothing."

Nora clenched her fist and struck herself in the chest. I was across from her, the bottle of scotch and the empty glass on the table between us. I got up and sat down on the sofa next to her. I put my arms around her again, and I sympathized with the husband who had tried to provide her with comfort earlier. An impossible job. She ripped herself away from me.

"I could have."

"Please tell me exactly what you could have done."

She straightened up. She reached for the scotch bottle and poured herself another one. She knocked it down just like the others. Drinking was what she'd turned to for survival. I waited.

She put the glass down again, composed herself, brushed at her skirt. She said, "I read a story in the paper about a teenage girl and her boyfriend. Maybe ten years ago, I'm not sure. I think it was—I don't know—in New York. The girl was sixteen. And I was sixteen when I read the article. The two of them—the girl and her boyfriend— got a gun and they shot her father. Killed him. The girl was arrested. She didn't care. She didn't talk. Not until she got to prison when she told the inmates what had happened. She told them her father had abused her. Then he stopped abusing her. He had turned his eye toward her little sister. So she killed him to protect her sister. She knew that what he'd drummed into her head—that if she told, no one would believe her—was accurate. They'd send her away for being a bad girl and a liar. I was told the same. I should have done to Sean what that girl did to her father. But I wasn't like that girl. I had no guts. Instead, I killed Kathleen."

"I think someone did kill Kathleen. But not you."

She turned her face to mine. "No. No one killed her. The detective is wrong. She committed suicide. Or she fell into the harbor because of a drug she'd taken. And I'm the one who caused her to become an addict. To become—"

"Nora, I believe you are capable of rational thought. You are refusing to think here. Do not claim responsibility to assuage your misery. Do not distract from what must be done to gain justice for your sister. You are surely entitled to denial. To misery and anguish. But justice must be wrought."

Her forehead wrinkled. Then she said, "I want justice."

I would take her at her word, but a new tack was required. "Do you know where the girl is who shot her father?"

"What?"

"The girl you told me about."

"I don't know. I hope she—"

"She's still in jail. What her father told her was a fact. The truth wouldn't have helped. And when she did tell the truth, to the women incarcerated with her—by then it was too late to save her. She didn't tell the truth earlier because it might not have stopped the abuse of her sister and she wouldn't take that chance. She chose jail by killing her father. In New Jersey, by the way. There was no death penalty in New Jersey at the time, though she surely would have accepted that too.

"Nora, considering who your family is, you'd have ended up in some hospital in a special locked ward if you'd killed your uncle. No one would have believed you, you know that. They would have chosen to believe your uncle. Besides that, it would have been difficult to kill a man in Sean Scanlon's position. Do you own a gun?"

"No."

"Have you ever fired a gun?"

"No."

"Did you have a boyfriend who might have helped you get a gun? Helped you to kill your uncle?"

"No. I was only eleven."

"Exactly."

Her voice had become a monotone. Her face was dead white. She ran into the bathroom and threw up the scotch. She hadn't turned to drink, after all.

She came back, the edges of her hair wet from splashing water in her face. She sat down again, only this time she leaned back into the sofa, rested her head against the big cushions, closed her eyes. Spent. I waited. Her eyes opened, she turned her head, her gaze directed at me.

"You believe Kathleen was murdered."

"Yes."

"Sean killed her?"

"I don't know that."

She turned her head away again. "Kathleen had nothing to lose, did she? Maybe she tried to get money from him or just get back at him. But . . . would he have murdered her?"

"I meant it when I said I didn't know. Since she was pregnant . . . unless Sean was the one who impregnated her . . . that would intro-duce another suspect."

She leveled her gaze to mine. "Sean doesn't have sex with women old enough to bear children."

I took in a big breath. "Nora, here's what matters now. At this time and this place. Not what mattered before, not what will matter in a year. Now. I need to know everything there is to know about your sister—her life, her friends, where she went when she'd run away, where she hung out, who she hung with. Everything. Maybe there were people she'd crossed paths with who had the motive to kill her—or scare her—and then maybe things got out of hand. I need to know this: Did your sister contact anyone in the family before she died? Once she was permanently disowned, if she was determined not to come home but needed something, who would she call?"

"My older brother."

"And if she wanted to come home again, who would she turn to?"

"I think I would have been the most likely."

"You never heard from her?"

"No."

"Okay. So think about all this. Distill everything you remember about your sister's life. What the private investigators found. Write it down. Can you meet me again tomorrow?"

"Yes, in the morning. The wake will begin tomorrow afternoon."

"You'll give me all you've written?"

"Yes."

"Then, Nora, you have to continue what you've only just begun. You have a couple of jobs to do, and you have the courage and the money to take them on."

"What jobs?"

"Cooperate with the law when it comes to your uncle. Tell the police what you told me. Detective Patel will support you. Help the Boston police go after him. Help them get him. Press charges. Don't hesitate even when you realize the damage to your entire family—to your marriage, maybe. Get counseling to help you cope with humiliating revelations. Get help, too, for the difficulties you will face, since they will still choose not to believe you. Right now they're concentrating on how to stifle Kieran. Do it while they've got their hands full."

She didn't say anything. She didn't raise her head from the sofa cushions. She was considering. No one had ever asked her to act before. She'd only acted in her imagination, shooting Sean over and over again. It was time to give her job number two.

"The other thing you have to do?" She turned her face toward me once more, perplexed. "Look up the girl who killed her father."

She sat up. "The girl in jail?"

"Yes. Visit her. Commiserate with her. Then go see her younger sister, probably of age now. Get whatever information she might be willing to offer you and take it to the DA's office where she was prosecuted. The imprisoned girl committed the crime of defending her sister in the only way she knew. Maybe you can get her a new trial. I can't; I wish I could. I find myself asking people to step in for me, people who have suffered like you. Then, after you find her, find the other children."

She was gaping at me.

I sat up too. "I have work to do. What time tomorrow morning?"

She came around. "Nine. I can do that much anyway. The first job." She gave me the saddest smile.

I didn't smile. I wanted her to understand how serious I was. "You can do whatever you choose to do."

She stood. So did I. She said, "I'll be here in the morning. My husband's a lawyer. He's actually a very good one. I'll talk to him."

"That'll help."

"But I am his second wife. The trophy. I'm supposed to sit around and gleam."

"Nora, is he at all aware of the real you?"

"There is no real me."

I walked with her to the door. "You okay? Want me to walk you down?"

She turned. "No. I feel better. Thank you."

Instead of goodbye, I said, "There *is* a real you."

# 7

The next morning her husband was with her. His eyes were red. Good.

He said, "I don't know how Nora kept me from getting into my fucking car so I could go over there and break the motherfucker's rotten neck."

Perfect.

Nora said to him, "There are other ways to see his neck is broken." She handed me a file, maybe a dozen pages inside. She said, "What I remember. Names of the people my father hired as well. I'd have transcribed them but I don't know how to type."

I took the folder and glanced through the papers. Nora's writing—neat as a pin.

"I called Detective Patel just before we came here. I told him what I plan to do. In Massachusetts, as of late, there is no statute of limitations for child abuse. Sean will have no choice but to turn himself in to avoid a public arrest. I could have asked my husband rather than the detective if it were true—about the statute of limitations— but I needed to conserve my energy. I didn't want to listen to my husband discuss the ramifications of such a move on my part once he'd calmed down. But I needn't have worried. He hasn't calmed down yet."

The husband, whose volatility she'd underestimated, pounded the table in front of him with his fist. He smashed the table the way he wanted to smash Uncle Sean's face. Fine.

He said to me, "Listen, I'm a partner in my law firm, big firm, big litagators. I've made a ton of money. But I make the effort to do pro bono work. To do something helpful for the guy in the street. I have to do it in secret because I'm the Sullivan family's fucking pool boy. An attendant who does what's expected, takes orders, and that's it. The main order is, make money to see that Nora gets what she's accustomed to. I do what they want, act the way I'm supposed to act, kowtow to the whole fucking show. I do it because I love my wife. I've loved her more and more every day we've been married. Because of her wisdom and for the encouragement she gives. Encouragement to do what I know is the right thing. To do something beyond acquiring money."

He banged the table again.

"My wife will not be kept sequestered any longer. Not by them and definitely not by me. She can do what she wants to do. What *she* wants—not what her father or her mother wants." Then he threw in one last *fuck* for good measure.

Justified fury is chock-full of possibilities, as opposed to unjustified fury, which results in acts like murdering girlfriends who prove fool enough to become pregnant, fool enough to not agree to an abortion.

Nora had his hand now, not the other way around. But she wasn't comforting him, she was sharing his fury.

I said to him, "Your wife's family will no longer be busy keeping political secrets. They'll be shoveling personal dirt under their carpets instead. But somehow you have to beat them to that dirt before they hide it away. Confront them, Nora. Confront them as a group because, rest assured, they've been holding out on one another. Stir things up."

Nora said to me, "Then I guess that will be job number three."

Her husband said, "I'm still worried about job number two."

Now Nora spoke to him. "Until yesterday, I've had nothing whatsoever to do. I can use three jobs—more than three, even—to make up for lost time. Before, there was nothing I ever *wanted* to do. People always ask, 'What are your interests?' I didn't have any interests. Uncle Sean killed any thought I might have had as to interests. But I'm through hiding out. I'm through hiding what he did to me."

And to me, "You told me last night that I'd have to deal with humiliation. But I feel no humiliation. I felt it as a child when I thought all of it was my doing. Sean told me that. Told me I had to pay for *flaunting* myself. I didn't even know what the word meant."

Her husband's eyes filled up. Nora reached to him and touched his face. She said to him, "And when I come out of hiding, maybe I'll develop interests. Last night, you saw the wisdom in my having a purpose. You said that."

"I did. I do now. But you don't deserve what will come. You're going to be dragged through the dirt, Nora."

"I can bear it. I've been looking in the mirror a lot for the last twelve hours. I am seeing an adult, not the child who used to stare back at me."

Well, they could talk to each other later. "We must speak of Kathleen now. We must say all we have to say, remembering that she's beyond hurt."

They came back to my presence in the room. Nora said, "Poor Kathy." But her face didn't melt.

"It's been two years since you or any of the family saw Kathleen or heard anything about her. That's the official line. I don't believe it. Do you two want to be the first to come clean? It'll make things easier for you—it will make you tougher when it comes to saying what you need to say with the rest of the family. What you have kept to yourself is likely to force out their own secrets."

But the dead girl hadn't contacted her sister. Nora was firm about that. "Kathy never tried to reach me. That's because she didn't want me to suffer anymore. She was the mature one, not me. When she was in the house, I could barely speak, couldn't look at her. She knew she was a continual reminder of what had happened to us both. One of the reasons she'd run away was to allow me some peace. I've come to see that—the sacrifice she made."

Her husband coughed.

Uh-oh. Kathleen Sullivan had contacted her brother-in-law. I could tell by the quality of his cough. He saw me watching him. He knew I knew.

He said, "She called my office."

Now Nora's face did melt, a little bit. "What?" the one-syllable word just slightly high-pitched.

Her husband was a big and blustery man, gruff and bull-like. But his eyes were filling up again. He said, "I'm sorry."

Nora all but shouted at him. "She *called* you? My God, when?"

"She wanted me to tell you—"

I interrupted. "When?"

"Three months before she took her own—" He stopped. Time to stop repeating the memorized line. But he'd go there later. "Nora, listen, she wanted me to tell you she was getting better. She was making a new life. She said she wanted you to know that, and then she hung up. I told your father. But Hugh felt strongly that I shouldn't tell you. He was beside himself. He—"

His wife pulled away from him, got to her feet. She walked to one end of the room and then she walked to the other end. Back again. Several times. We watched her. I got ready to spring. In case she decided to pick up a lamp and break it over her husband's head.

Finally, she spoke. "You told my father instead of me?"

"Yes. I followed pool-boy orders. Like always. I'm sorry." He'd already said he was sorry. Then he told her he was sorry a third time.

"Sorry? You're *sorry?*"

Yesterday Nora had sobbed uncontrollably. I didn't think she could cry any harder. I was wrong. She became completely hysterical. She just slipped down to the floor. He leaped up; he scrambled over to her; he knelt down on the floor, picked her up, and rocked her back and forth in his arms. He kept apologizing over and over: He'd make it up to her, he'd follow whatever lead she wanted to take, he'd take a leave from the firm, whatever she wanted, anything. He'd do anything.

It took a little while before she was spent. He half carried her back to the sofa. During all that, I made coffee instead of breaking out the whisky. I handed her a cup. She drank it down. She must have scalded her insides. Then she asked her husband, "What did my father say? Tell me everything he said to you."

Now he didn't hesitate. "Hugh insisted that the main thing was that you shouldn't know she'd wanted to get in touch with you. That for some reason you blamed yourself for your sister's miserable life, and we all needed to bring you further and further from her memory. He wanted to protect you, Nora. He told me he'd hoped all along she was dead. He hoped that because—"

A sudden silence. I wasn't about to let him stop. "Why?"

"I don't know. I didn't know. He just kept insisting on what was best for you."

"He *knew,*" Nora whispered.

I said, "I doubt he knew while you were a child, Nora. He probably didn't know for a long time. For a long time, he repressed what was in front him. And then he saw it."

She looked at me. "He saw it so he wanted *Kathy* dead? Why didn't he want Sean dead? Why?"

"Because he was rendered impotent. Was Sean so strong he could control him like that? Obviously, yes. Another pool boy, I'm afraid."

Nora's husband said, "It's Rosemary who does all the controlling."

More coffee all around. They needed a rest. But there was quiet for all of thirty seconds.

Then Nora spoke. "I look forward to telling my father that his duty to protect me, to protect Kathy, was something he should have thought of a long time ago. And I'm not going to spare him any of the details of what he figured out."

Someone needed to instigate the public unraveling of that family. Nora would do it. I said, "I need everything. I want the private investigators' reports. I want the trails they found. I want to know where she was when she called, what she was doing before she died. And I need to know from you, Nora, if your father found out where she called from." I looked at Nora's husband. "You already asked him that, didn't you?"

"Yes."

Now *I* considered breaking a lamp over his head myself. Instead I said to him, "Let me make myself really clear. I need to know all there is to know. All of it." I said to him, "Why don't you start."

"She called from a phone booth in downtown Boston."

Oh, boy.

Nora ripped herself away from him once more. "She was here? She was near us all this time? You knew and you didn't tell me?"

"Honey, your father—"

She stood and screamed down at him. "Honey? Honey is what *he* called me!"

I leaped in. "Nora, here is what's going to happen. I believe what you said about humiliation. But there will be other debilitating things. Like this. You have to ride them out. We have to stay with where we're going here. There is no choice."

She started pacing again. Her husband tried to get up but she warded him off with a wave of her hand. "I'm all right. Okay, then. I'm riding it out."

She kept pacing. I said to him, "Your father-in-law knew she was in Boston?"

"Yes."

"Had she contacted him?"

"I don't know."

I had to get Nora back. I called her name.

She stopped.

"Nora, find out. Get him to tell you. I want to learn all the secrets kept over the last two years. Once you know them, call me and we'll meet again. As soon after the funeral as you can manage. Please. If you can't reach me, call the detective in charge of the case. Call Patel. He'll get to me."

∿

That morning, Kathleen's picture was on the front page of *The Boston Globe.* It was a mug shot taken in Providence when she was seventeen. There was another picture at the bottom of the page, of her as a child, in her First Communion dress. She was looking sideways at the fall of the veil as if she were trapped in it, looking at it as if she wanted to tear it away. She was seven, an angel just recently introduced to Hell. It was impossible to say whether or not she was a pretty child. As a teenager, the mug shot revealed an animal— stricken, starved, insane. She'd been arrested under another name. Lawyers took care of things, lawyers hired by Sean Scanlon. We found that out from a PI named in Nora's notes.

I didn't have to wait for Nora, wait for the funeral to be over. Hugh Sullivan called me just a few hours after Nora and her husband had left. The wake would not begin until two. Could I meet with the family again? Yes. They were all there. When could I come?

"I can come now."

He said, "This time I would prefer the detective didn't join us."

I said, "I need him there."

There was a pause. "I've been advised that there is no law requiring him to be at a meeting with a federal agent. You have not detained us; we are not under arrest. I make this request because I feel my wife will be more at ease with just you there, a woman. With the officer . . . well, never mind. Rosemary has done nothing wrong, and that's what I'm trying to make her understand. She was a fine mother."

The gentleman doth protest too much. Rosemary Sullivan had abdicated her duty and reneged on her responsibility as a parent to keep her children safe. Hugh had done the same. Such a difficult job, taking on the care of new little human beings. Some women are meant to be mothers; some are not. Delby. Delby's mother. Certainly not mine. Not me. And some men are not meant to be fathers, Hugh Sullivan for starters. My own never had the opportunity.

I told him, "If you want to speak to me, Detective Patel will be present."

He assented. I think he was glad. It was his wife who'd put him up to seeing Rocky wasn't there.

So Rosemary Sullivan wasn't in the parlor when Rocky and I arrived. This time, we sat next to each other. Rocky wasn't just some traffic officer and I wasn't there for show. Now they knew. They were gathered together, and the group included a couple of extras: a sister-in-law; the older brother's wife. A woman who apparently would not abdicate what she saw as her responsibilities within her husband's family. The couple had a baby with them, one who would remain in attendance at his mother's breast with no lovely hand-knit blanket covering their intimacy. Good for her. And good for the baby; during the course of events, when a free-for-all began to threaten, he was passed around to be burped. When a second loomed, he filled up his diaper and his mother plunked him on the carpet, got down next to him, and changed him and wiped him up while he beamed at all of us. A victory grin of sorts, I thought.

Kathleen, it turned out, had contacted all of them, all but her sister, who Kathleen wanted to shield; who understood how Nora was unable to offer her shelter. She'd asked her father for money.

"I hung up on her, had the call traced, increased security at my door."

Nice.

Same request of her older brother. "I didn't hang up."

He'd met with her—twice, actually. The first time at their Maine vacation home in the dead of winter, two years before she died. A caretaker had called him to say there were people in the house.

The older brother said, "Her and a bunch of druggie friends. I called the police to have them arrested, but she and one of them got away, a guy who looked like some . . . looked like a—"

"You have no idea who he might be?"

"No."

"You'd recognize him if you saw him, though?"

"Yes."

"And what happened after he and Kathleen fled?"

"Nothing happened. The rest of them . . . they were too stoned to know what was going on. I chased them off. I didn't bother to press charges. Why have it the papers? Why stir up embarrassment for the family?"

Indeed. Why stir up anything when it's so much more expedient to conceal it?

"The second time—"

I asked, "When?"

"Year and a half ago."

"Just before her death, then?"

"Yes." He hung his head. "A few days before her body was found."

Rocky said, "You could well have been the last person to see her alive."

General consternation led by the mother of the baby, shocked that her husband had never told her. And the baby was passed, ended up with his father, the elder Sullivan brother, who now had let out what he'd held inside. He patted the baby while he let out the rest.

"She asked me to meet her there again. In Maine. She told me she was alone this time. I went up there, to the place that was supposed to be our ideal summer compound. She'd ruined that. We'd stopped going there years before. Too many memories of her temper tantrums: throwing things, breaking dishes. As soon as I saw her in the doorway, using the house none of us can stand to be in, I lost my temper. I told her she'd ruined all our lives. I couldn't stop berating her for what she'd done." The baby whimpered. He handed him to Nora. "She ran past me. She had a car. She got in the car and drove away. What did she think I was going to say, *Hello, how nice to see you again*? It was a green Toyota Camry. I wrote down the license number, a Mass. plate, but then I threw the paper away. I was afraid she might have stolen the car. I didn't want to get involved. I didn't want to find her, and I didn't want my father to find her either. The license plate had two sixes in it. My birthday is May sixth, that's why I remembered the sixes." He fixed his eyes on mine. "That is the extent of the information I have for you."

I said, "How did she look?"

His eyes widened. I'd asked him a question he never could have expected. No rehearsed answer at the ready. He managed pretty well, though. "She looked good. Maybe that's what made me so angry.

How dare she look so good"—his eyes set on his surviving sister—"when Nora looked like hell. When all of us looked like hell."

The younger brother said, "I disagree. We at least didn't look like hell in public. Only Kathy was the one who always looked like hell. I don't remember what she looked like before. The rest of us always look good. We just *feel* screwed up. But we're not, not really. Our family has overcome my sister." His gaze flickered over to his big brother and back again. "Kathy called me too. At Exeter."

How wonderful that his mother wasn't in the room. She felt she could trust him to not create more damage than he had already. God only knows what manipulation she'd used on him. She had underestimated him entirely. Or if she had expected her husband to regulate him, she was wrong about that too. Hugh Sullivan was astonished at his son's revelation.

"She asked me for money. It was the day after my birthday. She said she wanted to wish me a happy birthday. But she knew I'd have gotten my present from Dad so she was really calling to ask me for money."

We waited.

"I told her no. I told her she should get a job."

First a silence, and then Hugh Sullivan spoke. He said to his youngest, "You *are* a spoiled little shit. Who the hell do you think you are to—"

The boy gave his father a stern look. He said, "It's what Mom said to say if Kathy ever called me and asked for money. When she called *you*, you hung up on her."

As if on cue, Mom walked into the room. Rocky started to stand but she waved him back into his chair. He stood anyway. They stared at each other. Finally, she said, "Please sit."

He said, "After you, Mrs. Sullivan."

"I prefer to stand."

Rocky chose to sit. Rosemary took the baby from Nora, whose

arms remained out longer than was necessary to pass the baby on. Rosemary put him on her shoulder, nestled her cheek against his burnished hair, and said, "Babies are so easy."

Right. But that's only when you have nurses and nannies to walk the floor of the house's far wing for the entire night.

Then she said, "I spoke with her too. Probably right after she spoke with my eldest son. Perhaps *I* was the last to speak to her."

The baby was roused from his reverie by the tone of her voice. He looked into her face and his little chin began to tremble. His mother got up to take him back again, sat down, picked up her shirt, and put her breast in his mouth. She and her husband moved together and made a place at the sofa for the Sullivan matriarch. But still she didn't sit. She preferred to be above us all. She touched the arm of the sofa, though, to ground herself.

"Kathleen called to tell me she was pregnant. Could she come to us when the baby arrived. Presumably, there was no father in the picture. Expected me to fill up with sentiment, open my door, and tell her to come home to us."

They all leaned toward her as if pulled by a string, all with the wide eyes the older brother had exhibited when I'd asked him how Kathy had looked.

Nora came to her feet.

Rosemary said, "Sit down, Nora. Call on some thread of maturity."

Nora started to shake. Her husband and her father came to her, helped her back down.

Rosemary continued what she had to say. "I told her neither she nor any illegitimate child of hers would be welcome in my home. Our older boy had just married. I told her he would be the one to produce our first grandchild. There wasn't room for hers and it didn't count anyway. I told her she should have an abortion as a way to begin the process of standing up again on her own two feet, taking some responsibility for herself and her ways. Then I hung up. I had suggested such a hideous thing to her because that girl was to blame for all but destroying this family. Now, even dead, she works to destroy us." She looked specifically at me. "My brother Sean felt nothing but love for my children. He tried to safeguard us when he refused to identify Kathleen's body. He shielded us even though it meant putting his integrity at risk. Never . . . *never* would he have done anything to hurt my children."

Nora's gaze was fixed on some point in space.

Now she looked to her youngest child. He was in the suit he'd be wearing to his sister's wake. She nodded at him, a signal for him to spout what they'd rehearsed.

He smiled an entirely fake smile. "I watch too much television. I was roped into answering the FBI agent's question with something—"

Rocky interrupted him. I wondered what he'd look for in terms of an opening. He had it. He said to the boy, "You made a call a week ago Friday from the phone booth on Quincy Street, Cambridge, at the corner of Broadway, to inform the Boston police that the body found a year and a half ago on Hancock Beach was your sister. How did you know that to be true?"

The color washed out of the boy's face. He stood and ran out of the room. His father called him back; his mother did not. Therefore, he didn't return.

Then Nora began speaking. She'd roused herself from her immobilized state. The level of her voice was a decibel above Rosemary's but her composure was what, in the end, silenced her mother. First she said to Rocky, "I'll find that out for you; how Kieran could know such a thing." And then she said to Rosemary, "Mother, you will not attend my sister's wake. That's not the way it should be."

Her mother looked around as if she didn't know where the words had come from. Certainly not from Nora. But her eyes came to rest on her. "What did you say?"

"I said you will not be at Kathy's wake. You don't deserve to be in her presence, even in the presence of her dead body."

Rosemary Sullivan whirled at her. "I will not honor such idiocy with a response," and she turned again, on her heel, and walked out of the room as her son had.

In my experience, only the guilty storm out of rooms.

Hugh Sullivan, shrunken now, slumped into his chair. He said, "I'm the one who doesn't deserve to be with her, Nora. But I have to be there to ask her to forgive me. Even if I have to ask it of her body lying in its coffin. And it is perfect that she won't be able to forgive me, since she's dead. Because I don't deserve it."

He sure as hell didn't.

Nora's eyes met mine. The time had come for her to contradict her little brother's backpedaling. But her mother had left the room and so she wasn't ready yet to say what she needed to say. She was signaling me, telling me she would wait for the right moment to inform them that she would go to the authorities and describe her uncle's crime against her and her sister. Nora came over to me and I stood. She touched my elbow and led me to the parlor door where the others wouldn't hear what she had to tell me. My interpretation of her gaze had been accurate.

Rocky's phone beeper went off. He identified himself and listened, and then he hung up.

He said to all of us, "My department is receiving calls—many calls—from people who have recognized Kathleen's picture in the newspaper and on television. People who were aware of her whereabouts just prior to her death. I have to leave. I'll get back to all of you when I know who your sister came to be—from the time she escaped from you until her death."

# 8

One of the callers was a fellow who owned over a hundred porno-graphic Web sites. He called because Kathleen Sullivan owed him money; she'd borrowed against her salary and then disappeared. Since she was dead, he intended to collect what he had coming from her family. He was summoned for questioning to his local police station. Rocky and I went there as soon as Rocky collected Nora's elder brother, who agreed to come with us simply because of the look his wife shot at him. We hoped he might recognize who the tawdry webmaster and porn producer was, perhaps one of the group he'd seen at his family's defunct summer house in Maine.

The guy inside the precinct claimed he had nothing to hide, didn't try to. In fact, he called the local television stations, who had their crews outside waiting for him. When we arrived, Rocky diverted them, fed them some sound bites so they didn't have a chance to scrutinize our trio, wouldn't realize Kathleen Sullivan's brother was with us.

In the precinct, just outside the doorway to a questioning room, the eldest of the Sullivan children peeked through the one inch of space the door had been left open and turned back to us.

"That's him."

"One of the guys you saw with her in Maine?"

"Yes. The one she drove off with."

"You're sure?"

He added a little disdain to his tone. "How many people have that tattoo around their necks?"

Couple of million, but I let it go, told him he could be on his way. After all, he had a funeral to attend.

Rocky and I went in and sat at the table. We were informed that the man had already pointed out to the assembled officers that his Web sites were legal and that he and Kathleen had a good time making them. He said she wore disguises for the pictures, "wigs, sunglasses, hats. Stuff like that. Didn't want to be tracked down. She didn't wear anything else. Only her doctor would have recognized her." He laughed. "And me, naturally."

I said, "How much did you pay her?"

"Enough to keep her happy. She owes me eight hundred bucks. Owed me, I guess, is a better way of putting it. I didn't know her folks were rich. Like, I was clueless. I mean, that house in Maine belonged to them? So now I just want my due."

Kathleen had posed for him for over a year. They'd had a fight over her pregnancy. He explained to us that pregnant women didn't exactly entice customers. He said, "Then she just took off."

I reminded him that she hadn't taken off.

"Oh, yeah. No wonder I couldn't find her. I looked. I looked for a long time, just so you know. "

"When was the last time you saw her?"

Same time as her brother had, just before she died.

I took out Sean's picture, a recent one taken at the new Sullivan baby's christening. Nora had given it to me.

"Do you know who this is?"

"I do now."

"You've seen him before?"

"Yeah. Last time I saw her."

I don't know who tensed up more, me or Rocky.

"She'd gotten some job. She wanted to give me a hundred dollars. I took it. Then I followed her around a little. It was tough. Lost her. But I kept looking because I wanted the rest of my money, and one night I did see her at one of our old places where we'd hang. She was at a table with an older guy. Kind of a fat guy. Looked like he had money. Okay, I figured, so she had a sugar daddy. Good. I could maybe get my money out of her after all. I didn't hassle them. Planned to get her alone some other time."

I kept the excitement out of my voice, asked him if he had any idea how Kathleen had come to drown.

"Beats the shit out of me. Probably stoked, you know?"

I looked over at Rocky. We'd found out more than we ever hoped for. But then, the world of a homicide is a small one, just like the world of most everyone else. We would let the cops at the precinct question him further. But I had one more thing to say.

I stood up and leaned into the pornmaster's face. "You don't want your eight hundred dollars. You're not stupid enough to go after this particular family. You're just building up publicity for your Web sites. You'll be adding a screen credit, I imagine. Something along the lines of STARRING KATHLEEN SULLIVAN."

He laughed. "You got that right. Lady cops are like, *whew!*" He took in Rocky. "Hell of a lot smarter than the rest of you dudes. I'm going to get what's owed me and then some, and I'm going to do it all up front. Yeah, I'm adding her name to the sites, now that I know it."

"What name had you known her by?"

"We called her Murph. Red hair and all."

Rocky and I left. Perhaps Nora's husband could come up with a way to see to the porn sites. I could only hope.

Outside, Rocky said, "It would have been a lot simpler if some teacher had seen them together instead of that scum."

Well, yes. "Rocky, the police will find out when and where he saw Sean and Kathleen. Maybe a teacher happened to be in the bar that night."

My phone was vibrating.

Auerbach.

Sean's DNA did not match the fetal markers. I was disappointed but not especially surprised. In the back of my mind—a fairly dark recess—I'd wanted to think Kathleen planned it all, got pregnant by Sean in order to bring him down. But even dead, she would bring him down. And so she did, but in her own way, not according to my bleak fantasy.

I gave Auerbach's news to Rocky and his face turned glassy. I could practically hear the cogs in his brain struggling. I assured him we'd find out who fathered Kathleen's child and that Auerbach's findings did not preclude Sean's possible guilt as to Kathleen's death. He was looking at something over my shoulder, but there wasn't anything over my shoulder except the leafy branches of a maple tree across the street.

I said, "What the hell's the matter with you, Rocky?"

He came back to me. "She was a housekeeper at a parish church."

"Who was?"

"Kathleen. Most of the calls we took today came from parishioners. I'd thought the guy in there would be more promising."

"More promising? Jesus, Rocky. He placed Kathleen with Scanlon right before she—"

"Yes, I know. I meant insofar as who she was pregnant by."

"Well, I want that as bad as you do." Him, me, and Danny O'Neill.

He said, "We will talk to the pastor of the church."

"Is it a church here in Boston?"

"One of the largest in the Boston area. St. Lawrence O'Toole's in South Boston. A blue-collar area—poor, in fact."

"And Rocky, priests have cars, right?"

He was completely preoccupied. It was as if I were speaking too softly for him to hear. He just stared at me. But then he said, "Of course priests have cars. Are they supposed to hitchhike?"

What *was* the matter with him? "Rocky, the idea is to see if we've got any Toyotas with sixes in the plates. Then you can get the list of parishioners—church employees—and see what they're driving. Maybe she used the priest's car. How far is this church?"

The detective didn't hear me. His face looked a little gray.

"Rocky?"

"I'm sorry. What?"

So I asked him again.

"It's not too far."

"Then let's go."

The color returned to his face, but his features were set like plaster.

"Are you going to tell me your problem, Rocky?"

"There is just one priest running that parish."

"That should make things a little easier."

"He chooses to have his parishioners act as his assistants rather than other priests."

"So? What's that got to do with anything?"

"It's heresy."

I almost said *So?* again. But there was a note to Rocky's voice—a new note I'd never heard before. "Rocky, what the hell are we talking about?"

"I know the church. Fairly well."

Oh.

"May I tell you of this church?"

"It's pertinent?"

"Yes."

"And is the heretic priest pertinent?"

"Yes."

"And is his car pertinent?"

I watched his chest rise and then come slowly down. "I remember that it's a Toyota. I don't remember whether it's a Camry or if it's green."

There was a good deal of traffic between the police precinct and the ghetto. I would give Rocky time to think this through. But rather than think, he began to talk a mile a minute.

"St. Lawrence O'Toole is directly in the middle of a terrible fallen-down neighborhood. The place of the terrible busing incidents in the sixties, seventies. When this priest arrived there five years ago, the church had a crumbling spire that was about to fall over and a cross on top that was a chunk of rust. The inside of the church was full of rat droppings, and the four chandeliers had about seven lights among them. It was as though the church had been flooded by an overflowing river, the waters receded, and everything left as it was.

"In five years, the priest raised four million dollars for renovation—now it's a showpiece, as you're about to see. But first, before the money came in, he renovated the spirit of the church. He invited those outside the neighborhood to join his poverty-stricken flock, and they came. He raised people's consciousnesses. The money poured in."

Interesting. On many fronts. "You obviously admire this priest."

"Yes. The St. Lawrence O'Toole neighborhood was once my neighborhood—where I grew up. I left, of course, when I could afford to move to a more pleasant place. Last year, I married a Catholic, a confused one. Disgruntled more like it, but loyal. I converted to her religion because it so relieved her family and because she didn't go to church anyway, and my conversion does not make me any less a Hindu. Then, not too long ago, just when I thought she was about to throw in the towel and agree that if we were to practice religion we should consider joining a New England church painted white with no crucifix and no stained-glass windows—more in keeping with my own spiritual needs—my wife wanted to give it one last try: St. Lawrence O'Toole's. Its growing reputation for good works appealed to her. I told her I'd consider.

"And then there came a young man, the first to officially—publicly—press charges against a priest for abusing him when he was a child. It was the pastor of St. Lawrence's who gave this man the sustenance he needed to take such a courageous leap and stick through what was to come. The pastor is a hero. And so we joined his church."

"You know him."

"Yes."

"Shit."

"Yes. Shit."

"He hired drug addicts, then? Like Kathleen Sullivan?"

"He did. First, though, when he'd just arrived at the church, he replaced the two priests serving there with laypeople. He felt the two priests had never come to terms with the renovation of church altars, turning them around to face the congregation. They were pre–Vatican Two priests who preferred to keep their backs to the people and their faces to the wall. They were happy to leave him and his ideas, which went even beyond Vatican Two. So now the church has twelve thousand active members—soup kitchens, battered women's shelters, hospice care, all of it."

"And the name of your hero?"

"My hero is Gandhi. I have no living heroes at present. Please do not aim your sarcasm at me, Poppy."

I apologized to him for the second time in a day.

He said, "The priest's name is Tom."

"Tom?"

"Thomas Connealy. Monsignor Thomas Connealy. But he insists everyone call him Tom."

"And what's a monsignor? A bishop?"

"No. It's a title gifted by the pope. If the pope decides to personally honor a priest, he makes him a monsignor. In Tom's case it happened upon his ordination. Very rarely is the position bestowed upon ordination as was the case with Tom. Such a priest holds a lifelong elite membership within the church."

"Membership to what?"

"The papal household. No jurisdiction, just special privileges."

"So who is chosen to receive the honor?"

"The way I heard it, anyone whose family has the wherewithal to write a check for—I don't know—five or six figures. Not Tom's doings. His parents'. He has a doctorate in sacramental theology from the North American College in Rome. He could have risen in the ranks. But he wanted a parish. A flock. His parents were the ones with illusions of grandeur, not him."

"Rocky, you're a member of this church."

"I said that, didn't I?"

"Yes, you did. And you didn't recognize Kathleen Sullivan—her body—as the rectory housekeeper?"

"No. I never saw the housekeeper. They tend to be ghosts. The hierarchy doesn't like to play up that priests have live-in servants. But they do, a time-honored tradition. A priest should not be expected to sully himself with mundane domestic duties, even Tom."

Oh.

"Poppy?"

"Yes?"

"I notice you sometimes have moments when you are inexpressive."

"I do?"

"Your inexpressiveness lasts only a fraction of a second. Just now, for example."

I was impressed, yet again, with this detective. He was like a bloodhound, noticing the expression I must reveal when I decide to move on. I said, "I believe that when I realize there's no time in my life—in my job—to go on with a conversation no matter how interesting, I think, *Oh,* and then I skip ahead to what's important."

"You are magnificently disciplined."

"Thank you." What I do go on to is often a question that steers away from the topic for which I have no time. As in this case. "Rocky, so he's a good guy and he lent Kathleen his car. Is that what's bothering you?"

"Yes. But I have a much greater thing bothering me. He's Irish."

"Who isn't around here? I mean, besides you?"

"Poppy, Irish from Ireland. He emigrated when he was a young man."

"Oh, boy."

Rocky's eyes stayed riveted to the road.

"Do you know where specifically in Ireland he came from?"

"Galway."

"Jesus."

"Jesus, indeed."

"When did he get here?"

"I don't know."

I pointed to his radio. He picked it up and told the dispatcher to find out. The dispatcher said, "Jeez, Rocky, who the hell do I ask?"

"Try the archbishop."

I let Rocky drive a few minutes more before I said, "We should find out about the car too, shouldn't we?"

His lips parted but the answer didn't come out. Sometimes silence means no, sometimes it means yes. It can also mean the answer is obvious.

Rocky flipped on the radio again. "Here's an easier one while you're working on the first. I need the make, model, and license plate number on the car Thomas Connealy drives over at St. Lawrence's. The color."

"Don't tell me the pope's trying to get his license pulled."

"Just get it."

"Sure."

Took a minute. A Toyota Camry. Green. There were two sixes in the plate.

Several more minutes were required for the answer to the original question to come through, but it did.

"Nineteen-seventy-two."

I said to Rocky, "Ask him what month?"

"Do you have a month?"

He did. The monsignor had arrived in the United States three months after Nuala O'Neill found the dead Irish girl.

Rocky clicked off his radio.

I said, "I wonder why he waited. Why didn't he flee as soon as he'd killed her?"

The detective was gripping the steering wheel a little more tightly now.

So then I said, "Because maybe he didn't kill her."

"There is no need to patronize me."

"I'm not. Just stating what must be stated before we grow too prejudiced, what with the facts we're getting here a mile a minute. Maybe he hid himself in Ireland and came over when he had a window of opportunity. After events surrounding a girl gone missing had settled down. Still doesn't mean he killed her."

Maybe Rocky did need to excuse himself from the investigation. I kept talking.

"According to Nuala O'Neill, there were no missing girls back then that anyone knew about. What if she was in the same situation as Kathleen Sullivan? Disowned? Some men thrive on damsels in distress. But once the damsels are on their own two feet they don't kill them, they leave. To find a new one, another distressed damsel. Maybe Tom Connealy fits the bill. Maybe he—"

He interrupted me. "We'll ask him. Not whether he thrives on damsels in distress, if that's all right with you, but whether he knew of the incident of the drowned girl in Ireland. For starters."

"Rocky, we need a middle. Right now, you want him to be totally innocent; who could blame you? But at the same time you want to prove your objectivity by forcing incrimination. So we can't ask him that yet. We can't even mention Ireland. We have to wait. We have to see what happens once he reveals what he intends to reveal about our Boston girl. About Kathleen Sullivan. We have to listen to him, and we have to watch carefully for contradictions. There may be no chance of finding enough evidence to get a court-ordered DNA test. So if he was Kathleen Sullivan's lover, we have to get him to admit it so we know he could have gotten her pregnant. Then we have to convince him to have his DNA tested to see if he is or isn't the father. If he is, we spring the Irish girl on him."

He looked over to me. "I think, perhaps, that you are crazy."

"No, I'm not. I grasp at anything. You told me he's a hero, a hero with a mammoth sense of responsibility. Isn't that what you said?"

"Yes."

"So if he admits he and Kathleen were intimate, he may well volunteer to have his DNA tested. We'll appeal to his sense of responsibility. The thing is, can you deceive your friend? Can you play at this charade, suck up to his reputation? Manipulate the man?"

"He's not my friend, he's my pastor. I can do my job, whatever it requires. I am emotionally conflicted but professionally I remain steadfast. We will try your methods, since they are my own."

We rode the rest of the way through South Boston, both of us reflecting. Time for me to get into a new mode, gear up for a session with this priest. Tom. Tom Connealy. When I'm present when suspects are questioned, I pay careful heed to their words and I watch the minutiae of their physical reactions. One of my favorite training courses at the Bureau was body language. Various forms of fidgeting are highly expressive. Nervousness shows in the way a person strokes his hair into place when it's already in place; the way he shifts from one foot to the other, or if he suddenly asks to use the bathroom. Mostly, it's the eyes, although a mouth can give a lot away—like when a hand goes up to cover it. And shocking news can cause the pupils to dilate and immediately contract again, as if a flashbulb has gone off.

Then there's the giveaway inherent in facial muscles. Forty-four of them. Facial muscles can be deliberately pressed into service. When you want someone to know you're kidding, you wink. That's when you want to be unsubtle, but sometimes an expression can be formed for effect: frowns and grimaces, the dramatic looks of despair and sadness. It becomes almost comical once an investigator knows what to look for. And once you know what to look for and you find it, anything a guilty party says as to his innocence can become clearly implausible.

I thought of Rocky noticing what he called my momentary inexpressiveness. I said, "Rocky, have you had the facial-muscle course?"

He said, "No need. I studied the art of cartooning."

"Excuse me?"

"In college. For fun. I learned a bit. I learned to narrow a face's lips to show anger. To show stress, just raise the inner eyebrows. Bad smell or repulsion, wrinkle the nose. Those are the easy ones. Oh, and if you want to have your character kill someone, rearrange his face to the look of a snarling dog. Bare his teeth. I extrapolated from there. But you took such a course?"

"Yes."

"What did you want to get from it?"

"I wanted to find out how to tell when the spoken word is likely to be different from what the body is signaling."

He smiled. "Such a talent reduces the need for intimidation. Which so often gets a peace officer in trouble."

I smiled too. We understood each other. "I figure this priest you've been describing is not susceptible to intimidation."

"That's right."

"So how come you're not a cartoonist?"

His grip on the wheel was loosening. "I prefer to employ my ability to decode the face for more pressing use. And I simply enjoy searching for the lies within a face more than the enjoyment I receive drawing such faces."

"You don't mind if I change the subject, do you?"

"I was about to suggest that very thing."

"We'll need backup officers, obviously."

"I'll get them. But we won't need them."

"Rocky, I have to be honest with you here. He's your pastor, yes. You don't want to think he is involved here, we've established that. Therefore, I'm worried—"

"No, Poppy. I will not let my hopes that he has had no involvement with Kathleen overtake me. Not in the face of where he came from and when he came. But I am convinced that, even if he was involved, he won't bolt. He will not try to escape from what he knows he has to do. That is his personality. But all the same, the man might be a killer. Who can trust personality in such an instance? I will call for our backup."

Good.

Realistically, though, it is rare for the suspect—whether innocent or guilty—to simply bolt, to run out the door into the arms of the cops assigned to prevent flight if the need seems appropriate. An innocent party tends to become rooted, unable to move upon hearing the suspicion. A shrewd guilty party will also root, though his eyes will shift from doors to windows and then back to his captors. He takes the quick glance at you—not the vacant glance we might give a stranger but, instead, an assiduous, especially rapid contemplation. But sometimes they're not shrewd, and we all have to be on our toes, primed for the bolt, hands moving toward our weapons, so the cops outside won't be put at risk if at all possible when we shout "Freeze!" which is the signal for them to come storming in.

Rocky called for backup. He looked over and smiled at me again. "You treat me gently. That is very nice of you, Poppy. I can only hope my words and actions from here on no longer make you feel the necessity to do so."

I had been treating him gently with just a couple of slips, which he chose to put behind us. Because Rocky Patel exuded gentleness, which is obviously contagious, as I am not normally gentle.

~~~

We'd left rarefied Boston behind and begun driving through crowded and dirty housing projects. Rocky pointed out the cross atop St. Lawrence O'Toole's church, visible above the other buildings, its spire plated with glinting gold, a fancy spire with an intricate woven design like a filigree necklace. Or like a sword in a fantasy movie. Rocky took a turn off the main avenue, at a corner where there was a run-down Day's Inn, a gym next to it, and young black men hanging out on the sidewalk in front.

"I lived in that motel when I came here. I'm a Patel—we're more a tribe than a family. The Patels own just about every motel in the country; I don't know if you've noticed."

"I noticed they're all Indians."

He smiled.

"Once, as a boy, I saw a man—a motel guest—going to his car with a lamp in his hand, a floor lamp from his room. I watched as he struggled to fit it into his trunk. I ran to tell my father, but my father didn't want trouble. We had only just opened. So I ran to the street because several police officers were members of the gym and they knew me. A cruiser was parked in front of the gym, as I had hoped. I told the two cops of the theft in progress at my parents' motel. They came back with me and they grabbed the guest, who was then trying to squeeze the lamp into his back seat.

"My father came out from the office. He was watching from his window as the man stole our property. He said to the officers he only wanted his lamp back, that was all. The policemen agreed with such a course of action, and the thief was only too happy to hear this. But then the officers told our guest that the lamp was scratched. They made him give my father a hundred dollars for a new lamp. Then the thief asked the cops if that meant he could keep the *old* lamp. As I recall, one of the officers said to him, 'What are you, some kind of a fucking asshole?'"

I had to laugh—at the story, and at the incongruity of such language on Rocky's genteel tongue, which was not the same as when he'd whispered Jesus H. Fucking Christ at John's Bar on Hancock Beach, chanting those words like some Hindu prayer.

He finished his story. "The cops patted my head and they left. During my childhood, I wanted to grow up to be a boxer like the boxer I was named after, then there was the fantasy of being a cartoonist, but more than anything—since the day of the lamp—what I really wanted was to be a cop. So here I am. And I believe one of the reasons I went along with my wife's wishes to join Tom Connealy's church was because it meant coming home again. Here, to these streets where I had been a happy boy."

He swept his hand across the view in front of the windshield.

"Do your parents still own the motel?"

"No. Now my parents run an agency, procuring more and more motels for the tribe of emigrating Patels. They have taken advantage of the opportunities presented to them. They fulfill the American dream."

We slowed as we approached the church.

"Look how the exterior walls have been sandblasted. Look at the clusters of grapes hanging from vines, how they stand out so sharply."

I looked. The vines wound around the windows' Moorish arches.

He said, "They don't make churches like that anymore, do they? Even Catholic churches. Churches today look like hulking saunas."

He was right about that. The rectory was a large, lovely house on a street with trees so old their branches formed an arch over us. Aside from the motel and the gym on the busy corner, the street was full of other large houses that had once been lovely too—before the motel was built. Several were in the process of being spiffed up, returning from their rooming-house status. There was a sign on the newly clipped rectory lawn, like an accountant or chiropractor would have who works from home: ST. LAWRENCE O'TOOLE RECTORY. We parked on the street and so did the plainclothes behind us. There was a third car behind them, a technician from the local FBI offices. Rocky agreed we might as well take a chance and depend on our skills of creativity and persuasion, which would require a technician at the ready.

A woman opened the rectory door. She had a filthy rag in her hand. I hoped she hadn't been drying dishes with it. The detective said, "Hello, Jean. We've come to see the monsignor."

Rocky certainly knew *this* housekeeper. I felt a little flutter of doubt about him. Was he too enmeshed after all?

The woman was unsure what to do. She dreaded the appearance of a cop, but she recognized this particular cop and didn't know if she should fear him.

"Did you have an appointment, sir?"

Very heavy brogue. Not long from Ireland.

Rocky said, "It's official police business we've come to see him about."

She caught her breath, grabbed the rag with the other hand too, and clutched it against her chest. I remembered the words of my body-signals trainer: *If a perp performs a physical action like he's been shot, you've got a man whose worst nightmare has just occurred.* In this case, a woman's worst nightmare.

She said, "I'll have the secretary call him," and she trotted away, leaving us standing there in the foyer.

The detective spoke to me, voice lowered. "That's Tom's sister. She'd been here for a visit. Tom brings her over for a couple of weeks every year. But when they lost their housekeeper, she filled in. Glad to be useful. He introduced her from the pulpit." He raised his eyes to the ceiling. He whispered very softly, "I can't believe this." He hadn't needed to confide that last thought to me. But he did, and the flutter in my heart resolved itself.

We waited. While the detective took in the ceilings, I perused the five portraits hung upon the walls. There was Jesus, sitting in a chair surrounded by children; the pope, in gold and white robes and miter; St. Patrick, similarly arrayed, driving the snakes out of Ireland with a long wooden staff; John F. Kennedy; and a smiling fellow who looked like Van Morrison in a Francis of Assisi–type outfit who I assumed had to be St. Lawrence O'Toole. Van was perhaps a descendant.

Rocky noticed my perusal. He pointed to the print of Jesus with the kids. "Tom added that one. During the recent debacle."

A man came into the foyer, very young, too young to be our priest. He wore a cassock, no collar. He smiled at me and then looked to Rocky. "Detective Patel, isn't it?"

"Yes."

They shook hands. Rocky said, "This is Agent Penelope Rice from the Federal Bureau of Investigation. Poppy, this is the church deacon, Robert Mahoney."

The deacon's face fell. With the forty-four major muscles of the face, human beings can make around ten thousand expressions. In the case of huge emotional deflation, all forty-four become completely flaccid.

I shook the deacon's hand, feeling an urge to shake it really hard in order to pump him up again, but he managed to pump himself up and put on a pleasantly curious expression made from concrete. It needed more muscles than he was using for it to be genuine. "From the FBI?" he asked cheerily, his voice cracking.

"Yes."

"But the police have been here. With a picture. We told them she'd been our housekeeper."

Rocky kept it simple. "Robert, we came to see Tom."

"Well, all right then. Please come into the parlor."

We followed him.

"Make yourselves comfortable." He gestured toward the sofa and chairs.

The detective said, "We'd prefer to stand. We need to see the monsignor now."

Punctured again. "I will tell him that." He left the room and was right back. "Tom is coming."

The deacon didn't know what to do, so he chose to sit in one of the chairs himself. Couldn't depend on his knees for support.

# 9

The monsignor appeared in the doorway, same cassock as the deacon but with a collar. He appeared unassuming, pleasant-looking, middle-aged. An air of resourcefulness. Average height, just a bit stocky. Same black hair and blue eyes as Danny O'Neill, though Monsignor Connealy's hair had just a few streaks of gray. He was calm and unsurprised because he'd been expecting something. Perhaps not us, but he'd anticipated something beyond a request to identify the face of a dead woman in a photo. With the recent headlines, he expected another visit from the police but certainly not— I didn't think—the parishioner who happened to be a homicide detective.

"Hello, Rocky. It's always good to see you."

Deacon Robert leaped to his feet. "Tom, Rocky has brought along a member of the FBI."

Member.

Rocky said, "Agent Penelope Rice, this is Tom Connealy."

The priest shook my hand, taking me in, still calm but wondering. "A pleasure it is." The Irish in his voice was not so strong as his sister's, but still unmistakable. Then he shook Rocky's hand.

The detective kept things simple. "Tom, we've come to ask you some questions concerning the disappearance and death of Kathleen Sullivan."

Tom's eyes didn't shift, his pupils didn't dilate. But he closed his eyes for a longer moment than a blink takes.

He said, "It is difficult to think of her as Kathleen Sullivan. She was Maureen to us. But I cannot tell you how grateful I feel to comply with that request. It's quieter in my study. We get a lot of visitors. Less likely to be disturbed there. Come."

He turned and we followed him out, as did the deacon. The priest was indeed the shepherd, leading the flock. Without looking back, though, he said, "Robert, you may go on about your business."

With that, the deacon slunk away.

The priest's study was lined with books—every wall—with room left only for the windows and doors. There was a large desk with a chair, a few cabinets, and two wing chairs facing the desk. He sat down behind the desk. Unassuming, but he would reign. And right off he could not contain his curiosity as to the presence of the FBI.

"What is your role, Agent?"

I said, "I'm acting as consultant."

"Has Maureen's death met the criteria necessary to involve the agency?"

"Kathleen Sullivan's death, yes."

"Kathleen Sullivan." He paused. "Then that's good. More chance for me to understand where I failed her. I am grateful for the opportunity to tell you all I know of her. All that transpired between us. I have made my confession to Christ's representative as to the relationship I had with her. My penance was to tell the law authorities what I told my confessor. I had the opportunity to do that earlier, but I found I could not. I have just now been praying for the strength I need: the strength to go back to the police with what I have to say." He smiled again, sadly, not benevolently. "But God has sent the police to me."

There was a knock at the door. Good thing. I like things to happen fast, but this was a lot to take in. My brain cells—and I would guess Rocky's too—were frantically regrouping.

Deacon Robert opened it and stood there. A vassal is supposed to act subservient in the presence of the master. But the deacon was determined to make an effort at taking on some sort of command.

"I'm sorry to disturb you, Tom. I hope you'll excuse me, but I have called our legal offices and they have reminded me that my job is to look after you. I haven't done what I should have. I—"

"Your job is to do my bidding."

Rocky said to the priest, "Excuse me, Tom, but a lawyer is a good idea."

I'd agree with that, for all our sakes. At least we were on the books, Deacon Robert's book anyway, as acknowledging the need for a lawyer.

The monsignor shook his head. "I have grown miserably tired of lawyers of late. I'll call if I need anything, Robert."

The deacon slipped back out.

The smile was gone from Connealy's lips altogether. "Kathleen Sullivan—our Maureen—was an inspiring young woman. She was driven to turn her life around and would let nothing deter her from the course she'd set. I was completely taken with that determination. I mistook my admiration and good feeling for love. Romantic love. At first I thought I'd fallen in love with her. But I had deluded myself."

He became still then, glanced downward, and thought for a few seconds, or maybe he was fitting in a quick little prayer. Rocky and I both gave him time to fill in his silence, though we both were brimming over with the need to ask questions—to keep up with his willingness to confess. Then he said, "Let me make clear, first off, that I did not sexually abuse her. There was no seduction here, either. I did not seduce Kathleen Sullivan, as some will come to believe, and she did not seduce me, as others will put forward. But in looking back, I see we each suffered from our own delusions: she, that a trustworthy man would see her through her intentions; and I, that I could return to a life I was perhaps meant to have. One that I'd not been permitted to lead.

"And so we conducted an affair, an affair of desperation, not love, though we felt affection for each other; God knows that was true. I understand the difference between feeling kindly toward someone and falling in love because I did fall in love once before, as a very young man in seminary. But there was no departing the seminary. It was not left to me to decide the validity of my vocation, but to my family. My worry at the time as to the suffering I would surely cause my parents made me weak—and the girl, desperate. She fled to negate my having to make a decision. As Catholic children we learn that sacrifice is all."

How I wish I could have cut the scene like a movie director. Or, better yet, ordered an instant replay. I was desperate to ask, *Is he saying what I'm hearing?* I could only glance at Rocky, to find he was looking right back. We continued to let the priest spill his insides.

"Maureen—excuse me, Kathleen Sullivan—and I enjoyed each other's company. But I was supposed to be a father figure, not a consort. So now I will place myself at the mercy of my parishioners—and the police too—as I have placed myself at the mercy of God."

Another knock at the door and a man barged in, a fat man, huffing and puffing. The deacon was a few steps behind, his look agonizing as he tried to follow conflicting orders. The fat man carried a briefcase.

"Monsignor," he said, and bowed his head.

Connealy stood. "I have told my deacon—"

The man turned to us, interrupting the priest. "I'm Attorney George Walsh. I represent the diocese. I will have to ask—"

Connealy said, "You will ask nothing. I am not being held against my will. I am speaking freely to these officers of the law. I have made the decision to—"

"Excuse me, monsignor, the death of Kathleen Sullivan is now considered suspicious. You might say something incriminating, and then—"

"So be it. I accept the consequences of what I say. All the same, I am asking you to leave."

And then we all three got to see the face of a certain breed of lawyer, not a criminal lawyer but a corporate lawyer, the kind the Church employs to run roughshod over the pathetic complaints of anyone fool enough to accuse a priest of anything untoward. He squared his shoulders.

"Under these circumstances, you do not have the authority to ask me to leave. The archbishop reminds you too, through me, that you are an independent contractor. He is under no obligation to offer you legal counsel, courtesy of the diocese. But through his good will—"

Now Rocky interrupted. He said, "Mr. Walsh, the next time I go to confession, I'll think of you and say, *Bless me, independent contractor, for I have sinned.*"

A very small smile played on the monsignor's lips, and he spoke before Attorney Walsh could regain his footing. "Yet again, Mr. Walsh, I will ask you to leave."

Walsh was actually relieved. He had performed his duty. Corporate counselors hate getting involved in criminal law. If a large corporation discovers the bookkeeper is stealing funds, they fire the bookkeeper but they don't press charges. Stockholders might get antsy. Of course, the bookkeeper goes on to another job, gets caught stealing again, and moves along to yet another corporation. No one has the gumption to blow the whistle. White-collar crime can translate to steps up the ladder of corporate success, no matter what the specialty. I've always felt capitalism was great as long as you didn't mind associating with moral pygmies.

The lawyer had said what he'd been hired to say. The rest was to be knee-jerk advice. "Just one thing then. A scandal is inevitable. But the scandal will be more widespread if you do not—"

Connealy stood, pointed at the door, and said, in a booming voice that sounded as though it were electronically enhanced, *"Go!"* A pulpit sonar boom used for hell-and-damnation sermons.

Walsh was out of the room, not quite knocking into the deacon, who dashed after him. The monsignor came around his desk to shut the door and sat down again.

He said, "Kathleen Sullivan came to me, and not only did I fail her, I made things worse for her than they were already. She said she was pregnant. When she told me that, a huge wave of happiness passed through me. A child! I asked her what she needed, what she wanted. Whatever she wanted, I would do. But she wanted nothing, only her baby. She told me she would leave so as to keep the child and our relationship secret. I said, no, absolutely not; I would leave the church. I would marry Maur—I would marry her. She said no. She said no because our feelings for each other were based on need, not on the love that marriage requires.

"I told her we should do it for the child. And in any case I would support her financially and there was no need for her to hide. I still intended to leave the Church because I would make my paternity known and would owe it to my parishioners to leave.

"I wanted to be part of her life. And the child's."

Again, he brought his fingertips together, looked down at them, thought his thoughts, said his prayer. We waited.

"Then she was gone. Run away, is what I thought. So as not to cause the great trouble that lay ahead if she stayed. I looked for her, but she'd disappeared off the face of the earth. Because, as we've found out, she'd killed herself. I was wrong to think she'd simply fled to be noble, but thinking that was the easy way out for me. I believed it because my experience with women from the time I was thirteen until I was forty-five and became a part of this parish was—it was limited. In fact, it was all but nonexistent."

Time to steer him. I asked, "Just why did you think she'd fled? What did you at least deduce from the fact that she was a woman, even if your experience was limited? Why would she have run?"

He raised his eyes to me. His face had become haggard. The misery that he'd at first tried to keep in check now overcame him. He said, "Perhaps, deep down, I simply wished that. She could see through nobility."

Human nature. An honest answer. Unless he'd killed her. Then it was a lie. But there were no flickering indications on his face of a lie.

He said, "The woman who'd recommended Maureen for her job here . . . both of us made what effort we could to find her. We told the police she had run away and that we were very worried. But as they pointed out, she was over twenty-one. They reviewed her background with us."

This time I hadn't corrected him when he referred to her as Maureen. "And when the body washed ashore?"

He swallowed. He said, "An officer called me. When he told us the body had very short hair, it was what I wanted to hear. The woman from the shelter—we were both so relieved, so grateful it wasn't her. We wanted to believe Maureen was all right. Not . . . dead. I'm sorry. I'm stunted, Agent Rice. I'm a priest who missed out on large segments of the usual life most people experience."

Now I corrected him. "There was no Maureen, Monsignor. She lied to you as to who she was."

His face reconfigured, grew stern. He reverted to philosophy. "The way of the world—the world outside the seminary, the rectory—the Church deliberately removes that world from us priests as young seminarians. The world is purposely obscured. We are benevolently brainwashed to be noble, heroes whose purpose is to devote ourselves to saving souls. The priesthood attracts many young boys who choose to take advantage of the opportunity to partake in such a fantasy and to be sheltered from all they are afraid to know. Can you understand that?"

I couldn't but Rocky could. He immediately said, "Yes. In fact, a Christian cousin of mine entered the seminary after he saw his first pornographic pictures. He was fourteen. He told me he was repulsed to learn that girls had pubic hair. He decided he would be a priest so he'd never have to see a naked woman in person. He'd been fanatically overprotected—human nudity had been hidden from him. He said he thought a naked woman would look like a statue. Like an angel."

Hard to believe. "I find that pretty extreme."

The two men gazed at me. Then Tom Connealy said, "Perhaps now it would seem extreme because of the permissiveness of society. But fear of sexuality is not an uncommon motivation to a vocation. The priesthood can be a refuge for those who are afraid of sex or, as with Rocky's cousin, revolted by the thought of it. Or who understand that they are not attracted to women but to men and therefore must suppress their sexuality via an acceptable celibacy."

"Or attracted to children."

"Yes. To children."

"Until you become independent contractors. And then you're out there."

His nostrils flared the tiniest bit, an automatic reaction to sarcasm. But he went on. "I have brought about this digression myself, haven't I? I am not making excuses for my behavior, for my actions. Let me tell you what happened, how it all began when the director from the homeless program our church supports called—this was two years ago—to tell me about . . . Kathleen Sullivan, who called herself Maureen Murphy. She told me the girl had been making strides in removing herself from drugs. Kathleen Sullivan had come to understand that first she had to remove herself from the people she got the drugs from, from the people who joined her in the taking of drugs, her street family. She told our director that she couldn't rely on family—not her street family or her real family either, as she put it—but had to rely on herself alone to stop the terrible slide she had been taking for so long a time. The woman said to me she felt Maureen—she felt *Kathleen* at some point must have reached the bottom of that slide. And she had made the decision to climb out rather than stay down there. She came to our shelter.

"Kathleen Sullivan did not tell the director about her real family, the one that abandoned her or failed her, or about the dysfunction that caused her to flee to the streets. We only knew she came to the shelter with a purpose, and its director knew I needed a housekeeper. And just as the people at the shelter had promised, the girl we knew as Maureen was both determined and industrious. I found that she was also especially intelligent, owning an intellect that could not be denied. What she told me was that she had finally come to understand, and to believe, that none of the self-destructive actions she had taken since she was very young were her fault. She said she would not take responsibility for them, as all her previous counselors and health care professionals had demanded that she do. She was a victim of circumstances beyond her control. She wanted to make new circumstances for herself, and she would be responsible only for them. Frankly, I found that made fine sense. I was full of respect for her trust in her own authority. She was audacious.

"But what I couldn't fathom were the terrible words she spoke to me one evening after she'd been here a time. She said—I can hear her words now—she said to me, 'Tom, I have not experienced a happy moment since I was seven years old.' We talked late into the night. Memories of happy moments, the ones she'd known as a very young child, were returning to her. Moments with her father. With her baby brother. With a sister. As she slowly recalled memories of happiness, she wanted more, wanted to make up for happiness denied her. She kept thanking me for giving her a chance within the parish. And I kept saying it was nothing. But she'd received so little charity in her life she thought I was a saint, which I am anything but.

"With all that—her determination, her genuine sincerity, her thoughtful intelligence—I lost my head. I made a choice, the wrong choice. My role was to counsel her, not give her affection. I developed an infatuation based on huge admiration. And so we made love. She told me she couldn't become pregnant. She was mistaken."

"Or she simply lied as she'd lied about who she was," I said.

He took a deep breath. "Perhaps, perhaps not. But now, because of the choice I made, she's dead."

I am much used to the *I-killed-her-though-I-didn't-really-kill-her* speech. Nora had made just such a confession. The guilt-ridden assume the responsibility; although there is another slant, that of the husband who beats his wife to death and says, *I really smacked her around so she wouldn't leave me—so she'd know I loved her—but she died.* An accident, if you will.

In the circumstances of the death of Kathleen Sullivan, the confession the priest made arose from grief, guilt, confusion, and some dreadful long-past interruption of normal childhood development. Yes, he was grieving the death of the girl who was Maureen, but he hadn't loved her as her sister had, hadn't known her long enough to truly love her, and he realized it. As I felt little fingers of sympathy rise up, I had to remind myself that if this man impregnated two woman and both died suspiciously soon into their pregnancies, he must have killed them.

The priest continued to talk. "I didn't love Kathleen in the way a man loves a woman. It was what I wished I could feel, but I knew what that love feels like. I'd experienced such love for another girl when I was just a boy, before I was a priest. A girl Kathleen Sullivan so reminded me of."

I had to give myself an order: *Ignore for now what he just said—save it, Poppy.* Rocky was rubbing his chin with the back of his hand, forcing himself to do the same. I kept to my pitiless tack. "Monsignor, in admitting to the relationship you and Kathleen had as penance, and if Kathleen Sullivan's child wasn't yours, then a scandal will be averted. And if the child *was* yours, *you* will become the perceived victim. Isn't that what you want here? To keep your station within this tragedy?"

I elicited the contempt I needed him to feel. He said, his voice quiet and dark, "The child was mine. I will fight off any supposition that I was bewitched by her."

"You say you hadn't known her long. You say you came to understand the life she led. You—"

"I didn't come to *understand* it. She told me of it. She told me *why* she led it. She trusted me. And I . . . I cared about her. I thought—"

"Excuse me, but she took on a man forbidden to her. As a long-time addict, she'd learned to survive because of her talent to manipulate. She used you to go after what she wanted: a secure little setup, a future cash cow. But unless you followed her around twenty-four hours a day, saw what she was up to every minute during the time of your sexual relationship with her, you don't know for a fact that you are the father of her child. Maybe she had several men she was working on in addition to yourself."

A flush of color suffused his cheeks.

"Monsignor, I would ask you to consider allowing your DNA to be compared with the DNA of the fetus. We have to start with the facts. Only then can we move more quickly to the truth: how Kathleen Sullivan came to die."

He had lost control for a fleeting moment, a microexpression of disgust that lasted as long as the flick of a camera's shutter. But the last few words of what I'd said hit home. He said, "I know the facts. The facts are not what you describe. The child could only be mine because of Maureen's dependence on me, the trust she placed in me. *Mis*placed, I am ashamed to say. I will at least do that for her—prove that I am the father of our dead child."

She was Maureen again. She had come back to him. Good.

He put his face in his hands. He *had* loved her, he loved her now, but he didn't know it because he was stunted. He thought he was betraying the first girl, Nuala's girl, by loving Kathleen. Rocky reached out across the desk. The priest felt his touch and pulled back. He brought his face up to us again. He had no more to say. The man was spent.

So now I used my professional, nonjudgmental voice. "Monsignor, your offer to provide a sample for DNA testing is absolutely necessary and I am gratified for that. But will you give evidence as to what Kathleen Sullivan told you about the crime perpetrated against her by a member of her family when she was a child? As you have encouraged others to do? You know who and what drove her into the streets. Will you do that as well?"

He was unable to respond or he chose not to. I guessed the latter, though I didn't know why he wouldn't.

"Monsignor," I said, my voice a lot softer, "your failure to do what was right by Kathleen was not what killed her. I need to know how she came to drown."

He came back. His shoulders rose. "I am afraid to know."

No kidding.

"I am a Catholic priest. I am here, in Boston, at ground zero—if I make the kind of accusation you have suggested, they will see only the hypocrisy."

Aha! "There is nothing to be done about that."

Rocky said, "What people think, Tom, might be a problem for you. Not for us. If it's scandal you are referring to, I am unable to empathize. The avoidance of scandal is simply a dreadful church psychosis, nothing more."

The monsignor's chin lifted. His face strengthened; his shoulders rose too. He said, "And might I ask if you understand the Church's aversion to scandal? Where it comes from?"

The detective said, "From the word of the Lord."

"Yes, from all four of his chroniclers—Matthew, Mark, Luke, and John. If you sin and you repent, you are forgiven. If you incur sin in others—even without intention—your sin is far more grievous since you are inherently responsible for each of the spreading sins.

"Jesus was explicit. *Woe to the man through whom scandal comes.* The sin—a priest forcing a child to have sex—does not compare, in the eyes of the Church, with the gravity of revealing that sin, which sows the seeds of scandal, each seed blooming into new sin. Hence, the person who makes the revelation is guilty of vast multitudes of sin, sin feeding upon more sin."

I hadn't listened to a sermon in a long time. I found myself becoming fairly rapt.

"In fact, the church teaches the peril of scandal to our very young children. When they are seven, when they attain the age of reason, they are warned that if they approach the altar to receive the sacrament of the Holy Eucharist but then recall a sin they neglected to confess, even if they deliberately didn't confess it, they should still take the host. If not, the people in the church will begin to wonder why they didn't and perceive something that never existed, which might lead to false accusations, to—"

He stopped. He interrupted the rhythm. He came down from the pulpit and back to us. "For a long time I felt it would be disloyal not to support this interpretation of Jesus' words. But then I found I could not suppress thinking that what such an interpretation is saying is that if a child reveals he's been sexually abused, he becomes the greatest sinner of all because of the scandal he's created—all the idle rumors, which serve to spread the sin further and further. And worse, because he has scandalized the Church in the process. I began to realize that this warped interpretation laid the groundwork for our children's victimization. At which point I became so filled with fury that it was time to take my dissatisfaction and confusion elsewhere."

Now he sighed. Now he would confide in Rocky and me. "I took a year's leave just before this assignment here at St. Lawrence's. During that year, I came to see that my doubts meant one thing—that I was a pretty good priest. I had given myself the time not only to study the scriptures but to contemplate them. Jesus, the man, was not a complicated fellow, he was—in a word—compassionate. The woe he wished upon one who created scandal was meant simply to prevent *gossip*. A hurtful thing gossip is, never innocent. That's all Jesus was telling us when he lamented scandal.

"I rethought, I reconsidered everything, and then I came back to my pastoral duties. But I came back too soon, before I found solace in myself. And so I looked for solace elsewhere. In a sweet girl."

Not the first and surely not the last to make that mistake. Rocky said, "Monsignor, the point here is that—"

"I know what the point is. Kathleen Sullivan's child was mine. I am only happy to prove it."

I dropped my bomb as casually as I could, hoping it would pass for simple FBI routine. "We weren't sure, Monsignor, if you would feel this way or not. But if so, we didn't want you to have to go to a laboratory. The most reliable sample, most easily obtained, is a cheek swab. There is a police car outside, unmarked. We have a technician in the car."

The monsignor was impressed, an admiring expression in his eyes. "Then let's get it done."

Rocky whipped out his cell phone. While he spoke, the monsignor said to me, "Something we all learn as teenagers when introduced to biology—that the cells inside the cheek are easiest to collect and will remain alive for several minutes. We get to look at them squirming around under the microscope. A teenager is always so happy with instant gratification."

"Yes." And I remembered my own high school biology class, the proof of the pudding there in front of us in only seconds. I said to him, "It is only the long dead whose bones must be pulverized and liquefied for DNA to be extracted."

I can be a slave to my pet peeves. I am easily annoyed when criminals, even possible criminals, rely on friendly chitchat to place themselves on an equal level with me. He turned his face away.

From beyond the office came the most hideous sound, loud and inhuman. What with the accoutrements of my surroundings, I couldn't help but think it was the devil himself.

Tom Connealy got up, threw the office door open, and ran down the hallway.

I said to Rocky, "What the hell is that?"

"It's the sound of Irish mourning."

We dashed out and found the housekeeper collapsed in the arms of the monsignor and Deacon Robert on his knees reciting the Lord's Prayer very loudly, I guess in an attempt to drown out the keening. To no avail. The woman's mouth was wide open and the cry issued forth.

There are many kinds of howls, all unique. The howl at news of a death, the howl at the sight of a dead loved one, the howl when someone learns he has been undone. But this? This series of howls developed by the Irish was the worst. Connealy's eyes met mine. He said, "She refuses to accept what I've admitted to. She begged me not to reveal what is the truth. When you arrived, she could see that I would not be stopped."

And then he began to say her name, to repeat it over and over and over: "Jean, Jean, Jean. . . ." Eventually, he calmed her. A shot of tranquilizer from our technician would keep her that way for a while. Robert led her away. And then the monsignor stepped into another room and donated living cells from the inside of his cheek to the FBI crime lab.

~~~

In the morning, Tom Connealy's sister went off to the editorial offices of *The Boston Globe* to tell them there was a rumor that the monsignor was the father of Kathleen Sullivan's child, but it was not true even though the girl had tried to seduce the priest. Her next stop was a police station, where she confessed to murdering Kathleen Sullivan. Jean Connealy was arrested.

As soon as the paper hit the streets, several hundred people marched on the residency of the Archbishop of Boston, demanding that Tom Connealy remain their shepherd in spite of the scandal.

That same day, I said to Rocky, "Let's go visit Nora. See if she's made any decision."

Nora was home and smiled when she saw it was us. Sad smile, though.

"I'm glad you came. It makes me understand that all this is really happening. But still, I'm a wreck."

I said, "You're entitled."

"Is it true what the priest's sister said?"

"Some of it."

We told her which part was true, a truer interpretation of Jean Connealy's statement.

"Do you think my sister was pregnant by the priest?"

"Yes." We certainly didn't bring up the Irish girl.

She smiled and shook her head. "My sister meant business. Chose to have a child. A priest was as close to doing it all by herself as she could come."

I said, "Nora, he was in love with your sister."

She lifted her chin.

Rocky said, "Yes. It is not how it sounds. He loved her. He is desolate."

"It still doesn't sound very good, Detective."

"No, it doesn't. We are not helping you to feel better, are we? Though that is what we are trying to do."

"I think maybe some tea would help me feel better. Would you like some?"

I wouldn't, but I said yes.

Rocky would, and he said yes too.

"I'll be right back."

Nora's art was her home. Elegant. She'd surrounded herself with warm, serene beauty. No children to disturb the artistry. Perhaps there would never be children, considering her own childhood. I know someone who once told me she'd never have children for fear she'd hate them as much as her mother hated her.

Nora returned. She was agitated, yes, but she stood straight. She said, "We'll go sit on the back porch, is that all right? And have our tea."

Everyone should have Nora's back porch. Rocky and I were transported. Big raffia-woven furniture, big cushions, big orchid plants all around with long stems weighted down by blooms that looked like giant obscene butterflies about to take flight. Other plants had buds so large and fat, I hoped they wouldn't open while I was there because Thumbelina could well hop out. There was a crocheted hammock with a book lying in it. Nora actually used the hammock.

Rocky and I waited. She brought out a tray. She poured. Cloves floated to the top of our cups. Once she sat down again, we raised our shell-thin teacups to our lips.

I said, "Where exactly were your mom and dad while your uncle was forcing you to have sex with him?"

Nora didn't bat an eyelash. The reminding had already taken place. She knew the encounters themselves would never happen ever again even if she thought of them, even if she spoke out loud of them. She gazed through the windows onto her lawn and garden, walled off from the rest of Boston by vintage bricks.

Rocky was still, blending into the tiled floor.

She looked back to me. "I have learned that your tactic is to say the unspeakable in order to unlock words probably never spoken before."

"Yes."

"You cause a lot of pain in your job, don't you?"

"Yes."

"But in laying claim to the truth, pain is unavoidable."

"Yes."

She looked to Rocky. "Do you do that too, Detective Patel?"

"If the person I am questioning needs unlocking. But only if that unlocking will lead to a resolution of an injustice. Neither of us do it because we think it is good for the person we are questioning. We are not psychotherapists."

I said, "It's justified fury that gives us the stamina to steamroll over people who deserve only to be soothed. I'm sorry, Nora."

"Coping with being steamrolled—it's really nothing. Not for me. Not after what I've spent half my life coping with."

"I'm sorry."

"In fact, for many years I've had to steamroll over my own fury— crush it—so as not to give anything away."

Neither Rocky nor I spoke.

"It was during my parents' weekly business meetings. There were two rooms in our house where they conducted business, the business of politics. Every Tuesday night." She placed her cup in its saucer.

She folded and unfolded her hands lying in her lap. Folded them again. She certainly couldn't trust herself to hold a teacup. "Tuesdays. Damn, damn, damn Tuesdays . . . Adjoining rooms, big French doors in between. These were political meetings of the crew of kingmakers. Two jobs would be going on at once: in one room brainstorming, in the other, strategy. My father led the ideas people, my mother the strategists. Sometimes people left one room and exchanged places with those in the other room. Or people would have to go out to phone someone, use the bathroom, leave for another obligation and then come back. Uncle Sean would leave the meetings for twenty minutes or so. I have no idea what he told them he was . . . doing."

A tiny blaze came to Rocky's eyes. Controlled fury.

"Nora, did you tell your parents such a detail when you confronted them?"

"I tried. But my father almost immediately began weeping and my mother spoke over my words, telling me how twisted I was."

I thought of something. "Are the Tuesday meetings still happening?" Today was Tuesday.

"Yes. A tradition. They keep up those meetings in the face of anything, and they will meet tonight. I don't know if personal failures carry the same weight as political failures, but I should think the gang could well be contriving to take my parents down. They must be, what with all this. And my mother has to be aware that they could turn on her for their own survival. But nothing stops her, nothing. Just a matter of cleaning up the blood." Her eyes raised to the leafy tranquil scene outside the window. "Once—I guess I was fourteen or fifteen—my little brother and I came home from school and we had to help my mother clean up because there was a meeting that night. Kathy had sliced her wrists.

"My sister got to go to the hospital for that particular Tuesday. My therapist tells me that my two brothers and I are probably able to weather the worst crises after growing up in that house. She's right. My mother is an emotionless robot. I guess we are too."

Rocky said, "But you are now weathering crises in a human way, not like a robot would. I admire your fortitude very much."

Bang, her eyes filled with tears. No one should require the kind of fortitude forced upon her. So I said, right away, "What time do your parents' meetings start?"

"Eight o'clock."

"Consider stopping by, Nora. You're in the middle of what you have to do. Make your revelation public tonight."

＊＊＊

As she later would tell us, Nora arrived at her parents' house about seven-forty-five that evening, just in time to welcome their guests.

There was nothing her parents could do about her presence. Her mother had no choice but to be pleasant, though her father looked at her as if she were a dying dog. "He actually brought me a glass of water," she said.

It was a warm night. Before the meeting began, the members of the Sullivan cartel drank vodka and tonic, lots of lemons, while Nora stuck with her glass of water. Then she began to speak of the Tuesday nights of ten–fifteen years ago and reminisced with the group about various legislators whom they'd decided should be ousted and those who could continue to count on their support. They chatted as if nothing was happening in their lives out of the ordinary. Nora said she felt her mother growing calm, gratified for the shift in focus from what she feared the evening would be like to the group's successful work.

But then Nora, out of the blue as she put it, said, "My Uncle Sean was a big part of Tuesday nights for me. And for my late sister, Kathleen, whom you all mourned along with us. Back then when

I was a child, while you were here in my home, week after week, discussing various legislators, Sean was in my bedroom, his hand pressed over my mouth, raping me."

She said the ensuing silence lasted just a few seconds, and then panic set in—a glass dropped from someone's hand, shattering on the floor. Her mother began shouting at her while her father stood nearby, frozen in place. Nora walked out. She doubted if anyone so much as noticed her departure.

# 10

I'd gotten the swab directly to Auerbach, posthaste, by messenger, via a commercial flight, while Rocky Patel carried forth an equally pressing job. He issued a warrant for the arrest of Justice Sean Scanlon. Nora Sullivan had told her story to the police and pressed charges. She'd had her brother Kieran by her side. Rocky was there. He called to fill me in.

"When she finished telling us what she'd come to say, Kieran followed. He admitted to making the phone call. He'd had a tiff with his uncle after deciding to look into the documents of the family trust. Kieran discovered the fund was dwindling. Sean was executor. Kieran said Sean was fairly drunk when he confronted him. Sean threatened him—told him to shut up about his damned trust or he might end up at the bottom of the harbor too.

"So it looks like the boy had taken to wondering. He knew Scanlon had been called to identify a body, remembered feeling so relieved when it hadn't been his sister. So he decided to verify what he'd been wondering. He made the call. As Nora explained, he wanted to get back at Sean. There were no higher motives."

Rocky also reported that the porn webmaster had led police to another acquaintance who had seen Kathleen with Sean around the time she died.

Rocky said, "The statute of limitation concerning child abuse has been dissolved. Sean Scanlon is wanted for the crimes he perpetrated against his two nieces, and now for questioning in the suspicious death of the younger of them."

I congratulated him.

But *The Boston Globe* moved that particular headline lower down on page one. They suddenly had a replacement for the prime spot. Uncle Sean had been forewarned of the charge, no doubt by one of the many who owed him. He skipped.

Rocky Patel was a basket case, so upset that I went to his precinct and sat in a chair in his office while he paced. "Dear God, they'll probably find him in a cheap Las Vegas hotel room feigning a psychotic illness."

He knew whereof he spoke. Judges who break the law have a penchant for that kind of thing. After a judge is found, he says he's suffering from some obscure brain disease that developed into a Jekyll and Hyde personality, forcing him to embark on a hideous double life. With that, people will believe the man has a good side and a bad side, the good side exemplary, so good that obviously the bad side was something he was unable to control. He was powerless.

People end up saying, *He was a sick man, poor fellow.*

And his family would be photographed circled around him, a blur of loving compassionate faces. He'd serve time, for sure, but not much time, and not at some prison farm working the fields where fellow prisoners might break his nose with a hoe if he crossed them. He'd be someplace where he could write a book in peace, the crux of which would be a defense of his inability to control the terrible illness that had beset and overtaken him. Though he'd be very, very sorry about the embarrassment to his family, he would never take responsibility for what he'd done. And then he'd walk out of prison and into the loving arms of his family while all the law enforcers who'd busted their tails trying to see justice done would be hoping he'd cross a street and get hit by a Mack truck.

I'd said as much once to my friend Joe Barnow, who as an ATF agent way up in the ranks has seen it all. And he'd said to me, "Poppy, you're not considering the devastating impact the traffic accident would have on the truck driver."

That translated into: *Those who are treated as though they are above the law need to have the rug pulled out from under them. We can't just hope they'll be killed crossing the street.* I knew that, but I'm human. I'm still hoping a lot of people out there get hit by Mack trucks, one a Texas killer who was able to rearrange the muscles of *her* face as if she were her own personal plastic surgeon.

I tried to reassure Rocky. "Uncle Sean's situation is different from the judges you describe. He didn't commit larceny or wire fraud. Ask the average man in the street what larceny is, what mail fraud is, and he'll shrug his shoulders. But the man in the street does know what sex with a child is, especially a man in the streets of Boston. Ground zero, as the monsignor put it. So when you find the good judge, even though his wife will stay glued to his side right up to the sentencing, he'll serve hard time. In a field, detective, where a hoe will be issued to him.

"Or maybe it'll be worse for him. Maybe Sean Scanlon is the person who killed Kathleen Sullivan. Maybe the monsignor's support inadvertently gave her the wherewithal to confront her uncle. Maybe Nora's instincts were right on the money. Kathleen Sullivan put her uncle's career, his standing—everything—in jeopardy. So maybe the judge did it."

"But could he have taken the step from anger to murdering her?"

"People make that step every day. Forget his position. This man took steps to act on his sexual aberration. Part of that aberration includes the pain inflicted on the victims. I mean, Rocky, the children *cry*. The only way to find out whether he killed Kathleen is to bring him in. Do that. Any backup service you might need, you'll have. You'll have the FBI at your disposal starting with me, okay?"

Rocky had calmed himself. He said, "I still vote for Las Vegas or a version thereof. You have jarred me, Poppy. I will now stop sniveling."

Whatever. And I'd worry about procuring the services of the FBI for him later.

~~~

My man Auerbach said, calm as a cucumber because he had the same amount of faith in me that I did in him, "It's official. Those mucous membrane cells you sent me contain the DNA markers that match those of both fetuses."

"Draw up a report right away then. Now, okay? Fax it to me."

"The report's being written."

I started to thank him. For dropping everything and putting his lab into a spin. But he'd read my mind.

"Don't thank me. I'm just doing what I do."

He sees reading minds as doing what he does, anticipating requests, setting everything in action before the request even comes, risking the ire of budget committees.

Then I called Rocky Patel, who also knew what I would have to say. Who knew his pastor friend would officially be under suspicion as well as Sean.

Rocky said to me, "Then this is a gift for the judge. A priest got his niece pregnant. As to what Sean did to her as a child, I still worry he'll walk. All part of the disease he has."

"No, Rocky. Nobody will buy any such disease story." Then I said, "Ready to go break the news to him?"

"Yes. I'll be right over to get you."

We drove to St. Lawrence O'Toole's, this time led by a marked squad car packed with uniformed bolt preventers. The typical scenario would be to ask the monsignor to answer questions voluntarily and his answers would not be held against him in a court of law. If he refused to answer, we'd have to place him under arrest or give it up. If he attempted to leave and we prevented that, he was automatically under arrest without our ever having to say so. We'd go directly to Miranda. Hence, the threatening pack of bolt preventers at our beck and call.

Poor Deacon Robert. He escorted Rocky and me to Tom's office. Tom wasn't there. We found him in his church at the altar, kneeling under the cross, praying, and the deacon left us there and then scurried away—my guess, to call Attorney Walsh.

We walked the length of the aisle, then stood off to the side, in front of the pews where a groom and best man normally take up position to await the bride. The bulbs in the chandeliers were dimmed, the banks of candles in their red crystal cups on either side of the altar flickering. The monsignor stood and turned, and the soft heels of his shoes made no sound as he walked across the vast, glowing marble field of the altar floor and down the steps to meet us.

Connealy said to us, "My sister killed no one."

Rocky took a step toward him. "I'm sorry, Tom. The bail will be reduced if her confession is considered faulty. But we're not here to talk of Jean's plight. We're here to talk about you."

"The DNA results."

"Yes." It was not necessary for Rocky to tell him the results, at least so far as they pertained to Kathleen Sullivan. All the same, he did.

There was not a shred of vindictiveness, or humility, or pride, or anything else in the priest's expression. He merely said, "Because of your test, because of my lack of humility in agreeing to it, my sister is in jail. But she saw herself as performing her duty in protecting me, the priest in her family, her free ticket to heaven. Her priest, right or wrong. No one will look at the absurdity of her confession until they've got someone else. If Kathleen was murdered, if she didn't commit suicide, I imagine I will become the chief suspect."

Now I waited for Rocky to tell the man he was, in fact, already under suspicion, for two deaths, not one. But the detective was having a hard time. It's one thing to take down an enemy. Taking down a friend is another altogether. He needed a few seconds to gear up. Then he spoke very quietly and calmly, in the same tone the monsignor had used in the defeated delineation of his sister's tragic actions.

Rocky said, "Those same DNA results also show you to be the father of the fetus of an unidentified woman whose remains were found in Ireland, in County Galway, in 1972."

I studied the priest's eyes, watched as his pupils dilated and then contracted, waited to see what his eyes might reveal next. Emotions travel directly from the stomach to the eye—shock, fear, doubts, a thrill. Fear is what I was hoping for. Wrap it right up. But he looked from the detective to me without fear, only befuddlement. "I don't understand . . . remains?"

His shock was not manufactured. It was the shock of hearing paralyzing news. But it could also have been the shock of simply hearing something he thought would never be forthcoming. I watched him carefully because that latter sort of shock belies an arrogance, an arrogance that releases an ensuing babble of denial. No babble ensued. His shock was not the calculated shock of a sociopath. It was not the shock of the trapped, whose eyes dart about, trying to figure out how to disappear. The monsignor's shock reflected utter astonishment, the clear unmistakable shock that appears in the innocent. But I would not fall into that trap. An investigator must presume guilt, not innocence. Capture those presumed guilty—trap 'em, wrap 'em, ship 'em, and that's that. Proof of innocence is left to the court.

The monsignor breathed again. The truly shocked stop breathing just as he had. I have seen such a deprivation of oxygen culminate in a crumbling faint. A criminal who is a fairly good actor can mimic that, pretend to pass out, and one who is an exceptionally fine actor knows enough to hold his breath and musters a genuine faint.

A church holds a special silence, heavy and dank. When the silence is broken, it seems almost a physical thing. The priest's words rent the silence in two. "She's *dead*?"

He'd begun blinking and the blinking didn't look deliberate either, but rather in sync with his words, the muscles of his cheeks pulling taut as wires. "She died? But she—"

He stopped. His eyes closed. I stepped closer, afraid he might faint after all. But he was simply waiting, waiting in hopes that our presence and our words were some kind of hallucination. He breathed very deeply. He was a public speaker; he knew what to do when feeling faint. His eyes opened and he said, "Dear Mother of God. She was pregnant?"

There was no need to answer either of his questions. He believed us. The Irish girl was dead and she'd been pregnant.

And then the church doors flew open, slamming against the walls, the noise reverberating, spreading across the church like a gunshot. Attorney Walsh came pounding down the aisle. The legal office of the archdiocese of Boston is not nearby. He had gotten advance warning that Rocky and I were on our way to St. Lawrence O'Toole's. I leaned in to the detective. "Better find out who your leaks are."

He whispered back, "Maybe an angel."

Walsh's shoes were not soft-soled. The thudding of his heavy heels echoed. When he reached the place where we stood, Rocky said to him before he could speak, "Monsignor Connealy will be requiring a criminal lawyer. Please do something useful and see to that." Strong words, but his announcement was quiet; he was in church, after all.

The lawyer's words bounced off the marble. "You've *arrested* him?"

"No. But he is under suspicion. We're questioning him informally."

"Under suspicion of exactly what?"

I said, "The DNA results show that the monsignor fathered the Sullivan woman's fetus—"

He put his hand out to me, palm forward. "Enough. Monsignor, I must advise you to—"

"—and they have shown, as well, that he fathered another fetus, the fetus of a woman who drowned thirty years ago under unusual circumstances in Ireland. Those unusual circumstances were identical to those of the Sullivan woman's death."

The lawyer said, "What the hell are you talking about?"

"I'm talking about Monsignor Connealy's . . . *children*." I'd opted for dramatic effect. "The children were drowned along with their mothers. Women who were the monsignor's lovers."

He said, "What *lovers*?"

I stayed the course. "Both babies carried the DNA of one man. This man, your client." As I was speaking those words, I was thinking: *Please don't say what Delby said.*

But he did. Almost. "Well . . . maybe these women were cousins."

Heaven forbid that the same man would have had sex with sisters, I guess. If only this idiot were to represent Uncle Sean.

Best to ignore him. "Monsignor Connealy, what was the girl's name? The girl in Ireland."

His eyes filled with tears. He was thinking her name already. He said, "Maeve."

"Her last name?"

"Doyle."

Before the lawyer could say something stupid again, the priest said, "Agent Rice, Rocky, will you allow me to pray? For just a few minutes before we go on with this?"

Why not? The stunned Walsh had to understand what was coming down so he could find a real lawyer for his client. The detective started extolling such a necessity to the man again while Tom Connealy ascended his altar once more, strode to the kneeler where we'd found him when we arrived, walked right past it, and disappeared through the wall.

I drew my gun and ran. Rocky was right behind me, his revolver out too. He blew a whistle to alert the cops outside.

Rocky and I practically killed each other, trying to run through the narrow opening in the wall of marble that led off the altar into the vestry. Inside, there was an exterior door and two closed interior doors. The detective ran outside while I opened a closet full of vestments and then the door to the basement of the church. I ran down the stairs. The basement was kind of a spare church, a dark and gloomy one, full of places to hide—altar and pews, aisles and confessionals. A uniformed officer from the squad car appeared; he had run in from another set of stairs at the back of the lower church and was scrambling down the aisle toward me.

I shouted, "Stay here! Search. And draw your gun, officer, we have a dangerous man in this place."

I ran through another door into an underground passageway probably a hundred yards long, threw open the door at the opposite end, and nearly ran over two nuns who were standing at the rear of the auditorium of the St. Lawrence O'Toole Elementary School. Their wide eyes traveled from my face to my gun and they both shrieked. Six hundred children on their first day back to school knew enough to dive for cover. Watched more TV than the nuns, I guess. I ran through the rear doors of the auditorium and ended up in a playground, where I stood looking at the swing set and the slides, the jungle gym, and the chain-link fencing that the monsignor had scaled. There was no sign of him.

<center>~~~</center>

Deacon Robert told us—voice dry, his face without any color whatsoever—that Tom had taken the same route I had, into the school via the corridor used for the purpose of allowing the children to file into church without having to put on their coats and hats. With a weak and cracking voice he told me that fifty yards down the street behind the school was the MTA station. Monsignor Connealy had taken the T to a destination unknown.

Then Deacon Robert fainted. Genuine faint, the real deal. I could see it coming. I caught him.

# 11

I called my friend, a shrink. I go to him for advice I don't need. But he has X-ray vision, sometimes saving me as much as an entire day of working out psychological motivation since he can see into people's brains. We're nuts about each other, me on a professional level, he on the same, plus an emotional one besides. Being a shrink, he knows it's up to him to cope with that difficulty, not me. He's at Stanford, having ripped himself out by the roots from his work in London at Scotland Yard and from his home in the Cotswolds, which is literally a castle. In England, he was a profiler, their best, but he burned out. He wants no more of actual crime, so instead he teaches grad students everything he learned on the job. For excitement, he goes to Las Vegas periodically and plays baccarat. When a seriously high roller visits Vegas, he's treated as if he's James Bond. I told him once that there was no such thing as James Bond. He said, "A few days of fantasy living renews me."

I couldn't reach him at his office. In fact, there was no way he could be reached at all, according to the secretary. "He'll be back tomorrow at four. I'll have him call you then, Agent Rice."

Okay. To a gambler, the academic life is an enabler.

He tended to leave the tables around 2 A.M., whether winning or losing, which differentiates him from all the other gamblers who, if winning, wouldn't leave until they'd lost their winnings, or, if losing, wouldn't quit, in hopes of turning their luck around. A high roller, cleaned out and exhausted—often drunk—tends to be escorted back to his room around dawn. My shrink sees himself as a disciplined gambler, which he feels justifies his spells of fantasy, such as they are.

I called the Bellagio at two-thirty.

He picked up. I said, "Did you draw a lot of nines?"

He laughed.

"I need to kibitz."

"Then let us kibitz in person. I've lost so much money at this place they've given me a five-room suite. I haven't been in two of the rooms yet. We could go exploring." I let him babble a little more. "In the entry to the suite is a copy of Canova's *Pauline Bonaparte.* In her perfect nudity, she doesn't measure up to you."

"Thank you." I no longer bother with my lecture about how his money could be better put to use aiding humanity. His argument is probably valid. He told me he gives a fortune to charities and if he didn't have fun throwing another bunch of it away, he wouldn't donate what he donates. He'd put it in the futures market instead and do his gambling there like other rich men who do not give to charities.

I let him go on a little about how we all deserve some fun once in a while. A psychiatrist can rationalize with panache.

Then I said, "Listen, I just might find myself in Vegas."

"Really? Lucky me. When?"

First, I told him about the sleazy judge whose penchant might have been, after all, to head for Nevada. Then I went backward and told him about Nuala O'Neill, right on through until the priest's bolt. I said, "A guess based on the shock he showed. But they were probably murdered."

Then I told him they might have committed suicide or had an accident but I doubted it. That I would be working on all that since I could be wrong about Connealy not being the culprit.

And I said, "This priest's sister confessed to killing the Boston girl. Now she'll no doubt confess to killing the Irish girl once the DNA story gets out. If it's out, she's probably confessing as we speak." Actually, I learned later she was doing just that.

Finally, "So what do you think?"

His turn.

"The root of your question is grounded in Texas. The insecurity you developed there when you allowed yourself to determine whether or not a woman was guilty or innocent. You've forgotten that this is not up to you."

"I'm doing that?"

"Yes."

"But I've always done that."

"Not to the extent that it hinders you. Poppy, there is a suspect. The Boston PD made that official. They asked for help from the FBI. Your job is to go after him. That's it. And here is what I think. Same as I always think. You have to know your man. Then the unavoidable guesses and premonitions as to whether he could kill or not will not interfere with your proven prowess in bringing an offender to justice."

I felt myself deflate.

"Poppy?"

"What?"

"It's a fairly typical syndrome in a law enforcer. A sort of slump. Everyone has slumps. You just keep swinging the cricket bat until you find your form again."

Cricket. This shrink can make me laugh no matter what. "Okay, then, I certainly haven't stopped swinging. Let's return to the business at hand."

"Let's."

"How can one know a priest? A priest's family is cut off from him from the time he enters a seminary as a twelve-year-old. He has no wife and children. He has no friends because his fellow priests are too encumbered with their duties to be friendly, and the parishioners are too in awe to be pals. With our priest, a sister has anointed herself protector, the old-world spinster-variety sister meant to care for family members as she ages rather than have a life of her own. All I know, and this from my Boston homicide detective cohort who happens to belong to the priest's church, is that his family had money and that not too long ago he made a sea change in his priestly career, moved to Rome, came home again, and turned a disaster-area parish into a showpiece. Antagonized the now-deposed cardinal, who was loyal to medieval aspects of the Church. And as we all know, the priest succeeded, along with other more direct causes, the result probably far more astounding than he'd ever imagined."

"Meaning the great scandal."

"I think if I hear the word *scandal* one more time I will puke. Aiding and abetting sex offenders brought the cardinal down."

"Yes. You're right about that. Not one to let anyone cloud the facts, are you? No need to answer that, Poppy. Rhetorical. Dearest girl, obviously you know a lot already. The spinster sister in custody— she'll have a storehouse of family lore as she is the ultimate martyr. Don't put off talking to her. Let her whine and moan to you, even though I understand that it's difficult having to question someone so self-destructively neurotic. She'll know what you need most—his habits—since obviously she never lost track of him. Maybe she's been visiting him over the years. She was familiar with his life in Ireland. Get information from her. Your priest is a lone wolf. But he didn't become a lone wolf until after the Irish girl was gone from his life so many years ago."

"Too bad I can't chat up Jesus."

"That *is* too bad."

"By habits, you're suggesting . . . what?"

"His ways. In order to figure out where he ran to."

"FBI field offices, to say nothing of the Boston PD, are doing just that."

"But the thing is, why would he hide? From what you've said, he's admitted to everything all along. If he didn't kill anyone, what's he doing?"

"I don't know."

"What did his professional life require? Priests do many things besides celebrate mass. Maybe the Church gave him a job where he helped track down missing parishioners. Or missing wives, or missing children. Priests do that, Poppy. Right now, if you're feeling he's innocent of killing the two pregnant women, I'd have to say—"

My shrink friend loves to drop a ton of bricks on my head when I need it. Today, two tons. The first having to do with a complimentary round of personal analysis, the second with aiding me in separating the wheat from the chaff.

I said, "Shit," and then I told him I had to go, and he said, "I know that," as I was hanging up.

◆◆◆

I called Deacon Robert and identified myself. Then I interrupted him in the middle of his asking how I was. "Robert, have you been in the monsignor's rooms since he . . ."—since he what?—"since he left?"

"Yes."

"Did you see a packed suitcase?"

"Yes. It was by the door."

Tom Connealy had intended to leave even before we told him about the Irish girl. The monsignor wasn't on the run, he was going after the judge. It had been patently probable, and the shrink, being a gambler, thrived on probabilities. He'd adapted the lessons of foibles—foible, singular—to his life's work.

Lucky for me.

Next call—to Rocky—and I told him what I thought. He said, "But what does Tom expect to do with Sean Scanlon once he finds him? Ask him to confess? To repent?"

"Maybe Tom intends to strangle him. That's what I'd like to do to him."

"No. Tom is a gentle man. But Sean Scanlon is not. It's Tom who is in jeopardy here."

"A desire for revenge is a personality-altering cataclysm, Rocky, as any count from Monte Cristo will tell you. They're both in danger."

Rocky wasn't really listening to me. Which is what people do when they don't want to hear what you're saying. So that's why he said, "Poppy, if he finds Scanlon before I do, here's what will happen. Tom will call me."

"He will? Listen, the monsignor blames himself for the death of two women. Two women he loved. The death of two unborn children is on his conscience too. You can't expect him to behave rationally. When we spoke to him in the church, I asked him if he would reveal what Kathleen told him about Sean. He didn't answer me, remember? That's because he already had another plan."

This annoyed the detective. "Do you always make suppositions based on cynicism?"

"Of course. Listen, Rocky, first thing, has he taken some oath of poverty? Does he have his family's money?"

"Nuns take vows of poverty, not priests. I wouldn't doubt that the money he inherited has multiplied over the years. Considering his facility in raising five million dollars for the parish in a very short space of time."

"Then it's time to officially divvy up. We've got to make a plan for you to go after your local priest and I'll go after the federal judge. We'll call in to each other once a day. And we'll hope that one of us is successful and that we all four don't end up in the same place at the same time, because it might be a real messy place to be."

He said, "Divvying up sounds very good. I need a break from you, Agent. You're a bad influence on my optimistic nature."

"Since when do cops have optimistic natures?"

"When they have Shiva in their bloodstream but Jesus in their hearts."

Oh.

"Poppy, forgive me. What have I been arguing? I don't need a break from you. I need to calm myself and talk further with you, make the appropriate plan. Let's do that."

"Makes much better sense to me, Rocky."

"I'm sorry I said what I said."

"No need." Though I admit to feeling a little hurt.

"In fact, my wife has wondered if you would like to join us for dinner, a relaxing break. From upheaval, not from each other. We think you must be yearning for a home-cooked meal. I know I have been."

There is no food in my home. I said, "That's very nice of you, Rocky, but—"

"Poppy, let us have this respite as we think of what we must do. Something other than a meditation. As a Catholic I know there is more to faith than contemplation, even though Jesus himself had Hindu leanings. During his long missing years, he traveled to find Hindus, to study our religion, to appreciate the value of silent isolated thought. I believe he traveled across Persia until he came to the land of the Gujaratis. He studied with the most renowned Yogis. They taught him the art of miracles. My parents alone know several Yogis who can walk on water."

He did need a break. Me too, I'd say, since I was going right along. "What about the loaves and the fishes?"

"Jesus had his friends to help him with the more complicated miracles."

"Jesus was a fraud, then."

"No, he was a convert. But as to dinner. This evening, then. No buts. My wife says I am to take no buts. I will let her know we are coming."

I hate to see a man get in trouble with his wife. "All right, Rocky. A respite does sound good. I'd love to come."

"I am so happy then." Either Rocky really liked me a lot or he was scared to death of his wife.

～～

The wife had taken it upon herself to learn to cook the dishes of the Gujarat state of India. I could smell the spices out on the street.

She and Rocky were the same size, small and slim, eye to eye. Dark, too, but she was olive-skinned with big brown eyes. Surely didn't look Irish. Her name was Lucy, and Lucy was as personable as Rocky.

Every one of the two dozen or so bowls and platters covering the dining table were full of things outstandingly delicious. I recognized lamb saag, one of my favorites. I told her that, and after a taste I told her, too, that it was the best lamb saag I'd ever had.

"I love lamb," I said.

She said, "Me too."

Rocky the vegetarian said, "I wonder that you do not imagine little fluffy lambs gamboling in a meadow while you are washing down your lamb saag."

His wife said, "Rocky, when you put on your shoes, try to imagine cattle trapped in pens."

"I was pulling Poppy's leg."

She smiled. "I know."

Then he reached over and brushed a strand of hair from her cheek. I vicariously enjoyed his gesture of affection toward her. I tried not to wonder what it would be like to have sex with a man shorter than me. Then I said to Rocky's wife, "Who taught you to cook? Rocky?"

And now she touched him. The back of his hand, tapped it with her fingertips. "His mother taught me how to do all this. But my own family taught me the basics."

Rocky said, "My wife is modest as to her skills. She is now chef at the family restaurant." He named the most beloved Italian restaurant in Boston, owned by the same family for three generations. Turned out his father-in-law was the Irish one. His wife looked like her mother. Perhaps her temperament was her father's, as Rocky had mentioned understanding the Irish temperament, not the Italian one.

Lucy said, "Rocky was a regular at the restaurant. He is a connoisseur of pasta, as long as it doesn't involve meat sauce. When my mother realized that the two of us had something going, she said to Rocky, 'What is this title you've got, detective first grade?' And Rocky said to her, 'There are fewer detectives first grade in all the United States than there are cardinals in the Church.' That's all it took. She decided she loved him too, so much that she invented a sauce with yogurt in it. Come to the restaurant, Poppy, and try a bowl of Penne Patel."

"I'll try to do that." I took a break from shoveling huge forkfuls of aloo gobi and vegetable jalfrezie down my throat. "So Rocky, is your mother as crazy about your wife as Lucy is about you?"

"No. She is devastated."

We all three laughed. Rocky's wife said, "But she doesn't let on to me—stiff upper lip."

Rocky said, "Perhaps when a baby is coming."

Surely.

My evening with the two of them *was* a good break, a gracious break. A little civility is just what I needed to regroup, to prepare for a much-needed chat with my director. It was difficult, when I got to my hotel, not to lie in bed and call Joe after enjoying the affection between Rocky and his wife. Joe said one time to me, "Poppy, you sure give good phone."

He's a funny guy when he's not lying. But no, it was not time for Joe. I dialed my director at home.

∿

He was three things: reprimanding, consoling, and apologetic. He led with apologetic. About not knowing that one of the Sullivans was a federal judge. Only then did he segue into the reprimand segment. "It's bad publicity, isn't it? Two men suspected of murder are now both on the lam because trust for their position in society gave them a window of opportunity to disappear into thin air." Reprimanding, yet empathetic: "The office," he said, "doesn't necessarily make the man."

Finally, he consoled. "Figures in authority paralyze the best of us, Poppy."

I'd been momentarily paralyzed by the majesty of a figure in black, kneeling in prayer in a dim but soaring church, warm candle-light all around, Christ on the cross looking up to his father in anguish just before he was about to expire. I was feeling my own anguish, guilty of the worst sin in our profession—complacency. *Misaligned trust* is what Patel said. "We can only trust each other, Poppy," is what he said later. "That's it."

I'd said, "And even then."

Now my director said he was working on a logical argument for the manpower I'd asked for. "But that's my problem, not yours."

True, so I let that go.

But our press wasn't as bad as the press given to the window openers enabling the bolt of Justice Sean Scanlon. *The Boston Globe*'s headline: TRUSTED OFFICIAL FLEES JUSTICE.

"You see, Poppy?" Rocky said. "All explained by misaligned trust."

Yes. Sean Scanlon was in the lower reaches of the judicial chain, not known outside his milieu. More help there as far as enabling a bolt. And all was overshadowed by the monsignor's sister confessing yet again, this time to killing the other girl, the Irish girl. "I killed Maeve Doyle, the wretch who started it all," was the quote the media loved most.

⌁⌁

Maeve Doyle. We hadn't needed the navy brother after all. The detective and I were on the way to an interrogation room. I said to Rocky, "Use the siren." Meanwhile, the gardai now had her name. So did Danny's mother, who could search out the girl's parents with greater ease.

We were met by Jean Connealy's lawyer. He said to us, "My client is deranged." Then to me specifically, as he shook my hand, "An honor, Agent Rice. I hope your questioning takes you where you want to go, takes you to Tom, poor fellow. But meanwhile, I'm going to get Miss Connealy some psychological testing and she'll be out of here." Then he introduced us to the younger man at his side. "From the firm. Good with this sort of client."

I assumed he meant a deranged one. When the hotshot counsel slipped off to another more challenging client, Patel said to me, in front of the substitute lawyer from the firm, "To retain this gentleman's boss"—he smiled at the substitute—"you have to deposit thirty-five thousand dollars into his checking account before he'll even talk to you on the phone." He asked the young lawyer, "Who's paying, Tom Connealy?"

He didn't say, but the answer was a given.

Just as we were about to go into the holding cell, the gardai arrived. Well, one garda, a chief inspector. He said to me, "I am here merely to observe the proceedings; then I will decide, along with my superiors, the next appropriate step. I will not be interfering in your interests in this investigation. I have my own."

Meaning, his interests had no connection to Sean Scanlon.

He meant to observe from the other side of the two-way mirror.

"I do not wish Miss Connealy to see me. She will not cooperate with you if she senses who I might be. An Irishman who becomes a part of the law is a traitor to her. That would be how she sees the likes of me."

I said, "I have no problem with your observing."

Rocky said, "Nor I."

"Then go to it," he said.

The sister didn't appear any worse off in prison garb than she had in her housecleaning garb at St. Lawrence O'Toole's rectory the first time I'd laid eyes on her. She probably looked the way Danny O'Neill's friends envisioned his mother when they imagined a char-woman.

When we asked her if it were true that she'd killed the woman in Ireland, she raised her eyes—not to us, to Heaven. "Those girls were handmaidens of the devil, and the Lord saw to giving me the weapon to slay them so I might protect my brother, him one of Christ's shep-herds. My brother will not be sacrificed."

"You will, then?"

Her eyes lowered to earth. She didn't respond.

"Your brother told us you didn't kill Kathleen Sullivan, that you wouldn't kill anyone even to protect him. But you would confess to a murder if need be. Would you say that's an accurate assessment?"

She said, with confident reason in her voice, "My brother is a babe."

"A babe in the woods?"

"Yes."

"You mean that literally, don't you? Now that he's fled."

"I do. There wasn't a need for him to go. There is not a thing to run from. I killed both the girls."

I asked her how she killed them, and could she start with the Irish girl.

She didn't hesitate. "At Salt Hill."

"What is Salt Hill?"

"A neighborhood sittin' above Galway. On the bay. A resort for all to enjoy, rich or poor." Her look became wistful, her eyes distant. "A prom to walk, little places to have a lovely lunch, the golf course. Tourists, too. A carousel. A casino." She stopped. She wished she were strolling the prom at Salt Hill.

I said, "The golf course. Is it the same golf course where a killeen was found?"

"Yes."

"Go on."

She looked up at me. Blank.

"How did you come to kill Maeve Doyle in Salt Hill?"

Jean Connealy remembered what she'd gotten herself into and climbed back into her story. "I invited her there. I asked her if she would come and talk to me and she said, yes, she would. We agreed to meet on the north end of the prom. Not too many walk that far. The shops thin out. But she wanted to see me because she thought I wished to speak to her in a friendly way."

"Did you wish that?"

"No. It's only what I led her to believe."

She stopped again. When an actual killer is confronted and tries to establish an alibi, he'll describe everything he did on the day in question. He remembers it all, down to the tiniest detail. He's worked it out carefully—what time he woke up, what he had for breakfast, exactly the clothes he put on, the weather. But when he approaches the time the killing took place, he becomes circumspect, stops using the pronoun I. "There was a good movie everyone was talking about. Decided to see it. Can't remember the name. That actor—what's-his-name—was in it. Nope, not sure of the theater." And then, after the time of the killing, he returns to minutiae and the more specific pronoun. He'll say, *"I remember stubbing my toe on 34th Street around ten o'clock, ten-fifteen. I found a quarter on the sidewalk just a few minutes later. I bought a pack of gum from that vendor on the avenue. Then I went window-shopping for an hour or so. Then at eleven-thirty I saw a guy selling knockoff watches, and I asked him how business was, and he told me he was having a good year because he'd found out where he could get Patek Philippes. At noon, I—"* and so on.

An innocent party can't remember much of anything that might have happened on a Wednesday a week earlier. Politicians learn this early on. They make a point of having to consult their calendars or secretaries when they get in trouble. But someone who decides to confess to a crime he didn't commit goes beyond the time frame, brings in a broader picture, as does the actual criminal. But he gets details wrong since he's inventing. We go on to check such details and then discredit the fiction.

"A prom is a boardwalk, then?"

"A promenade. It's a wide sidewalk, and curvin', not straight like a boardwalk."

"What was the reason you gave her? For wanting to meet her?"

"I needed no reason. She knew who I was. She knew I found out what was going on between her and my brother. I told her that when I spoke with her on the phone."

"In a friendly way."

"Yes."

"Perhaps you led her to believe you would try to help her and your brother."

"Yes."

"But you intended to kill her?"

"Not at first. I intended to press upon her the evil she'd wrought. The sin—encitin' him away from the Church. But—"

"What was she wearing?"

The woman reached into the pocket of her sweater, took out a handkerchief, unfolded it, spit into it, balled it up, and thrust it back into the pocket. That was her answer.

I waited. Silence is such an effective prod. Rocky took notes, a ploy of his own. He was just scribbling. Jean Connealy looked from one of us to the other and, since no question was coming, she volunteered the flowery elaboration one expects from a false killer. "She wore a whore's costume. It were a sailor dress, a dress meant for a two-year-old, but she had squeezed herself into it."

Rocky's pen stopped jabbing its way across his notebook. He raised his eyes from the page to me. Nuala's girl, who'd come ashore dead on Inishmore, was indeed the girl Jean had met, Maeve Doyle.

"Until I saw her in that dress, I thought I'd just speak to her, convince her to release my brother, but when I saw her flauntin' herself, her legs exposed like that, I knew I was actin' the idiot."

The friendly phone call hadn't fooled Maeve Doyle. She knew she'd be meeting a wolf in sheep's clothing. Street smarts, I wondered, thinking of Kathleen Sullivan. The Irish girl had worn the dress as a show of defiance, the strength of her will.

Interpretation is all.

Jean kept going. "She told me my brother would marry her. That his vocation was not true, that he wanted to marry her too. That she was pregnant, though she hadn't told him yet. I didn't believe her—that she was pregnant. But I was sure she'd told him just that. My brother was so young. In so many ways. She was workin' to entrap him."

"Are you saying your brother was too young to have sex?"

Her eyes narrowed as she took me in. She wouldn't answer.

"Is it only now you've come to believe her—that she was pregnant?"

"It took until now, yes. She was pregnant as she'd said. But my brother was not the sire."

Rocky's pen stopped again, at the word *sire*.

I said, "The DNA testing has shown—"

"It shows the work of the devil."

I couldn't resist. "And his fairies."

"Yes. But the banshees who warned me were stronger."

Wonderful. Danny O'Neill would have to fill me in on banshees.

I left the mythology behind. "So back then, at Salt Hill, when did you decide to kill her?"

The corners of her mouth turned up a slight bit, the muscles put in use the ones that belie a haughtiness. She couldn't wait to tell the story, the semi-truths of a false confession.

She said, "When I saw her there, in the distance, standin' on the old quay, waitin', there was almost no light, except which came from the stars. Her legs were white. I saw those legs, and I wished more than anything that she would die right then. That God almighty would send forth a bolt of lightnin' and strike her down. But He didn't do that, instead seein' to it that I would understand the ways in which He works. He brought about such a fury in me that I couldn't control my actions. I went straight up to her and she said what she'd come to tell me, all lies. She flung the words at me. So with my two hands I beat her chest, pushed her. Shoved her. She stumbled backward. She tried to catch herself at the pilin', but she fell off the pier and into the water.

"I waited for her to come up. Where she fell was only a few feet deep. I believed I'd soon see her standin' in the water. But she had disappeared. I went around into the water. It came just above my waist. The water was black as pitch. It took me a long time but then I felt her. I pulled her out. She must have struck her head. She was dead."

"Her death was an accident then?"

"No, it was not. I wished her dead, and I felt glad when I saw she was."

"There are shades to killing. The law says that when a death is caused without intention—"

"There are no shades to *sin*."

"God was your weapon. Part of the blame would go to God then, Miss Connealy?"

She looked away from me. She looked at the door. She'd said what she wanted to say and now she was ready to leave. Too bad. No telling yet which threads of the story were true, which she'd forgotten after thirty years, and which she'd made up.

"What did you do next? After you pulled her out."

She thought for a moment. Then she said, "There were small traps roped together there. For tourists. It was the place where the vendor keeps them at night. I untied one and pulled it into the water. I dragged her into the trap. I rowed out into the bay until my arms were too tired to row further, and I pushed her into the sea."

"You were able to row out? I understand Galway Bay is a rough sea."

"Not in summer, not so much directly by the shore. I didn't have to go out far because the tide was recedin'. A strong, swift tide we have. It would take her out beyond the bay."

"It took her to Inishmore."

"I only just learned that. Before I came to visit here."

"Before?"

"Yes. There was a rumor, set into play by a loudmouth. By a troublemaker."

"Who was that?"

"Someone who could have let it be. Not tried to find out who the body was. For all our good."

"No. Just your good. Who are you talking about?"

"You wouldn't know the person."

"I would like to know who had information that the Irish authorities do not."

"Nuala O'Neill is the name."

Of course I already knew that.

"And why exactly would this Nuala O'Neill want to find out whose body it was?"

"She hoped it was the body of a troublemaker like herself. An IRA woman, a woman maybe killed by those in authority."

I immediately went to pulling the rug out. "Did murder come more easily the second time?"

She cringed. Thinking of yourself as the smiting hand of God is a fantasy; to think of yourself as having murdered someone is disorienting. Jean Connealy was not deranged. She almost censored what she was about to say next, but she didn't because I wouldn't release her from my gaze. An investigator needs the talent of a superb second-grade teacher who can hold the focus of twenty-five children all at once. Psychology is such a valuable tool, especially important ever since interrogators were ordered to stop beating prisoners into an admission.

So she answered me. "Yes. Work in the defense of the Lord is very hard, but it becomes easier."

"Your brother isn't the Lord. I thought you were defending your brother."

"He is the Lord's earthly representative."

"Basically, then, you repeated the crime. Enticed Kathleen Sullivan to some pier."

"Yes."

"What pier?"

"I don't know."

"The pier at Hancock Beach near Revere, isn't that right?"

"Yes."

There was no pier at Hancock Beach.

"You didn't kill Kathleen Sullivan."

"I did."

I stood so I could look down at her. If she looked heavenward again, she'd find my face blocking the view. I said, "Kathleen Sullivan was killed, and your brother didn't do it. You have not protected him, you have protected someone else. You diverted the police from acting responsibly. A cold-blooded murderer is free out there, and we have to find him. A perilous job. Did the Lord ask you to do that too? Lie through your teeth and consequently loose the devil?"

She sucked in a big breath and let it out in a well-practiced or maybe inbred way, producing that miserable, nerve-grating wail again. She began to rock back and forth. I shouted into her face.

"The devil is loose and guess what? Your brother is chasing him, trying to find him, and if he does find him you will be the one responsible for putting him in grave danger."

She had arrived at that very conclusion or she wouldn't have been keening. I'd just needed to yell at her.

Then I said to the young lawyer who was good with this sort of person, "She's not deranged. She's a selfish bitch." I don't know if he heard me, since he'd clapped his hands over his ears. *She* heard me, though.

Outside, the garda was gone. Drew his own conclusions, didn't want to talk with us.

Rocky didn't beat around the bush, he was right with me. "You'll tell me what the fire marshal will have to say."

"I will."

"And Poppy, have we another word, perhaps, for *bitch*? A word that might not have been so—"

"I said bitch to be sure she'd understand the untold damage she's wreaked."

"Aha. I prefer *louse* for someone who behaves as she has, but that wouldn't have suited."

"No, Rocky, it wouldn't have suited."

Then I had to laugh. Which was what he'd meant for me to do. He patted my shoulder, relieved that I hadn't become deranged.

I said, "Thanks, Patel."

"Ah, such a sincere though still unnecessary thank-you when one uses the last name."

"Why don't you just say, You're welcome."

"Yes, why don't I? You're welcome."

The feelings I'd been experiencing when I thought of Lucy, Rocky's wife, had a name. Envy.

～～～

Rocky dropped me at my hotel. In my room I listened to a message from Danny O'Neill asking me to call him. Very convenient. He left a long list of phone numbers—he wanted to make sure I would reach him. When I did, he sounded more tired than usual. He was just back from Ireland.

"Poppy, while I was there, the name of the Inishmore body came out in the newspaper. I came back. I need to talk to you."

"And I need to talk to you, Danny. Your mother's name came up in the interview I had with Tom Connealy's sister, along with the name of the Irish girl."

We met at the bar again on Hancock Beach, halfway between his house and my hotel. This time it was full of fishermen. Fisherwomen, too. Obviously not wives or girlfriends. They almost looked like clones of the men. Their baggy canvas waterproof clothes and boots hid their bodies. They had short, stringy hair or a long single braid down their backs. Just like the men. The faces were female, though, and like the men all were merry and totally worn out.

Danny said, "They've been up since four this morning, and just back from twelve hours on the water. Having a beer before they head home. So content to do what they do. We can identify, can't we?"

"Yes."

We watched them. Impossible not to, so animated, so exhausted. When I'd arrived in DC, I was never more content. But then, once behind a desk, I became a fish way out of water. The new director understood entirely, and I got a new assignment, becoming one of his handful of independent agents, usually choosing our prey though once in a while assigned a topflight project, as in the blossoming prostitute-killer situation. He had my sympathy, fighting threats of terror while at the same time refusing to abandon the federal laws the Bureau oversees, having to butt up against the pressure from Congress to overshadow police forces on what are state-level laws: tracking down deadbeat dads or keeping members of rival street gangs from killing one another. Shouldn't be our responsibility. I was glad to be outside.

My director will sort it out because he's a moral giant and knows how to command from a desk. Didn't need me or anyone else to assure him of that.

Now here I was with Danny O'Neill, who only gazed at the Guinness in front of him as if the glass were too heavy to lift. He looked as exhausted as the fishermen. Jet lag among other things. He said, "Poppy, I told a small lie. That's why I didn't want to talk on the phone. Sometimes I need a face."

"Danny, a *small* lie? Between a fire marshal and an FBI agent, any lie is a big one."

His eyes came up to mine. "Yes. You're right. I know you're right. Let me sort it out, though, okay?"

Sort it out. I wasn't in the mood for parables, but he had already started.

"I found out who the Irish girl was because the gardai had the information. They'd kept it from the public on the excuse that they wanted to use it to flush out perpetrators of what they saw as more important crimes. Internal ones. I talked to them. My mum doesn't know I did. I don't carry the antagonisms she does: old antagonisms, Irish antagonisms. I'm an American. I trust authority. My mum never will. But here I am the authority. There are investigators in the gardai able to separate out politics in order to solve crime. So they put me in touch with a priest."

Yet another priest.

He saw the cynicism that came to my face. He smiled. "In Ireland, Poppy, there is a priest at every table. Part of the wallpaper. And here is what I learned from this priest, an old old man: He told me that thirty-odd years ago, it was impossible for the gardai to identify the body washed up on Inishmore because she had no family. Now that she has been identified, this priest was able to explain to me that there was only Maeve and her brother, no one else.

"Their mother left them when they were infants, abandoned them. The children were separated and cared for in foster homes— good homes—good people. The two found one another as teenagers while each was searching out the other. This priest handled birth records and he'd been asked to help them—asked by each independently of the other. He told me when he gave them the news of their relationship, it was the most joyous reunion he'd ever seen, the happiest day not only in their lives, he said, but in his own. He meant it too, I could see. But then he had to give them the particulars of their background, which sobered them to the point where the brother decided to make a huge change in his life.

"The brother emigrated to the place where their mother had been born—here. She was an American. The sister, who was two years younger, was not so decisive. She didn't know what to do. The priest got her a job, a job near the seminary where Tom Connealy was studying with the intention of becoming a priest, cloistered like all the rest but with money at his disposal plus the roots of the displeasure that came to mark him. He would bribe his way in and out of the seminary walls when he felt the need.

"The girl came back to visit with the priest a year later and told him she was in love with one of the seminarians. He told me he felt great envy when she described the love and devotion she felt. He said to me he was envious of the boy as well as the dear girl's affection for him. Told me he wondered what his life would have been like if he'd ever had the opportunity to so much as *meet* a girl. He had been a bright boy, but his family had no money, no other way than the Church to see to his climbing out of poverty."

Danny dipped his lip beneath the foam of his Guinness and took a swallow.

Well, this was all very touching.

He went on. "In the meantime, her brother in America had joined the U.S. Navy to avoid the draft—since he knew of the sea— and he was to sail for Vietnam. She came to the States to spend some time with him before his tour, and then she went home again. The priest told me it wasn't long before news came of the brother's death, and shortly thereafter she left her job. She went away. He couldn't find her. He didn't know who the seminarian was who she'd loved. He wished he did know, so he could offer solace to a boy who surely must have needed it. Then, since I figured the truth of it would eventually find this priest, I told him who the boy was and his present circumstances."

He sat quietly, drinking more of his beer. I waited too. Then he said, "There's more. But nothing to do with Tom Connealy, so I'll quit there. Now you can tell me what you wanted to say about my mum, Poppy."

I let that go for the moment—his quitting part—and instead gave him all the details that had come from Jean Connealy. About her invitation to Maeve Doyle. The details as to what happened at Salt Hill.

Danny listened, and when I finished he said, "Impossible."

"Which?"

"Some."

"Which?"

"There are no little rental boats left to lie on the sand at Salt Hill. The height of the tides is unpredictable. Unexpected storms can be fierce. Boats might wash away without warning. And no matter what Jean Connealy says, she couldn't have rowed out far enough for the currents to take a body to Inishmore. So if she pushed Maeve into the water and Maeve drowned, she'd have had to get help to get rid of the body, and I doubt she recruited four men in a curragh. She got someone with a motorized launch to take the body out to sea, and she's protecting the person who helped her. Maybe Tom Connealy. Maybe he simply helped her dispose of the body of Maeve Doyle as opposed to killing her himself."

Maybe. "Danny, the connection with your mother. It isn't really outside all this, is it?"

"Not entirely. But from your standpoint—"

"Let *me* determine what my standpoint is. Jean Connealy told me your mother spread the rumor about the body in Inishmore."

"Did she?"

"I reminded her that it wasn't a rumor. She said your mother could have left it alone, not tried to find out the identity of the woman. Not now, not at such a late date. It would have been for the good of all if she'd minded her own business, is basically what she said."

"Her own good?"

"That's what I said. But now I'm thinking it would have been for the good of people beyond just her and the monsignor. But not for the good of your mother. So Danny, what did you want to tell me about your mum? You decided to skip that part. Why did you change your mind? Redefine my standpoint."

"I shouldn't say anything until I have some proof. About a connection." Another long drink of beer. "My mum was never pushed from the ferry as she'd told me. She lied."

He wasn't as exhausted as the fishermen. He wasn't suffering from jet lag either. He was in the middle of serious distress. "What did you say?" But he didn't repeat what he'd said. So I asked, "Why?"

"I don't know."

"And of course, Danny, my next question would be—?"

"How I found out she lied. My godmother called me. She and the other ladies in my mother's circle were on the ferry with her, but belowdecks. My mother told them she was going up for fresh air. If you live on Inishmore, you get more than enough fresh air. Tourists are the ones on the upper deck, not islanders. But this was the first morning boat from Inishmore to Galway; tourists don't leave Inishmore early in the morning. So Peggy Ann went up top to see what her friend was about, wondering why she was behaving oddly, just in time to watch my mum throw her boots over the side and then jump in. That's what gave her away. Boots aren't just heavy, they fill with water immediately."

"Your mother *jumped* overboard?"

"Yes. Shocking, I know. I thought Peggy Ann had had some sort of stroke or something when she spoke those words. But no, she told me my mum had good reason—the reason was to see that I'd be involved in all that has come about. She intended to stir up as much trouble as she could. My mother is as closed-mouth a person as I've ever known. She prefers to rouse people secretly and in devious ways. She started the rumor that the dead woman she'd buried was killed because she was part of the same cell my father was. Peggy Ann said my mum wanted my help, and even more she wanted the attention of the gardai to fall upon her."

"Why?"

"I have to go back and figure that out. While you and Patel find that miserable scum of a judge, to say nothing of Tom Connealy. The monsignor is somehow connected to my mother. The connection lies in whoever helped his sister dispose of Maeve Doyle's body, because I don't think it was him who did."

"You don't believe Tom Connealy killed Kathleen Sullivan, do you?"

"No."

"What about his sister. She killed the Irish girl?"

"She may have killed both girls. I don't know that."

"Or would Sean have been the one to kill the Sullivan girl to shut her up? If Kathleen confronted him. Or would the monsignor have confided in his sister, innocent of her involvement in the death of Maeve, and caused her to go to Sean to suggest a way he could get rid of Kathleen?"

He drank more beer. Then Danny said, "Who knows? Maybe both girls committed suicide after all."

"Well, that would be neat. A man gets a woman pregnant so she throws herself into the sea. Then, thirty years later—new girl and the whole scenario repeats itself, except we go from the Victorian to the asinine. Meanwhile, Monsignor Connealy figures he's responsible for the death of the two women. The second girl he sees as having been set upon twice, once as a child and then again by him. There is nothing he can do for the first girl. So back to the Victorian. He will assuage his guilt by avenging her death. But we're talking about a priest, and a priest lives in an insular world, not the real one. Perhaps he won't be able to find the judge, who has led a double life for some time. If he does find him, though, there is no predicting what the judge might do."

"The priest could well have found him already."

"Why would you say that?"

"Rocky Patel says Connealy has tracking skills."

"What is that supposed to mean?"

"I checked in with Rocky today. That's what he told me."

"How come he didn't tell me?"

"He just found out. He tried to call you. I told him you were on your way here to meet me."

"What tracking skills?"

"I didn't ask."

Then Danny said, "So, before you go back to work would you like to revisit my apartment and have another tour?"

I didn't answer him. An image of Joe was fluttering in and out of my line of vision, the first such flutter since the night we'd returned from Block Island. Felt like a hundred years ago.

Danny smiled. "I didn't think so. Someone has a grip on your heart, Poppy. If you're ever out of the grip, I'll be here. Anytime you want to sit at this very bar, have a Guinness with me, just let me know. All right?"

"All right."

I smiled too. Soon I would get my personal life in order, straighten out a few things with Joe when I got back to DC.

But first, Rocky. Just as I took out my phone, there he was in the doorway of the bar.

# 12

Hello, Detective."

"Hello, Agent."

"I'm all ears."

"Let me see if I can get some orange juice first."

He settled for Bloody Mary mix, carried it back from the bar, and sat in Danny's vacated chair. I leaned forward in mine.

"You've got new information, according to Danny. Something about priestly tracking skills, of all damn things."

"Yes. I have been so anxious to tell you. You weren't at the hotel, so I tried the fire marshal. I got here as fast as I could. Poppy, I talked to a few parishioners who have worked closely with Tom. I have found that during the year Tom was lost in the desert—as with Jesus, he'd gone to find himself—he started with a desk job."

Definitely the place to find yourself.

"He had been given a temporary appointment to the chancery's tribunal, where he was assigned the duty—"

"Hold on. Chancery who?"

"The chancery is the diocese archives and record office. The tribunal is a court of justice therein."

Oh.

"Rocky?"

"Yes?"

"You'll have to slow it down a notch."

"It's a kind of court, a Church court. Made up of priests trained in canon law. Tribunal hearings are not public, accusers are not allowed to attend. The victim is represented by a priest. That priest's title is Promoter of Justice. He's also the prosecutor. He describes both sides of the argument to the tribunal, all under the auspices of the Congregation for the Doctrine of the Faith."

"And what the hell is that?"

"Once known as Inquisitors. The Congregation resides in Rome."

"There are still inquisitors?"

"Yes. But they don't burn people at the stake anymore."

Now *there's* something.

"His job was to handle requests for marriage annulments, very boring work. The assignment was a punishment. Tom came to see it differently. He was not bored."

"Meaning?"

"He was required to find wives—rarely husbands—named in annulment proceedings. Because once in a while, they hide."

"They do? Why?"

"With an annulment, all issue are considered bastards. The assignment to Tom Connealy meant getting around fathers who had no qualms as to denying legitimate parenthood to the children at stake. All the husbands cared about was getting rid of their first wives so they could acquire second ones, and to hell with the children. His job was to see that the first wives signed the required documents. But some scorned wives avoided the annulment proceedings because they couldn't abide their children being considered bastards. Some actually hid.

"So Tom took it upon himself to find the wives in order to advise them to file for divorce. Imagine. He's a dedicated and thorough man. After he found them, he would then advise them to threaten a lawsuit against their bishop for attempting to deprive their children of legitimacy."

Imagine, indeed.

"And so Tom was punished further. He was demoted to the lowest level on the job scale. He was ordered to run a miserable defunct parish in a poor neighborhood, all black except for one family recently arrived from Gujarat, India. The latest of my tribe running the Day's Inn."

"Why didn't the man just *leave* the Church? Since he was so against its beliefs."

"Not beliefs. He was against the dogma. He didn't leave, Poppy, because his vocation is true."

"All right, fine. The main thing is he'd had experience finding people who were lying low."

"Hiding."

"Hiding. But based on what you say, the man had no experience in hiding himself."

"I would have to disagree there. He wouldn't hide from the wrath of his superiors, as we know, but he had maintained two separate relationships with two women during the course of his life. No one ever knew of his involvement with either. He could hide himself well."

"All right, then, Detective Patel, the race is on. You concentrate on the monsignor while I'll see if I can pinpoint Sean Scanlon. We're both trained carefully in the art of ferreting out people in hiding. Surely we'll be a lot better at it than someone who worked at the— what did you say it was called?"

"The chancery tribunal. Though Poppy, let me remind you, the tribunal goes back eleven centuries. And in those days, in their quest to root out Jews, they were so adept at hunting they could trace a family back many, many generations."

Rocky was good at making his points.

Then he said, "The Spanish took up Ireland's cause against England during the Reformation. Perhaps there is something spiritual here. Perhaps Tom has Spanish blood."

Not a good point. "Rocky?"

"Yes?"

"The spiritual is wasted on me."

"Nothing is wasted on you, Agent Rice of the FBI."

~~~

So what was the odd thing about Sean Scanlon that might help me in my search? That's what I needed to know. The detective asked around for me. Sean had three brothers and two other sisters in addition to Rosemary Sullivan. Six siblings and a wife, but no children of his own.

I said to Rocky, "Then he recognized his bent. Did not intend to control it. Knew he shouldn't tempt himself with little girls of his own—or their friends—running around."

Rocky sighed. "Poppy, I detest that we must verbalize such things with the kind of clarity you have just exhibited."

"I don't detest clarity. How can you rid society of the detestable unless you're clear as to what detestable is?"

He smiled. "I muse aloud. I am not meaning what I just said. My wife finds this very annoying, my musings. My friends, my fellow peace officers, do too. It disrupts their own trains of thought. So I'm always surprised when people outside my circle respond to my musings because, you see, the people who know me have developed tin ears, and I'm not aware when I do it."

"Well, Rocky, you could fix that if you wanted to. Become aware.

Obviously, you choose not to. Presumably, you like to annoy your wife and buddies. Either that or you like to have them cater to your demands. Or you simply don't care."

His chin lifted. "More the last. The trait is too important for me to give up. Musing aloud is how I think. My wife has adjusted by developing an ability to keep me tuned out, although to have placed that responsibility upon her shoulders has been unfair, I know. But at the same time, I have also had to adjust to some of her—"

"Rocky?"

"Yes?"

"What else about Sean Scanlon?"

He readjusted, cleared his throat. Took on the expression of a homicide detective first grade. "Scanlon's wife isn't quite five feet tall. She probably weighs eighty-five pounds, if that. She has black curls that frame her face. She looks like the Disney Snow White. The man married a childlike woman. Such a situation reminds me of a police officer I know. He's gay, but he denies it. He is married to a woman who looks masculine. She dresses in button-down shirts hanging over her pants. She has a haircut like the late Elvis Presley's. She is a lesbian. They are apparently able to make accommodations."

"Elvis is alive."

First he frowned and then he immediately convulsed, laughing loudly and wildly. Smacked my upper arm. "And I am betting you've seen him, which is how you know."

"He's sitting at the corner table."

He turned to look, turned back. "You're right, it is Elvis. I know because he's eating a peanut-butter-and-marshmallow sandwich with bacon." Then he leaned in toward me, his old self before I'd criticized him. "Judge Scanlon belongs to the Country Club at Brookline. Elite, costly. I understand their carts are replaced twice as often as the carts at Augusta. He attends the club's social events but plays very little. From what I have found, his golf game leaves a lot to be desired."

"Who's the person to talk to at the club?"

"Chuck. He is one of the pro's assistants. Sean belittled this fellow one day in front of several people."

I took out my notebook and wrote down *Chuck.*

"You don't use a Palm?"

"No. I don't want someone grabbing it, leaving my life accessible to God knows who else."

"You have secrets?"

"Of course. Anything on the monsignor?"

"Yes. He has a BlackBerry."

"My God."

"He doesn't have a criminal record, Poppy, so he doesn't expect us to follow his e-mail exchanges. He's riding an underground railroad. He has a lot of friends—former priests who are now married. Who are school teachers. Insurance salesmen. Parents of children. Quiet and unobtrusive. We're having local departments stake out people he contacts."

"Where does it look like he's heading?"

"West. And none of the train conductors know his next stop. I give them details of what he's up to and how dangerous it is to be doing it—chasing a desperate man—and then they give me the names of other ex-priests they know. There are an inordinate number of ex-priests in this country."

"How far west has he gotten?"

"St. Louis."

Rocky's cell phone rang. He didn't say much beyond identifying himself, only listened. Boston PD had discovered downloaded child pornography on Sean Scanlon's computer, the one he used at the Federal Court Building. Meaning local, state, and federal offense. Nora would have an easier time when she brought her past to them.

And then Rocky's phone rang again. Logan airport security wanted us to come see some videos. Logan now has hidden video cameras everywhere, even in the bathrooms. We headed out to the bar's parking lot, and all the fisherpeople raised their glasses. They called, "See ya, coppah." And one voice: "Watch ya shadow, FBI."

I looked back. Their glasses were still raised, and they were smiling all.

~~~

The two of us bent over the security officer at his computer. We watched a film of a steady stream of cars pulling up to the American Airlines departure gate. The officer counted the cars aloud and stopped the video on the ninth one. "Rosemary Sullivan's car. Judge Scanlon's sister."

He zoomed in and paused again. Rosemary was behind the wheel, Sean in the passenger seat.

He reached over and put his hand on her shoulder before he got out. Squeezed it reassuringly, no doubt. He carried a briefcase, opened the rear door, and took out an overnight bag. He signaled for a porter while his sister popped the trunk. The porter lifted out two suitcases the size of gunships. Sean had to help the porter get them onto the luggage cart. Curbside check-in at Logan has not been resumed. Not that Muhammad Atta checked in at the curb, but never mind that. Sean and the porter disappeared through the sliding doors. Rosemary Sullivan's hand went up, a little wave that Sean didn't see. Then she slipped into the line of traffic.

Security went to a second tape. "This is from inside the terminal."

We watched as Sean approached the first-class end of the counter. "He traveled under a phony name, phony driver's license. You don't get a phony license of this quality overnight. He already had it. He'd used it before."

Security showed off a little. He enhanced and cleared the picture of the back of Sean's head at the check-in counter. He zoomed in. We could see Sean's photo on the driver's license and we could see the name on it: Franklin Devaney.

"Where has he used it?"

"To rent cars in Orlando, Scottsdale, Reno, and Puerto Rico. When he travels internationally, he uses another name and a phony passport. Scotland, Thailand. We're going through all the tapes. Thousands and thousands of feet of them. Our computers have been programmed to search out his face. Soon as it's found, we'll look into airline records and see when and where he's traveled over the last two years and what documents he used. We've got equipment now to access information at the FBI and put it together with ours. Automatically feeds to the state police. Boston too. It'll take a little while to get the whole job done. A few days."

Rocky said, "That's actually very good, isn't it?"

"As good as it gets, far as I know."

Not good enough.

I asked, "So where'd he go?"

"He took a flight to Las Vegas."

Rocky caught my eye. Told you so.

"And then?"

He ejected the video and put in another. "Arrived McCarran and was picked up by a private limo. Plates were angled so the camera couldn't pick them up."

We watched the new film. It was just as he said.

"McCarran isn't so advanced, technically. I can't zoom in to try and get that plate. That's because no planes from McCarran have been hijacked and aimed at famous buildings. So the next step is yours, Agent. Detective."

He showed us to another room where we could use a phone. I called the FBI chief in Las Vegas and told him what was coming down while the security officer was sending him everything we'd seen via tape and computer. Put us on conference with himself and a couple of other agents; they were looking at the Boston tapes within the minute.

"Okay, we're on it, Poppy. Call you back as soon as we have a line on him. Sorry about your accident in Texas."

"Thanks." I thought, Wait till he hears about the one on Block Island.

"You're all better?"

"All better."

"Glad to hear it."

Me too.

While I dialed my jigsaw puzzle man in DC, Rocky said, "You're injured?"

"Was injured. Not that big a deal."

Auerbach came on. I told him to find out where Sean Scanlon went in Reno, Orlando, Phoenix, Puerto Rico, Scotland, and Thailand over the past five years. What did those places have in common that enticed the judge?

First he repeated the place names aloud. He said, right off, "Golf is a guess except for Thailand. Thailand? Well, no need to expand on that. Travel in pursuit of cheap prolific sex. I've read what you have on Sean Scanlon. Along with a lot of men, he probably traveled there to have sex with children. Child prostitution rings exist in all those other places in a limited but specific way. The rings crisscross because they're all operated by the same people. That's what I meant by specific. There's actually a monopoly on child prostitution. An organized crime network runs it, out of Los Angeles. It took this agency of ours a long time to accept that crime could be organized. That there could be a syndicate. Well, we've got one here, Poppy, and we're getting closer to them as we speak."

Auerbach spouts forth information with very little discussion needed. Everything he learns gets logged into his computer. He maintains an index. He never uses the index because whatever he logs into his computer stays in his head.

I gave him the identities Sean had used.

He said, "We'll get this guy, Poppy."

Then I talked to Delby. She filled me in on local events. "I had no idea how regularly prostitutes seem to disappear off the face of the earth. And, Poppy, how we all like to think the girls found Jesus, quit, and went to MIT to become brilliant metallurgists or whatever. That's the Justice Department's conclusion, by the way. But the director will still be ready to sic you on whoever is disappearing them in a week or so. Pressure's on and growing. Good thing you like pressure, boss."

Good thing.

I heard from the Las Vegas agent put in charge of the Scanlon case at one in the morning. She has a reputation for never paying attention to whether it's day or night. She eats when her stomach growls. When there's a work lull, she leaves the office, goes home, sleeps, comes back. She's told me her body clock is tuned to commotion and lulls.

"Hey, Poppy, how is it?"

"It's good." I had just fallen asleep but why bring that up?

"Here's the info you wanted on Sean Scanlon. First, new identity as soon as he left the airport. Before I get to second, I have to ask you: Does this guy work for the CIA and we don't know it? Maybe I'll check, since we're supposed to be attuned to such things. I say that because he's got sources at his fingertips that—never mind, it's peripheral. So he's not at the airport two minutes when he gets picked up by a particularly well known car company, well known for their drivers' abilities to rustle up a companion for you on a moment's notice. Scanlon gives the guy, the driver, his criteria. He wants the youngest call girl out there and make sure she's as flat-chested as possible.

"He checks into a unique hotel off the strip where you get five-star service sans lobby, sans casino, sans restaurants. Nobody sees their fellow guests. Sort of like a 1950s ranch, sprawls out across the desert, and each unit has a garage so if you drive, say, from LA, nobody even sees you walk to your door from your car. Manager comes to your room and checks you in privately.

"Melissa Breen. That was the hooker procured by your perp. She looks about nine. She's thirty-six; how the hell she does it I wouldn't know. Long bangs hanging in her eyes, wispy thin, the waif look—she gets it done. She says he asked her how much to shave off her pubic hair. Then she called him a dirty bastard. I told her at least he's using make-believe kids instead of real kids, which calmed her down somewhat. She told him a thousand, figured fuck it. She hates guys like him. Handed her ten hundreds on the spot, didn't even negotiate. Showed her a razor and an electric shaver. Like guys with really heavy beards have to do. She says he was a pig.

"When Ms. Breen left, your guy left right after. Just wanted a little tryst to tide him over, cheer him up. No calls to or from his room. Must have made the arrangements in Boston. Thing is, he's gone. We've lost him."

"I'm sorry—lost him?"

"I feel like such a shit."

"How'd you lose him exactly?"

"There's a way to get from each room to the manager's office. Your guy must have paid the manager to take him to wherever it was he wanted to go without our seeing. So we cornered the manager, made our accusation, and he was indignant. Naturally. He was appalled—naturally—when we informed him we were about to vacuum his car. He told us not to bother. He'd complied with Sean Scanlon's request to spirit him out of there when the judge counted out ten more hundred-dollar bills."

"And will it help to know where the manager took him?"

"No."

"I didn't think so."

"He took him to the Venetian—two miles away—where he didn't check in and had no reservation under any of the names we're looking at. The manager helped take the luggage out of the car and left. But Sean immediately had it put into a taxi and then he was driven off to a location unknown. We're working on it, but I suppose you can imagine how many taxis there are in Vegas. Plus unlicensed cabs too.

"But we're looking. Real hard. And we're looking at passport copies of the ones he uses. We're at McCarran scrounging around for anyone who comes here and then goes to that list of places you told us about. Trouble is, he could have gone from the Venetian to other airports—to private strips. He'll eventually surface with a good case of cabin fever would be my assessment. Pretty soon, the lam will become a tedious place."

I told her, "That's what I figure. He wants to get to where he's going and then stay put while he determines what the hell he should do. He thinks taking a roundabout route to get there will throw us off. It will. But not for long."

"That's right. Not for long. I appreciate your saying that. I will trace him. And Poppy?"

"What?"

"Our chief's worried he might get in a little hot water here."

"What for?"

"He's going to have to justify giving up an agent full-time—me—to go chase a guy when we're supposed to be putting full effort into finding the creeps who were supposed to fly a fifth plane, Vegas being a place full of decadent infidels and all. Could be the fifth plane's still coming."

"You want me to talk to him?"

"No, I'm talking to him. That the guy downloaded the stuff Boston found helps. You'll keep Washington happy, though, right?"

"Washington *is* happy. Crossing international borders to have sex with children is a federal crime. We're all doing our jobs here, okay?"

"Okay. Yeah."

Fifteen minutes was how long she took to get back to me. I'd just fallen asleep again. "Poppy, Scanlon hired a plane out of a strip at Palm Springs. What he did after he left the Venetian was to go to the near-est car rental service and get a car—under yet another identity—and drive all the way to Palm Springs. The plane took off right on time but hasn't returned. The pilots are independent—a bunch of cow-boys. So even though the plane was supposed to return, nobody's worried that it didn't. Of course, *I'm* worried. Soon as I figure this one out, I'll be back to you."

〰

In Boston, a charge was made against Rosemary Sullivan for aiding and abetting the flight of a suspect under indictment. She would be arraigned and released on a promise to appear in court on a specified date. Her lawyer would, for sure, talk her into some kind of plea-bargain arrangement wherein she could spill what she knew and they'd let her go with a slap on the wrist, if that.

Rocky had an outpost. When she arrived at Superior Court for the arraignment, he'd be tipped off. He said he planned to stay within six city blocks of the courthouse until he got the call.

Nora reached me. She needed to talk. I was, of course, indulgent.

"My mother drove him to the airport?"

"Yes."

No spark of fury. Just the dullness of resolve. "My father and our lawyer are trying to make her understand that she has to answer in person at the arraignment. That she will be subject to arrest if she doesn't turn herself in before the deadline. She has"—Nora must have looked at her watch—"just under twenty-four hours. I never thought I'd see my mother in this position."

"Nora, there are people who take refuge in tunnel vision. They're selfish, but if they want to live in denial at great cost to others, we can't do anything about it until they break a law. Then they have to be yanked out of their tunnel. I need to yank your mother at her court hearing. We'll have the right to question her."

"She'll deny everything, and she'll do it with authority. Imperious, regal authority."

"Imperious I can believe. But she won't be regal, Nora. Not in a courthouse where someone sits higher than she does. Not with everyone watching her squirm."

~~~

The next morning, Rocky did get a call, but not the one he was expecting. *The Boston Globe* got a similar one. We had to race to the DA's office and were relieved to see we were in time for flashes popping a mile a minute as a trio of lawyers got out of a big black car, surprised and blinded at the same time. This was supposed to be a meeting no one knew about. More popping flashes when Rosemary got out too and waltzed past, not squinting like her defense team, composed, regal, immune to what was happening around her as Nora had predicted.

Defense lawyers can request a meeting with the prosecutor when they fear or know their client is about to be charged with a crime; it's a way to find out if there is really enough evidence against a client to indict—when, for example, a hotshot business person has been found with his hand in the till. That's what I pointed out to the *Globe* reporter, who didn't understand such logistics.

He said, "That's not fair."

"Tell me about it."

The lawyers all knew Rocky Patel. They didn't know who I was. They found out, though, once Rosemary could see past the dots in her eyes. She told them in a clear voice, above the fray, "The FBI is following me," and pointed.

Once inside, the DA said, "I wasn't expecting Mrs. Sullivan." That made two of us.

The lead lawyer informed him that Rosemary wished to be present. It was clear why. The DA seemed to take a step back from her without moving.

She sniffed. "I take it no summons has been issued for my arrest."

Everyone began reassuring her at once while Rocky and I bided our time. When they finished their reassurance, the DA, for my benefit, demonstrated that he intended to do a job. "Even though there is no summons, would you agree to answer a few questions? Nothing can be held against you."

Her lawyers descended upon her like fruit flies around an old banana. I guessed the one in charge was the old-family-friend type, since he called her Rosemary. He acted protective, explaining to his client that they were working on a deal to prevent her arrest and that she was not required to answer any questions or even be at the meeting "as I have tried to make clear. You know what my advice is here, Rosemary. You must remain silent."

She said to him, "Well then, *leave*, because I am not taking your advice. I will not be silent."

She wanted to deny as forcefully as possible that she drove her brother to the airport. And so she did. When she'd exhausted her annoyance with everyone and finished exhorting us for our *nerve* in so much as suggesting such a thing, her lawyer advised her that she shouldn't be accusing an agent of my standing in the FBI and a detective first grade of the Boston PD of breaking the law.

That was when I chose to flash a few prints taken from the videotape Rocky and I saw at Logan airport.

At first she insisted the pictures had been doctored.

I said, "You'll probably have a chance to try to prove that in court."

So she sighed—regally—and waved her hand in front of her as if she were batting away a fly. "And if I did take Sean to the airport to catch a flight, well, there's absolutely nothing wrong with that."

I told her it was against the law to help a man under indictment flee the state.

She turned to face her apoplectic lawyer, condescending to address him directly. She said, "What do they want?" as if we were asking her a little too subtly for a favor and she wasn't exactly sure what that favor was.

I planted myself in her line of vision. I leaned into her face. I said, "I want to know where he is."

She said, "That's his business."

I said to her lawyer, "Counselor, perhaps you could explain to your client exactly what cooperation might mean for her."

The words he chose were: "Rosemary, for the love of God!"

Only now did she direct her gaze into my eyes. She said, "My family has been torn asunder by one of my children. And now another has taken up where the first one left off. Do you have children?"

"That's none of your business."

"It is my feeling that you probably don't. So you wouldn't know how difficult it is to be the mother of girls."

"I guess it *must* be difficult if the mother has a brother like yours."

Regal, no. Imperious, yes. "What you are insinuating is disgusting. He did not do what Nora accuses him of. She is a hysteric, made unbalanced by her sister. We're all caught up in vulgar times here; the world is a vile place. But Sean was nothing except good to them, nothing but good."

And if he wasn't good, blame the evil times we live in. One of the junior lawyers was bursting. His words exploded from him. "*Mrs. Sullivan,* if you agree to tell the authorities where he is, you'll be allowed a plea bargain. A plea bargain is all we can—"

The chief lawyer stepped in. "Rosemary, listen to me. This whole episode is taking on a life of its own. Did he say anything to you as to his destination? Do you have any idea?"

She chose to cross her arms and look away, her face a study in irritation. But she did respond. "I don't understand what is happening here, what my role is supposed to be," and with that, she turned on her heel and left, followed by the team of flopping, fluttering lawyers.

In the end, of course, she was arrested and I made haste to see a judge about a court date. He fit me into his busy schedule, then sat at his desk staring at me, trying to figure out what I wanted just as Rosemary had, but at the same time he was going to do his best to mollify me. Bail would be high because of flight risk. He said, "A symbolic gesture. To show her how seriously she must take these actions."

"When will the hearing be set?"

"What with the court calendar, I would guess ten weeks."

"Ten weeks is far too long."

He collected his papers and started organizing them into a tidy pile, as if disregarding me would preclude any further protest, would shut me up. Didn't work.

"Judge, when Sean Scanlon is forcing children to have sex with him during those ten weeks, or if he drowns another victim, the responsibility for such actions will lie with you, won't it?"

I'd woken His Honor up from his housekeeping act.

He glowered at me over the top of his glasses. "Just who the hell do you think you are, coming into my chambers and threatening me?"

I said, "They're not your chambers. These chambers belong to the people of Massachusetts, who you're supposed to be serving. So serve them."

I was afraid the vein traversing his forehead might burst. He put the papers down and lowered his head, his chin almost on his chest, in order to peer menacingly over the silly half-glasses. He said, "What do you want?"

Again, exactly what Rosemary had wanted to know, as if either of them didn't understand what I wanted.

"I don't want a damn thing. I'm simply advocating."

His fists were clenched. He hissed at me, "For who, the fucking FBI?"

"For the children of Boston, Your Honor."

He slumped. I waited. Then he said, "She will be placed under house arrest at the discretion of this court."

"When?"

"Now."

That meant she would be fitted with an ankle bracelet, a perfect symbol of her humiliation. And what was fast becoming her ruin.

Outside, the *Globe* reporters asked for comments. Rocky told them what the judge had decided. All but one jumped into their cars and zoomed off to the Sullivan home. The one who stayed hadn't missed the sight of Hugh Sullivan standing ten yards down the sidewalk. He was now walking toward me.

"Can we talk, Miss Rice?"

"I'm listening."

He looked around. He decided he didn't care who was listening. He said, "I have failed miserably as a father. Criminal failure is what I am guilty of. I have destroyed one daughter and hobbled another. There is nothing I can do to make it up to Kathy except to find out

all that she went though in her short life. To at least carry that bur-
den with me. And Nora. I will beg Nora's forgiveness. And I will do
all that is in my power to help you get to Sean."

He handed me a Palm Pilot.

"My wife's activities are on this." Then he gave me a couple of
disks. "She stores her past schedules and appointments on these.
Well, her secretary does. I don't know if they'll be of help."

Rocky said, "Where did you get these things?"

Rocky was really saying, *How* did you get these things? I didn't
see the relevance of the question. I didn't care how *or* where he'd gotten them.

He said, "From her purse. The disks were in her safe."

Rocky said, "Ah." He'd been curious, and he'd been right to ask—
for future reference when the need arose. His case. He'd be asked to
testify in court, not me.

I said, "Rocky, I'm seizing these as evidence."

I'd still need a warrant to search them. Rocky didn't protest,
because he knew such a warrant would be a lot speedier for me to get
than for him.

Rosemary Sullivan's husband said, "I don't know what she'll do
when she realizes what's missing. But I won't worry. You've rendered
her impotent."

I asked him, "Did she carry on e-mail correspondences?"

He smiled rather woefully and pointed to one of the disks. "The
last thing I did at home today—I copied her e-mail correspondence
onto one of those disks."

And with that the reporter, standing by, flipped open his cell
phone.

# 13

Rosemary Sullivan's schedule on her Palm confirmed the trip to the airport. As for the disks, they made clear that Sean headed up one contingent of the movers and shakers at the meetings in the Sullivan home. An extraordinary number of politicians across the country owed their careers, their success, their wealth, and their status to him and to his sister, who saw to the direction of the contributions, which were enormous—another case my director would be able to consider when assigning valuable manpower. Rocky Patel was looking into untoward activities as to the Sullivan children's trust fund, the results of which would be flagged in DC.

Without Sean's influence, the judge currently presiding in Rosemary Sullivan's case would still have been an unsuccessful commercial real estate lawyer. I suggested to Rocky that he might reveal this so the fellow could recuse himself. He agreed. He said, "I'm grateful to be the one designated for that job. It will take two minutes and it will be great fun." So few of our jobs take two minutes and fewer still are actually fun. Gratifying, yes, but fun? Hardly ever.

Between Rocky and me, we saw everyone in Rosemary and Sean's moving and shaking group. Journalists and photographers followed close at our heels, following up with calls to those we visited for comments as soon as we'd left their homes or offices.

All these men, who more or less controlled the Republican politics of the state, repeated the rehearsed speech to us. First, they contended that the meetings meant nothing, as Ted Kennedy was still senator. Really, they were a rather small juggernaut. I told them the governorship and control of the state legislature, plus the election of enough congressmen to help keep the U.S. House in Republican hands and effectively tip the balance of the Senate, was nothing to sneeze at. They shrugged at that. Wouldn't take credit.

They were more open, though, and a little more animated when it came to Sean. All agreed that Sean traveled quite a lot—on golf junkets. And all of them also agreed the few times they might have played with him was a sacrifice for them; the sight of his play reminded them of a large tree stump attempting to swing a club. Only his arms moved. His membership and activities at Brookline only served as a front for his junkets. To the query *So what did he do on these junkets?* the Massachusetts politicians resorted to shrugs again.

The lieutenant governor of the state hadn't shrugged, according to Rocky. "Poppy, he said, 'One could only guess,' and then he winked. Oh, how I wanted to blacken that winking eye!"

"But you're a Hindu."

"I'm also a Boston police officer."

"All the more reason for restraint."

I got a step further with a state supreme court justice after *his* wink. The justice said, "Fellows do that. Fellows who want women outside of marriage. *That's* the name of the game. The game is not golf."

I said, "You think the name of his game is women?"

"Yes."

I told him he was wrong. "The name of Sean Scanlon's game is seven-year-old girls."

Now I said to Rocky, "You know what his response was to that?"

"What?"

"He said, 'If it's true—and I for one am having trouble with it—that was then and now is now.' The guy wanted to assume that Sean had stopped. The fool. I told him Sean was out buying little girls in another country as we spoke. He said he didn't think about things like that; he was a family man. I told him he was also a supreme court judge with less backbone than a cardamom pod."

Rocky said, "Cardamom pod? That's what you said?"

"Yes."

"Well, it's true. I cannot wait to tell Lucy."

All the men we spoke to were adamant that they had never had an inkling of Sean's behavior. We made a point to say to each and every one of them, "By behavior, you mean the criminal abuse of children?" The answer was a reluctant yes. But one of our hosts' wives happened to stop by for a visit while Rocky and I were interviewing him, and she felt free to give us her reaction to the question. "Sean Scanlon has always reminded me of a ferret. When he moves, he stays close to the walls."

When I checked in with Auerbach, he had just finished combing Rosemary's Palm. "That thing was her alter ego; it represented her personal almightiness. All her contacts are on it—kind of a brag book." He provided me with some examples of those contacts, and I immediately authorized him to have a few local agents spend a day descending on each of the 257 doorsteps, including fourteen Republican congressmen and two senators, inquiring as to the exact nature of their relationship with Judge Sean Scanlon's sister, Rosemary Sullivan. The authorization would get me in fairly deep shit.

All 257 were as evasive as the law allows, each with legal counsel

222 / MARY-ANN TIRONE SMITH

at the ready leaning over them. Only one refused to see the agent: the President's wife. She called my director and told him that if the FBI wanted to speak with her, she would prefer it would be with me—she preferred to speak with the woman she knew to be in charge of the operation, if that was all right. Was it ever.

On the phone, my director said, "Fly back, Poppy. Time I had a briefing, no? Then go talk to her." He was quite calm. Still, I felt the need to explain myself.

"Sir, we all appreciate Auerbach's zealousness. But I didn't know the President's wife was one of Rosemary Sullivan's contacts. If I had, I would have—"

"I understand. As soon as you get here, I'll take a break from whatever meeting I'm in and we'll talk about it."

~~~

I got to DC and took a meeting with the director.

"Sir, I had a lapse. I should have gotten to you before Auerbach—"

"We all have lapses. And Auerbach . . . well, he's Auerbach. I accept his forthright mind-set. And I have surely learned to trust you to fix any lapses. But that isn't why I wanted to talk to you."

Uh-oh.

"As you can well imagine, I'm taking a lot of flak. Scanlon isn't big enough. His crime does not warrant the kind of—"

"Sir—"

"Let me finish. I'm here to take flak—large part of the job description. Poppy, you're about to talk with the First Lady, an event to make the most of. A chance to eliminate some of the flak that's beginning to really piss me off."

"I see." I surely did.

"In taking advantage of such an opportunity, you must be forthright with her and ignore your facility with oblique persuasion." He smiled. "Just the facts are all that's necessary."

"I know that, sir."

"Yes, of course you do. Meanwhile, I look forward to the *Post* tomorrow."

I smiled. I was about to have fun, too, just like Rocky Patel. So liberating not to have to be oblique.

The First Lady would not hear of being treated in a special way beyond her initial request of interviewer. And no, absolutely not, she wouldn't be represented by an aide. No, again; she would not give me five minutes as advised. She and I would determine the time required for her to hear and answer my questions. She told her husband's chief of staff that if she could be of help in an FBI investigation, it was her civic and moral duty to do so. She brought the administration to a halt as they tried to figure out how best to handle her. While they figured, her secretary called Delby and arranged a time to meet. Delby told me the secretary said, "I heard the President told his staff that if she's made up her mind, nobody's going to change it. He's right about that, believe me."

We met in a small conference room in the White House. We sat at one end of the table. This was meant to be business, no one but her and me plus a Secret Service man taking in the view over the Rose Garden.

She offered an explanation for her relationship with Rosemary Sullivan.

"I invite major female fund-raisers to tea, a duty that has fallen to first ladies for some time. The get-togethers are for the sole purpose of making the women feel important and indispensable, which, frankly, they are. The party needs people like Rosemary Sullivan."

I felt a little sad that the President's wife had to chat up someone as transparent and arrogant as Rosemary Sullivan. I told her that.

She said it could be worse. "Imagine having to chat up movie stars like the other side has to do."

And I said, "I'll take Benicio Del Toro over Rosemary Sullivan in a minute."

She laughed.

Then I got down to the task at hand. "May I tell you what underlies the importance of apprehending Rosemary Sullivan's brother?"

Her eyes flickered. "Yes. Do."

"The last department established by us—by the FBI, on our own—was the Child Abduction and Serial Killer unit. The unit required two new agents in every field office, which in turn required a huge budget increase. Worth every penny, was my vote."

"I would agree."

"And then Nine Eleven. We needed another unit immediately, a large unit, and there weren't funds yet to do it. So we began reassigning agents to the tasks of terror, and many of them are coming from Child Abduction. People don't understand that the unit encompasses many different kinds of crime against children. We have successfully cracked down on Internet porn sites, internationally. Each child in a pornographic DVD is a real child and people who pay to access the sites allow that child to be abused time and again, supporting an industry that seriously damages children, here and all over the world.

"Sean Scanlon has abused children, his own nieces, and perhaps is still acting on his pedophilia. He's not a suspect in fraud or larceny—although the Boston Police Department is looking into that as well—he is a suspect in the death of one of the nieces he abused.

"The director understands the necessity to secure the homeland. But he will not deemphasize protecting our most vulnerable. He will not deprive me of the force I need to bring Sean Scanlon into custody."

She was silent. Never fill a silence or you lose your foothold. How

I keep appreciating that advice. I didn't know if I had a foothold, but there was nothing left for me to say anyway.

She filled it. "I will speak to my husband."

Almost a jackpot. I went for the rest. "You could speak to the press, too."

She put an elbow on the table, her chin into her hand, eyeing me carefully. "No, I can't. No one elected me. I draw that line. But I will tell the President how much I wish I *could* do it."

I thanked her; she stood and so did I; we shook hands.

The Secret Service man never stopped scoping for snipers.

That evening, the President saw to it that the press was nearby when he boarded *Air Force One* for Mexico. He stopped briefly at a microphone. He lauded the efforts of all federal agencies in their battle against terror. And he mentioned the other work they were doing at the same time, bringing up the recent national thrill of an abducted child who had been rescued.

He said, "We will remain secure, but not at the expense of the war on drugs, or our vigilance of corporate fraud, or the *protection of our children.*"

He waved and was off, absent the trademark grin, remaining hard-faced.

Mission accomplished.

᚜᚜᚜

Auerbach said to me, "The most complicated call we had to make was not to the President's wife, Poppy, believe me. We came across a phone number to an international vacation club called Gentlemen Golfers. A phone number where no one ever talks to callers. The caller has to leave a message in code and gets a response in code. Took us a damn long time to find the source of that phone to get the code we needed."

"How long?"

"An hour."

Figured. Telecommunications leave clear fingerprints all over the place, all retrievable. "Are the codes hieroglyphics?"

"No." He'd probably checked out any hieroglyphics possibilities. "After the exchange of codes, a message comes on giving the weather conditions at six famous golf courses: St. Andrews, Pebble Beach, Palm Springs, Augusta, Royal Troon, and Olympic. But the actual weather at those places doesn't match up to the phone report. On three separate occasions, the recorded message said the weather at Palm Springs was overcast, chances of rain eighty percent with a high of seventy-nine and a low of fifty-eight. Palm Springs, situated in the Joshua Tree desert, never has weather like that. We're working up parallels. Each of those courses is a another code name for a different place. We got our heads together on this, Poppy. We're going to crack it and see which sham golf course matches the place where the judge, I'd have to say, has dug in."

"Then I'll let you go. Give Delby the code when she asks for it."

He said, "Sure," and hung up before I could praise him. My assistant was at the ready—a click from the departing Auerbach, then her voice. "Hey, boss."

"Delby, call that number Auerbach came up with; he'll give you the code to use. Leave an irresistible message. Use a cell phone from equipment. See that the home base for the cell phone is . . . well, come up with something."

"I'll figure out a place compatible with my message."

"Great."

She decided legitimate was best. Auerbach agreed; so did I. She ended up bringing the phone to the office of the guy who lines up her gigs; all he was required to do was what he did every day. He left the message, not Delby. His message: *I've got me a freelance singer*

*who does private gigs, arranges for a band herself, she'll go anywhere.*
*She's good and she's a fox.*

Delby only sang in DC, jumped in on bands coming through, so this was only a slightly exaggerated version of how he'd normally pitch her.

Delby informed him that a response from the number he'd called would go to an FBI line, not his. If there was a response to his message but from a different number than the one he'd called, Delby told him to say, "Could you hold?" and then he was to push the little red button on the phone we'd given him and the FBI would take the call.

He asked Delby if he could eavesdrop.

She told him, "Sorry, honey, once the phone rings from the number, or once you press the button, your own line is shut off."

I asked her if the guy was okay with all that.

"He'll do anything for me, Poppy. And I'm taking him to dinner, compliments of the Feds."

"Good."

I would leave a message on that number myself. They—whoever *they* were—would go nuts wondering how we'd found the code, how we'd known who the number fronted. I'd fly up to Chicago, check into a hotel, and actually make my call from there. I informed Delby and before I hung up, she said, "Boss?"

"Yes, Delby."

"I've got an envelope here for you. From the ATF."

"What in the world do they want?"

"I'd guess they don't want anything. The stationery is the Chief Field Adviser."

Oh.

"It's on your desk. He sent it today. Knows you're in town. What with the President's wife and all."

I went into my office and saw it sitting there amid the neatness Delby creates for me. It was a peace offering. Two tickets to the Stones tour, DC, that night.

I went back out, showed the tickets to Delby, and asked her if she could get a baby-sitter. She looked at her watch. "I can. But I think he probably wants—"

"I know what he wants."

"Yeah, I guess you do. Sorry."

"I'll pick you up at seven-thirty."

She had a kind of hangdog look.

"I'll call him."

She smiled. She said, "Meanwhile, what are you wearing?"

"The director's flak jacket."

I called Joe. Didn't take long to get him, either.

"Now isn't the time to see you," is what I said. "I'm taking Delby to the show."

So he said, "I miss you. I can't tell you what the sound of your voice is doing to me. Your normal voice, not the pissed-off one."

"I'm still plenty pissed off."

"You're entitled."

He said that like he meant it, not to act the good fellow.

"When I'm through with this case . . . we'll talk."

I felt him smile. "I can't ask for more."

"No. You can't."

⌁

Great show. They began with a song from their first album. My step-father always said no collection was complete without it. The audience rose and sang with them. Sang "She Smiled Sweetly," so plaintive, almost a lament. As far as I was concerned, a lament for two sweet girls, both dead and, it looked like, murdered.

# 14

The message I left at the encoded number Auerbach provided was: *Are you interested in little boys too?* I gave them the name I'd used when I checked in, and the name of the Chicago hotel. I'd wait twenty-four hours before reeling in and heading back to Boston. I used the time to study up on the prostitute killer, a folder full of information.

First call I got while studying was from Delby. There had been an immediate response to Delby's agent's query, a recording directing him to send videotapes of her performances to an agency in LA.

I said, "I hope you've got a tape of a really bad performance."

She laughed. "I told you a million times, boss, quit worrying. I am not a contender. It's my hobby. I like my day job."

She sells herself short, Delby does.

That night we staged a robbery at the LA agency. Our LA guys copied everything on the agency's hard drives, took pictures of documents and contracts, and made it look like kids had managed to break in, kids hunting for drug money. The kids took the contents of the petty cash drawer.

My man in LA said, "They had four thousand dollars in petty cash. LAPD said to the guy there who made the complaint, 'If this is the petty cash drawer, I hate to think how much you've got stashed in your safe. Are you nuts?' "

LA. I don't know how the cops there deal. People are operating in some parallel universe.

I asked the department chief in LA how many sifters they had.

"Until yesterday, I'd have maybe been able to set aside one for your stuff, Poppy. Now I can give them this assignment and actually have them sift for something that's real. They've been sifting their brains out of late and don't even know what the hell it is they're looking for. You know how many foreign students there are in this country? Way too high to count."

A response to my message left at the phone from nowhere came three hours after I'd arrived in Chicago. A man called me from the lobby. He wanted to talk about my proposition; he was coming up.

Okay.

Two goons appeared at the little glass hole in my door. The distortion enhanced their bored look as they set about their drudge job. I opened up, and the one leading the way in put the flat of his palm against the middle of my chest and shoved me backward. There was a small look of stupefaction in his eyes when I didn't fall. With the look still on his face, he and his companion were shoved too, from behind, and they did fall. The door was slammed shut and the two of them looked up into the barrels of my own revolver plus two Glock 8s, the weapon of choice of the Chicago PD.

They were arrested for an assault on a federal agent.

They said, "What federal agent?"

The cops pointed at me.

"We didn't assault her."

"We have you on video shoving her."

"Since when is shoving assault?" the leader wanted to know.

The cops were only able to keep them overnight. Their side of the story, via a lawyer who everyone kept asking for autographs, was that they were meeting up with a call girl. One of them shoved me with the idea that the hooker would know what kind of action they were looking for. Their own guns were registered. Their fingerprints gave us nothing.

I saw to it they were followed by a second-string FBI team, an easy job compared with what with the first team was doing—following a zillion Arab Americans. But whoever their boss was, the two goons never made contact with him, or him with the goons. For every hundred miles forward, they went five hundred laterally. They'd been given all the time we didn't have. Operation called off.

However, the reaction to the phone message I'd left—the goons— was so strong, so immediate, that we knew it made sense to begin another hunt. We had to pick up a money connection between Sean and the location of the unknown phone.

Sean Scanlon, shrewd enough to slowly and deliberately buy back stock in the Sullivan shipping company after they'd gone public, now pretty much owned it. Plus he had a ton of general family-type money that he'd shared with his siblings when their parents died. And, of course, he was stealing from the trust funds of minors in his family. We instituted a watch—on the company accounts, Sean's personal holdings, and his liquid money as well.

~~~

People who do five thousand ordinary things in their lives and then choose to do one unusual thing—commit a felony, say—should not assume the five thousand commonplace habits will conceal or disguise the one exception. Even if, as Auerbach put it, the unordinary one is hidden on paper.

He said, "I've got a guy who's totally devoted to working paper.

He thinks putting on a white suit with a screw-on helmet and rooting around in garbage is fun. So strong is his faith in himself that his tenacity precludes any effort to convince him to develop his talents in a few other directions. In a case like we've got here, Poppy, we're grateful we have such a dinosaur in residence."

Auerbach feels you're a caveman if you own a box of note cards or sport a mug of pens on your desk. But the more recent ploys, by fraudsters running companies for the purpose of bleeding the profits and making a lot of loans to themselves before declaring bankruptcy and firing all the employees, is to see that nothing they do is logged into a computer. They transact via paper and then they shred and burn the paper. This is especially useful, also, for small companies that exist to serve the needs of people with huge wealth who want to indulge themselves without anyone ever knowing about the indulgences. These sorts of clients flaunt their ownership of the latest impossible-to-get vehicle, but not the existence of a house where they do things they don't want people to know they do or take part in an activity meant to remain secret. Those needs often revolve around gambling and showgirls if they're over fifty, hunting for moose from a helicopter above a tundra if they're under. The youngsters leave the dead moose where they drop them. I asked one of these guys I'd met at a party what he does if the moose is simply wounded. Did he just let him lie there dying? He said, "No, we drop him food laced with antibiotics."

Oh.

Basically, the various fantasies of well-to-do married men can be fulfilled if they choose to fulfill them. The trouble is, casinos are no longer the exotic out-of-body experiences they once were, and as for a renewed sex life via a beautiful call girl, there has come an acceptable replacement—tossing aside wife number one and taking on a replacement who does things the first wife was perhaps too busy to do, what with raising children and seeing to the polishing and packing of the chandelier crystals every time hubby announced a promotion entailing a geographical shift. The type of fantasy a perverted man like Sean goes for is a different matter entirely.

Child prostitution flourishes in several places, one being Thailand where—surprise—one branch of Sean's club was located. Actually, the man-in-the-street can take cheap travel tours to Bangkok for that purpose. But the kind of wealth Sean had available meant specialized pimps anywhere could bring children to Sean by the hand.

Time to hit up my burnt-out shrink. I reached him at his office; he was back home again. I said, "Want to analyze someone for me?"

"Of course I do. In person?"

"No. A judge."

"I'm ready and waiting."

I told him all about Sean Scanlon, all I knew about him, all I'd been thinking about.

He said, "A fairly easy one here, Poppy. Perhaps your never having had siblings explains your needing some help."

"You don't have any brothers and sisters either."

"But I'm a profiler. I went beyond the introductory courses."

"Don't be modest." The man had written the preeminent book.

"All right. Modesty pushed aside. This particular sister—Rosemary—has that ever-so-wonderful ability to be a leader via gentility, authority, and alacrity. You've seen her in action."

"Yes. She's a disgrace."

"Well, there are some stations in life where intelligence is not necessary. The brother might be very clever but he wasn't blessed with her sort of je ne sais quoi. Therefore, she rose to the top.

"Now, in an unsubtle rivalry, the brother might plop a plastic gallon of milk and a jar of lemon curd on the table when she's invited someone she's trying to impress to dinner. But Sean, of the nouveau riche and no fool besides, couldn't dominate her in such a way. He has no opportunity to dominate her in any way at all, with one exception. He can dominate her by acting out his sexual proclivity right under her nose. And, in this heinous case, via her children. And she, in her gentility, is unable to act. Because if she did, she would have to admit to reality, which means she would be undone. So she chooses not to see. She has trained herself to be blind." .

"Blind, as in looking the other way?"

"Exactly. Isn't it amazing, Poppy, the sacrifices to integrity people will make to maintain power?"

"Integrity? We're talking Medea here."

"Perhaps worse. Medea committed her crime with deliberation, with motive. Rosemary Sullivan allowed hers to happen, choosing to stand by. In the end, in pop-speak, she came to enable her brother's proclivities. She knows what he's about. But better he does it in Thailand than risk getting caught in Boston. A continuation of not giving voice to the unspeakable."

Unspeakable. "I so hate them."

"Of course you do. They're scum. So find the bloody bastard."

Now enter Auerbach's paper man.

Sean Scanlon, he discovered, funneled a great deal of money to a company that was a ghost—Gentlemen Golfers. He paid cash and he used a messenger service. Then there were other sham companies he used to launder his money, which kept his transactions out of the computers. But he made several withdrawals from the companies' bank accounts that were kept on paper with one of his private accountants. This particular accountant's job was to make sure the IRS was chronically confused. When we raided him, he began eating paper.

Most organized crime cells leaping onto the Internet highway have to come to grips with the fact that their accountants can't gulp down disk drives or even flush them down the toilet. And they find out the DELETE button only moves things, it doesn't obliterate them.

So our paper man covered a wall with copies of withdrawal receipts and established a pattern. He determined which company account Sean would work next. Sean would keep to the pattern rather than withdraw a huge bundle and arouse suspicion from the ever-watchful IRS, despite the difficulty of their job when people are determined to hide their assets.

The FBI marked the money.

Sean deposited one chunk via messenger into an account held by Gentlemen Golfers. It was located in the Cayman Islands, where else? The company consisted of six Cayman Islanders—all women working phones. No computers there either. The women's job was to help the forty-eight members of the club make reservations at the six resorts known to the women only as: One, Two, Three, Four, Five, and Six.

During the raid, five of the six women managed to hit a button that canceled the calls they were taking, plus records of any calls at all. Being the Cayman Islands, the core venture that's way ahead of tourism is the art of concealment. But one of the staff was disengaged, ripped from her seat before she could do anything.

Our agent said, "It was because she was lighting a cigarette. A Marlboro gave me the one-millisecond advantage I needed. I told her to try the nicotine patch, not that it worked for me."

That call was traced to Orlando. To one Leland Jones. Our Orlando office took him into custody and Rocky and I flew to Florida.

〰

He said to us, "I'm a hotel manager, that's all. My clients want one thing above all else—privacy. What they do with their privacy is"—

he smiled—"private. They pay a lot for the company's services. The clients themselves own the company, make the rules, and, as individuals, see that the services they prefer are provided—at my resort here in Florida and a few others worldwide. I'm just one of the resort managers."

"What else do you do for your clients?"

"Nothing else."

"Do you provide illegal services?"

"The company provides the services, not me. I take reservations, that's all. I told you."

"How long do your guests stay?"

"They tend to stay a day—one overnight. Two at the most. They come to rest up before they have to face whatever it is their business expects them to do and gear up for the annoyances of recognition, as they're in the public eye. All the accoutrements of big-time power."

"What business, for example?"

"The business of world trade meetings, for example. Chairing a Senate committee for another."

"And these senators can stay longer?"

"Up to two weeks. That seldom happens."

"They're allowed to partake of these stints as often as they like?"

"To a maximum of two weeks at each site. But, as I say, they use the services sparingly because they don't have time on their hands. They come when they can squeeze a visit in. They decided this themselves when contracts were drawn up; wanted to make sure no one would take up permanent residence. They each own a piece of the corporation in the manner of floating property."

Sean had a two-week hiatus in which to decide what to do with his life. Unless he planned to take a hop around the globe every other Thursday, which didn't seem tenable.

I said to the manager, "In other words, a time-share."

He raised an eyebrow. He wouldn't bother explaining the difference. He did condescend to say, "Based on that initiating principle." Then he outlined the logistics of his corporation. "Each resort has a concierge for the six guests or fewer who are in residence in individual villas. With the exception of a waiter, the concierge is the only person a guest sees. Each villa has a private dining room. A waiter brings meals from the central kitchen whenever they want something, whatever they want. Several cooks rather than a chef are in residence, well trained and well paid. Short-term. It is a chance to make a great deal of money, work under ideal conditions. Of course, guests feel free to go off-site for meals. Some do."

The manager was looking at his watch. I said, "What about the housekeeping staff?"

"There is a housekeeping staff."

"On-site?"

"No."

Thought not.

"We'd like to visit the resort here in Orlando."

He didn't respond. He was cooking up a deal in his head. When he finished his momentary cooking, he said, "Listen, I'm curious . . . I have a contingency I would like to offer."

"What might that be?"

"I'm supposed to notify the members immediately, all of them, when there is an inquiry from the law."

"That's not going to happen."

"I can see that. Therefore, I have unofficially resigned from my job. I do not intend to be involved in whatever is going on here. I'll give you what you want if you'll give me a head start."

We made the deal he was after. First we wanted the addresses of all six resorts. He said, "I only know Orlando."

"The deal is off."

He gave us the addresses. He took Rocky and a local detective to the Orlando resort—the cop went along because Rocky and I felt the locals should be suspicious. I didn't go. No women allowed, is what he told me. "The club is for men only. Although women are welcome as guests." Wry smile.

I asked, "Could Tiger Woods join?"

"Of course."

Of course.

I had to wait for Rocky to return from his tour before I would know anything. I called a taxi and went to Disney World. It had been my understanding that everyone with children should make a pilgrimage there. I was pretty sure I'd never have any of those, but I needed something to do for a couple of hours. At the Tiki Bird House, I discovered how much I preferred natural wonders to mechanical ones. What cleared my head was the standing ovation the birds got. They weren't real birds.

When I returned, Rocky told me the concierge of the resort was entirely willing to accept the fiction that Rocky was the son of some maharajah, the cop his assistant. The man deferred entirely to the manager. "He gave us a look at the facilities and added a lot of very helpful information. The most helpful being that there are two sets of housekeepers. Two levels is how I would put it.

"After a guest checks out, a fellow comes in who the concierge expects but doesn't know. This man goes through the villa to be sure the client hasn't accidentally left anything that will identify him. Only then do the housekeepers come in to clean—illegal immigrants who just want to do a job, get paid, and disappear into the woodwork."

"So, first, any evidence of illegal activity is removed."

"I would say that's the idea."

It was obvious the manager was raring to get going on his head start. I told him we'd need him for just a few more minutes. The antsy Leland Jones said, "I'm only the reservations manager. I don't know anything beyond my duties. We're basically assembly-line workers. Employees who install the rear doors know nothing of installing the front doors."

"Where is Sean Scanlon staying?"

"I wouldn't know. I don't know any Sean Scanlon. Our clients use code, not their names."

"I want their codes then. Of every member presently using the resorts."

"You still won't have their names. No one does."

"Doesn't matter."

He sighed. He checked his watch again. "The members won't like this, but at the same time, who put them in charge?"

The man was obviously put out at perhaps being treated like the nobody he was. The servant class isn't what it used to be.

There were members staying at all of them. Most, just for the night, on their way to and from business dealings. Of the twenty-two present residents, seven had reserved stays of more than one night. Four in Bangkok, two in Scottsdale, two in Tahoe, and three in Dorado, Puerto Rico. I said to Rocky, "Then Scottsdale or Tahoe are the only places he won't have to use a passport." Using false passports had become far riskier of late.

"He won't have to use one in Puerto Rico either, Poppy. It's a U.S. subdivision, not a foreign country. Meanwhile, Tom Connealy's last known whereabouts was Denver, but somewhere along the way he took a flight to San Juan. He used his Irish passport instead of a driver's license, which gave him just enough of a jump for us to miss him. Then a possible sighting in Arizona. Maybe he's gaining ground. Shall we head south or west?"

"Both. We'll split up."

"Then why don't you go to Scottsdale, I'll try Dorado, and if neither of us meets up with him, we'll arrive together in Tahoe."

"All right. You like the Caribbean, Rocky?"

"I don't dislike the Caribbean. More relevant, I hate the desert. I have monsoons in my blood."

I have red and white corpuscles in my blood.

He said, "I only have to think of the desert and I feel myself drying up."

"Try to think of something other than your body, then."

He blinked a little. "You don't meditate, Poppy, do you?"

"No. I don't buy its purpose. It's a waste of time."

"But no. There is not meant to be a purpose. It's simply a gift, a gift to yourself. Meditation gives you just a tiny bit of time in your life to shut out everything except what emanates from within. That emanation then makes your conscious life richer."

"It does? I signed up for a Yoga class once. I told the instructor I was unable to keep outside thoughts outside. She said to tell those thoughts, firmly but not angrily, to stay away during my Yoga hour. But Rocky, my job won't work if I shut down thinking. In fact, if during Yoga I suddenly realize why a disgruntled employee is sending threatening memos to the CEO of General Electric—if I come to understand what the words in the memo actually mean, what clue about the sender they reveal—I jump off the floor, grab my mat, and dash out the door to get on it."

"Well, perhaps your attempt to calm your thoughts actually works to *direct* them. Allows you unexpected revelations as to the threatening memos."

"Yes, perhaps. But those same kind of revelations come to me when I'm painting my toes."

"There, you see? Meditation is a really just a simple ritual that helps us to become more attentive . . . heedful. Your vehicle of meditation is the ritual of nail-polishing. And I like the color."

He was looking down at my toes. I was wearing sandals.

"Thanks, Rocky."

"You're welcome."

"Try not to convert me anymore."

He smiled. "I, a Gujarati Hindu, was converted to Catholicism. Forgive me. I only recommend that you keep your mind open to—"

"Rocky, please?"

"All right, then."

We headed for the Orlando airport. As our car pulled up, there was a tremendous thunderstorm. I dashed into the terminal, but Rocky stayed outside, looking up, smiling into the sky, getting drenched, refueling.

~~~

I'd decided it was best just to raid the places. Rocky agreed entirely. He went to Dorado with an agent in Puerto Rico plus a couple of curious Puerto Rican cops. The first guest they contacted was an investment banker with a serious heroin habit. During his stay at the club he'd do speed balls all day; he looked upon his villa as his own personal opium den. The other guests in residence weren't into anything untoward beyond enjoying adult consensual sex, perverted though it might have been. One fellow simply enjoyed live shows rather than porn movies. He wanted more than the norm on a couple of levels. The actors he'd hired threatened to sue him when they were disturbed by cops and federal agents in the middle of Act III, Scene III, *Macbeth* in the nude—Banquo dead on the floor, Fleance escaping the three hired assassins, Lady Macbeth et al. offstage awaiting their cues—all of them naked. The guest had apparently guaranteed their protection. The actors calmed down when they were assured their identities would not be revealed. They were over twenty-one.

Rocky said the Puerto Rican cops did arrest the banker, who was very put out. "I had to remind him that the ingestion of heroin is illegal. He said to me, 'And don't you know that a man's home is his castle?' He is soon to find himself in other guest quarters. I told him I didn't know of a single prisoner who feels he lives in a castle."

"Who was the guy?"

"I hope to find out in the front pages of my local newspaper. The Puerto Rican force must first convince him that not giving his name won't help his cause."

Rocky said that when the arresting Puerto Ricans cop cuffed the banker, they made sure to speak Spanish only so there would be no further philosophizing from him.

My day in Scottsdale was calmer. The two guests there were ensconced with longtime mistresses, just getting away from it all. We still raided the place and used our raiding tactics to learn more about the workings of the resorts from the concierge. All he wanted to know was what he could do in terms of advising his supervisors as to preventing further drug raids. We suggested a rule: Say no to drugs. He just shook his head, resigned, and plenty glad his present guests weren't junkies.

So Sean Scanlon was not in Puerto Rico and he wasn't in Scottsdale.

I would get to Tahoe ahead of Rocky. The first hurricane of the season was keeping him in Puerto Rico a couple of extra days. The thunderstorm we'd experienced in Orlando had been a narrow band of that hurricane leading in from the southern edge of the Caribbean in a northwesterly direction. Damage to the airport tower in San Juan meant two days of repair before the runways could be opened to traffic again.

I could barely hear Rocky's voice over the crackling and crunching of the disturbed phone line. "The rain has been soaking. It's coming down in sheets. So wonderful. I can only hope there are no deaths or injuries related to the storm."

"Especially to you, Rocky. I need you."

"Yes. Forgive my selfishness."

"It comes with all that damn meditation. Have you thought about the people's houses, which are no doubt sliding down into the sea?"

"I'll hope against that tragedy as well."

"You're a real sport."

"Poppy, may I be serious for a moment?"

"Shoot."

"If we suspect Scanlon is at a specific residence, we must be sure of it before we do anything."

"Why? We go in, he's there, we grab him."

"But I have been thinking, which is not the same as meditation. If we do that and we are successful, in the end it will be his word against Nora's. Having downloaded pornography is not the same offense as the actual sexual abuse of a child. And her brother Kieran could again say he made his story up, go back to claiming he watches too much TV. With the tension built so high at home, Nora may run out of steam. What if there is never any solid evidence connecting Scanlon with Kathleen? What will he be arrested for? Simple evasion. He will plead the imaginary disease as we have discussed. He—"

"I know what you're saying, Rocky."

"I know you do. Still, let me say it. Let us voice what we detest voicing—a necessity, as you have pointed out to me. We need to arrest Sean Scanlon in the act. For the sake of the larger—"

"Absolutely not."

"But in taking great care, we can appear on the scene before the child is—"

"No."

"Poppy, in the act of procurement then. Let us aim for that."

I had to think, too. Perhaps I was meditating since I was staring at my fingernails, the polish just beginning to chip.

"Poppy?"

"We will aim for that, Rocky."

"I'm sorry. I feel the same as you."

I know. He did. That helped a lot.

# 15

The agent who met me at the Reno airport asked if I'd ever been out that way before. No.

"The drive from Reno to Tahoe is worth the price of admission. And I get to be your tour operator."

He offered me theories and tiny details concerning the Gentlemen Golfers place in his district while we climbed and descended roads curving through spectacular pine forests, dark green trees soaring into wildly blue skies. He hadn't exaggerated. It was breathtaking.

"I'm going to have to fill you in on the so-called club later this afternoon. Once you're settled in. It just looks like an especially large estate. Assumed to be a perfectly legal private hotel as far as we were concerned until your questions started coming in.

"There are six villas within the resort. Lavish is the best way to describe them. We made contact with the guy in charge. Concierge, he said. He has two guests at the moment. He doesn't know their names. The staff refers to them by the names of the individual villas where they're staying—Aspen, Willow, et cetera. He kept saying that what the guests were paying for was anonymity, so I asked him why that was. He said the club was more a retreat than a vacation. That high-powered men were under heavy ongoing pressure, and the club gave them an opportunity to unwind."

I told him I'd already heard that line in Orlando, and we were under heavy ongoing pressure too, and so what.

The agent said, "Yeah, so what."

"Did the concierge show you around?"

"The unoccupied villas. We saw everything you can imagine in a resort where money is no object."

"So who did he think you were?"

"He thought we were from the tax assessor's office. He enjoyed chatting me up, actually. Liked to brag that the golf *consortium*—his term—was happy to pay whatever taxes were due. Named a few contributions they'd made to the Tahoe public library, to town landscaping projects, to . . . let's see . . . high school sports. As if he made the contributions personally when his job happens to be wiping his clients' asses."

One way to put it. "Any sign of new guests?"

"We've had continual surveillance since we heard from you. Two guests have arrived in the last three days."

"Must be easy to hide your van in these trees."

"Not so easy. The club is at the most remote area of the lake, high above it, views that knock your socks off. At the backside of the club, the drive goes for about twelve miles before it hits a town-maintained road. There is armed security patrolling the drive and the surrounding woods. Four guys. All legal."

We rounded a descending curve, a complete horseshoe, and then Lake Tahoe lay spread out under us, emerald green here, turquoise blue there, aquamarine everywhere else. All the water, clear as gin. You could see patterns of rocks on the lake bottom as if the water were only six inches deep. I believe I said, *Whoa.*

"Told you." Then he asked, "Do you want to check into your hotel first or come visit our little station?"

"I'll take the little station."

We got to the little station, which was not a van hidden in the woods, via an unmarked motorboat. I left my suit jacket, shoes, and panty hose in the car and climbed in next to the agent. The little station was a nifty, compact yacht that could have slept six if it hadn't been jam-packed with equipment. The two agents on board glanced up long enough to give me a quick wave. A third agent was on deck fishing. Each would take a turn acting the normal role while the partners kept tuned in. They said they could go faster than any other boat on the lake. "Including that one," and one of them pointed out a boat that looked innocent enough.

Sleek and gleaming, it was moored at a dock at the base of a sheer cliff, the rock face hung with vegetation. Next to it were smaller boats and a couple of those things you paddle with your feet. At the top of the cliff, a hundred feet over the water, sunlight glittered on the mullioned windows of a house almost hidden behind trees and rock.

The Gentlemen Golfers Vacation Club.

"Both guests present have similar habits. They eat, they drink, they use their pools—each villa has its own—they take the sauna, they make use of their hot tubs. Neither of them fishes, neither uses any of the boats, both stay put. So far anyway.

"We borrowed the traffic helicopter from a local radio station and flew over the place. Station got a call complaining within two seconds. Station apologized: new pilot, didn't know his way yet. But meanwhile we got photos of each of the guests."

He put me in front of a computer screen while he tapped at the keys.

"One guy goes on runs in the woods, swims laps in the pool, uses the exercise equipment. That's where the guests differ. Well, there is one added difference."

"What's that?"

"First guy's brought his girlfriend along."

A photo came up of a swimming pool with two people in it, a man and a woman enjoying a splash without the encumbrance of swimsuits. "This is our exercise boy."

He gave me a closeup of the woman's face.

"Is that—?"

"Yes."

An actress. A famous one. Married to a famous actor.

"Won an Oscar," the agent said. "Won two."

How nice for her.

Closeup of the man's face. He looked a little familiar, not her actor husband. "Did he win an Oscar too?"

"He won an election. That would be our governor."

Oh.

Then he showed me a second photo—the other villa's swimming pool. A slack-muscled, blotchy-skinned man was floating in an inflatable chair. He was smoking a cigar and he had a drink in his hand. His eyes were closed, his faded hair wet and stringy.

The judge himself.

"Your guy, Poppy, no?"

"My guy all right. Too bad you couldn't have dropped some kind of depth charge from that helicopter and sunk him."

"Yeah."

"He's been alone?"

"The judge has been alone since he got here."

He tapped a key. Close up of Sean's face, so at peace.

"In the evening he watches pornography. He masturbates. Actually, his neighbors you just saw do the same. But their DVDs of choice are of the classic variety—group sex, lesbians in a bubble bath, the usual kinky kind of thing." He sighed. "Sometimes I wonder what happened to just plain in-and-out."

I had other things to wonder about. Like, "How do you know all that?"

"Tax assessor insisted on doing his routine check. Planted a few wires."

"You've *heard* what you're telling me is going on."

"Yes."

Now the agent's tone altered. "Justice Scanlon goes underground for his videos. They involve children." We never get used to it.

So I said, "What are we waiting for? Grab the films, figure out who the kids are, find out *where* they are, and get them into protection." Maybe we wouldn't have to take the route Rocky had voiced. Penalties for owning child sex videos had ratcheted up quite a few notches in recent years.

"Well, because by the time we'd get in there, the DVDs would be destroyed. Zapped into puddles of celluloid—or whatever it is DVDs are made of. There wouldn't be a trace. They're prepared for anything in there. They've got generators in place that could run a city. Lots of equipment. Our guy saw technical stuff that is unbelievable. Thought our people and the CIA were the only ones with stuff like that."

"Plus a few terrorists."

"Let's hope it's just a few. So we discussed staging a drug raid, but I'd like to talk to you about that."

"Good. I want to talk to you about the same thing."

"Poppy, I need to know that you understand why we might want to pussyfoot around. They'll see us coming, for starters. Your man will be warned off—no incriminating evidence left behind. So because of that, here's what we've done. Our tax assessor was able to leave a few lines of his own, tapped two of their outdoor surveillance cameras. Tricky as hell. But we can now see any vehicle that comes down the drive."

"And the vehicle's occupants? Will you be able to see them?"

"Yes."

"What if they're too small to see? Or if they're on the floor of the vehicle?"

He blinked. "One camera is at the resort's gate. That's where the occupants get out and shift to golf carts. We'll see them there if we missed seeing them on the drive."

All right then.

I said, "Did this tax assessor take a class with Auerbach at the crime lab?"

"He did. That's why he's so good."

One of the agents working the equipment took off his headphones, leaned back, stretched, and looked back at me. "LA's coming close to netting the ring that makes the kiddy-porn films Scanlon's got. Just so you know."

"How close is close?"

"At this point, they're telling me days. Otherwise, trust us, we'd have been looking for those kids ourselves. On our own time if necessary."

Good.

"Sean Scanlon's had no visitors? You're sure?"

"None. But you say he's probably staying another ten days. So we're not taking our eyes off him. We are on our mark. We can pounce on him in minutes if he's found a way to act on his proclivities. There'll be no warning him off."

When you decide to take a risk, vigilance plus an immediate plan of action is everything. I felt somewhat assured.

The agent who drove me from Reno said, "Poppy, why don't you go organize yourself, get comfortable. We'll have you out here right away if we see anything beginning to happen."

He was taking in my blouse and skirt. The agents were in T-shirts and shorts. Okay.

I checked into the hotel. Organized myself. But I didn't wait for them to come get me. I took a little inflatable from the hotel dock. A hundred yards from the boat, an agent had his binoculars on me. They weren't just being vigilant electronically.

The agent hauled me aboard his floating office. I felt the tension in his muscles through his grip. I got to loll about the boat the whole day, jumped in for a swim once in a while. The water was icy. The agents on board told me I made a great decoy. Besides, I was the only one who caught fish. Spend some time on Block Island, you learn to catch fish. That night, Rocky called me. He was calling from an airplane heading to Las Vegas. He'd left from a secondary airport in Puerto Rico, connected in Miami to a Vegas flight and after a stop there, he would come to Reno. He said, "I have no choice but to enter the desert. But I am wholly fortified."

"Wonderful. Why are you going to Vegas?"

"I talked to a Franciscan monk, Poppy. He's a missionary at a Hopi reservation in New Mexico. Tom stayed with him, said he was headed to Nevada. Where prostitution is legal and where most of the hookers, as with hookers everywhere, have children. He is following threads and rumors. He's looking for women who prostitute their children, in hopes of finding Sean. He doesn't know about Gentlemen Golfers, I would say.

"Also, he's in a car. The missionary says he doesn't know where Tom got the car, but it has California plates. We know the make and the color. I'm going to try to head him off. I'll find the car right away, because I called your assistant, Delby Jones. She said they'll have it under surveillance by the time I land."

"Rocky, Sean is here."

First, dead silence, then, "There? Is that what you said? He's *there?*"

"Yes. The agents have photos of him at the Tahoe club."

"My God, this is perfect. And . . . you're waiting?"

"We're waiting. I'm on their boat out on the lake now. These guys know what has to be done. They're watchful and they're listening."

"But everything is under control to the point where—"

"Under control. Listen, you find the priest right away, Rocky. With what he knows, what he's doing, there's a possibility his activities might tip off Sean. So find him. Tell him what's going down and why he has to stop his search."

"That's what I'll do. Yes. That is exactly what I must do."

He hung up. Something Rocky and I had in common. We hang up on people without even knowing it.

〰

When I have got a fly about to graze his wings against the thread of a web I've constructed, sleep is not an achievable goal for me. I put on a sweatshirt and stayed on board the station after nightfall. The lake was as still and glimmering as a mirror, the color of the water now uniform, royal blue, reflecting a couple of million stars. Orion lay backward across the waters in front of me. The wake we made as we trolled along created a line of wash that parted into two sets of ripples, which spread, unimpeded, until they were finally absorbed by the darkened shoreline. All the boats we passed were anchored or tied up, mostly empty. People vacationing in Tahoe tend to spend their evenings in the casinos. Except for lovers, who hang on boat railings, drinks in hand, just the way I was doing with one of the agents, only our glasses contained water.

The two agents in the cabin in front of the consoles were fresh replacements. One of them called out to us, a sharp quick call in the still of this magnificent night.

We dashed inside. They were on their feet.

"There's a car in the drive."

The two of them were staring at the screen's split picture—one of the drive and one of the club entrance. We leaned over and watched. The car was moving slowly and carefully, as if it were sneaking up on someone in the forest. Once it was out of sight of the camera, one of the agents shifted to the view at the entrance gate. There was a golf cart waiting to meet the car.

The agent said, "That's the concierge in the cart."

We waited. I felt perspiration forming on my top lip.

"Where the hell is it?"

"It's coming."

Finally, the car pulled up.

The driver and his front-seat passenger emerged, clones of the guys in Chicago. Maybe even the same guys. One of them opened the rear door. A woman and two little girls got out. The goon stood and watched while the children and their pimp got into the golf cart and were carried away toward Sean's villa, babes to the slaughter. I actually grabbed the sides of the computer console, trying to restrain what I could see was happening.

The agent at the screen hit a switch and shouted something that sounded like "Branson!" Then he shouted a string of numbers. Then he stood back. I couldn't move. I was screaming at them to do something when the noise of sirens arose from several places in the forest high above the water. The racket of helicopter rotors filled the rest of the night. The boat lurched forward. We sped to the club's dock, threw a line over a cleat, and the agents and I jumped out of the boat and ran up the stone steps.

By the time we reached the villas, a helicopter had already landed, several cars had made it up the drive, and the place was swarming with cops. The security guards were in check. The two goons—not the pair in Chicago—were in custody and had already been whisked off. The woman, also in custody—cuffed—said she was the children's mother. She was white, the children were Asian. The children, safe, were whisked away too.

The woman was explaining that they were there for a visit to a family friend. I told her to shut up. She was not a mother, she was a pimp; she was worse than a pimp. The Tahoe cop in charge of the assault pulled me over to him, told me to let her talk. She'd been read her rights. "Better she dig the hole she's in as deep as she's fool enough to dig it."

He was right.

The governor and the actress stood in their matching robes off to the side, gaping.

No Sean.

The concierge was mute, mulling over what he should do, what he should say. I put my gun into his right ear to help him. The cops cringed; the governor's mouth fell down to his collarbones.

"Show me how your members get out of here in this kind of situation."

He choked out an answer. "I press an alarm system that's wired to all the villas."

"And then what happens?"

"I don't know. I've never had reason to press it."

"Until now."

"Yes."

I didn't move my gun, just turned and ordered everyone to start looking—to spread out, to look behind every tree, under every shrub. There was a scramble. I said to the concierge, pressing my gun a little farther into his auditory canal, *"Show me."*

He knew enough to say "All right" and took me to a door in the lowest level of the house. Outside was a trail through the trees. "When the trail forks, go right." He gave me a key. "When you come to the château, open the old cellar door. It doesn't go into a cellar."

"Lead the way."

He chose not to protest.

The governor and his friend hadn't been about to go running down a path through the woods in the pitch dark when they heard the alarm, but Sean had no such qualm. I reached the little imitation French château in a few minutes and unlocked and lifted up the metal door that didn't lead into a cellar. The stone stairs inside were the beginning of a tunnel heading straight down. The passage was lit, a blessing, since I didn't have a flashlight. I could hear footfalls far below. Sean's.

I went running down the steps while the concierge went running somewhere else. Suddenly, the lights went out. Sean must have heard my steps and extinguished the lights once he'd reached the bottom of the tunnel. The darkness was as extreme as darkness could be. I put my arms out and slowed down.

The floor of the tunnel was dry. I speeded up. There was nothing I could do about the spiderwebs brushing my face, the ones Sean had been able to steer clear of. As I ran, I was reminded of a bedtime story my stepfather used to tell, about a child who visited an empty French château and found an underground tunnel that coursed beneath a hillside and came out near the child's own cottage. Her name was Nanette. She'd gotten herself into the tunnel, and the door behind her had shut. She wasn't strong enough to open it. A radish and butter sandwich, packed by her mother, fortified her until she found her way down through the tunnel and out. I just kept thinking of her sandwich, the crunchy radishes, the creamy butter. I thought of my mother. I thought of the prostituted children's mother. I ran faster and smashed face first into a wall. The tunnel had diversions.

I couldn't afford to get lost so I sat down, tried to stop the nosebleed, waited until I saw the beam of a flashlight. A Tahoe cop was making his way down the tunnel. He handed me a rag from his pocket for my bloody nose. The rag smelled worse than fish. Bait. He hauled me to my feet.

"I found that concierge guy running through the trees. I put my gun in his other ear and told him to show me where you went."

It took the two of us just a few minutes to emerge from the tunnel. We were behind a clump of trees, huge trees with enormous trunks, the lake shining beyond.

We could see the ripples, the last bit of Sean's wake to reach shore. He was out there amid two hundred and fifty other boats.

The cop called in with the information. The Tahoe police force got word to keep any boat from docking, to keep any boat from coming ashore. I said to the cop, "How many acres does the lake cover?"

He said, "A ton. It's twelve miles wide, over twenty miles long. Couple hundred private docks."

"Do you know how to start a boat without the engine key?"

"Sure."

We went to the lake. The surveillance boat was gone, out trying to head off Sean. I bent over, dipped my hand into the water, and splashed my face. I looked up at him. "Have I stopped bleeding?"

He reached out and held up my chin, looked at my face.

"Yep."

I returned his rag, quite a lot bloodier than before. He said, "You didn't break your nose, ma'am, but you'll have a world-class shiner. Maybe two of them."

"I know."

We hijacked a nifty little Chris-Craft. I asked the Tahoe cop his name.

"Willie."

"My name is Poppy Rice. I'm with—"

"Yep. Heard the name mentioned."

"How long have you been on the force, Willie?"

"About a year."

Thought so. He looked twelve.

He said, "Being the rookie, the guys make fun of me."

"That'll pass."

"It's okay. I got away with doing what you did to the guy up there."

"You won't be able to do it again."

"So I'll apply to the FBI." Then he said, "I'm hot."

He wasn't suddenly bragging about his looks. He was sweating from his run through the clammy tunnel. I was still shivering in my sweatshirt, from the shock of running into the wall face first. He pulled off his shirt and hung it on a brass hook on the well-appointed boat. His chest was as hairless as a baby's. He looked younger still.

We joined in the search. The cop called in to his dispatcher to identify the boat he was on. Then he paused before he answered the forthcoming question. "Stolen boat."

He hung up and told me there were four police boats, plus the federal boat, on the move. He said, "We'll stick to the shoreline."

Fine by me.

Willie piloted our boat toward the rocky outcroppings along the shore. We went in and out of the many pretty inlets that edged Lake Tahoe, all with moored boats, or boats riding at anchor, deserted. We searched every one of them. We looked inside all the places where boaters stowed various sorts of gear, food, liquor, and gasoline. No Sean on board any of the boats, not hiding in their holds. Just a few boats had dim lights lit inside their cutty cabins. With our guns drawn, we seriously frightened the few boaters who weren't off playing blackjack—the lovers.

I looked in the water around each and every boat before I let the cop take us on to the next.

He said, "Hoping to see the top end of a snorkel?"

"No. A hollow reed. Saw too many war movies when I was a kid."

He said, "Vietnam. Phew." I'd had old Humphrey Bogart films in mind.

We sped out onto the lake again, where we saw the *Tahoe Queen* on its midnight dinner cruise coming about, following orders to return to its berth. We pulled alongside and asked the captain if he'd seen anyone on the move in the last twenty minutes. He had, just before he was told to his cut engines and head back. He pointed in the direction he saw the boat take.

We headed again toward the lake edge, and then we spotted a boat idling fifty feet from shore. We could hear its engine. No lights in the cabin, no one visible on deck. We approached. It was the boat from the Gentlemen Golfers dock. The cop cut our engine, and we started to draw our guns for the hundredth time—which was why we went about it too slowly. Sean Scanlon stepped out of the cabin of the boat, a gun of his own leveled at us.

At the sight of me he squinted, and then he said, "You!" He had to use his other hand to keep the gun from wavering. Maybe his bullets would take the slice his golf balls did but I wouldn't risk my life on that chance. Neither would Willie. He gripped the wheel.

I said, "Justice Scanlon, you are wanted by the state of Massachusetts for the—"

He shouted, "Shut up!" Angry and frantic. A real menace. "I'm coming aboard your boat. Get it closer."

Willie edged in. I immediately and as surreptitiously as possible started shifting my weight left to right, right to left and the boat began to rock just a little bit. The rookie cop picked up on it and joined in.

Sean said, "If I feel myself falling, I'm going to empty this gun into both your heads."

I knew that risk was worth it. I only hoped Willie understood how prudent we'd have to be. But all Sean needed was his one free hand to step from the gunnel of his boat and onto ours. He didn't take his eyes off us, nor did we take our own eyes from his. The muscles of his face were lopsided. Alcohol saturation does that.

With appropriate training, a person observing the judge could recognize that his face seemed off-kilter. A person in this category of alcoholism is at the same time unable to focus his attention for too long, to remember quite where he is, or what he is doing exactly. Because he needs a drink. Even more menacing a state.

Sean said to the cop, "I want you to get me over there." He pointed across the lake. "There's a dock there. Take me to it and let me off."

To me, he said, "Do not move a muscle. If you so much as twitch, I'll shoot you."

And he would have.

Sean knew his own boat would undoubtedly be stopped if he tried to take it anywhere. He was able to reason this out despite the fact that reasoning irritates a drunk's brain. He'd be needing a shot soon. Sooner than I imagined. He took a flask out of his pocket and threw back a slug.

The boat's radio started beeping. Sean aimed the gun more at Willie than me. "Get it. Act normal."

Willie picked up a handset, clicked it on, listened. He repeated a call number. The boat's radio immediately came on. A dispatcher said, "That you, Willie?"

"I'm here." Willie hadn't taken his eyes off Sean the whole time. "I've got Poppy Rice."

"You do? That's a relief. We were wondering where the hell she disappeared to. At least we don't have some kind of hostage situation. Anything to report?"

"Nope."

"Neither has anyone else."

Willie asked, "How're the kids doing?"

That was a normal question given the circumstances, but not the normal Sean wanted to hear. He raised his gun an inch higher.

"They asked for hot cocoa with marshmallows. We had to break into Todd's grocery."

Sean waved the gun.

Willie said, "We got a couple boats left to clear."

"Soon as you're done, come in."

"Okay."

"Over and out."

The judge had two hands on his gun now, managing to hold it steady. "Speed up this boat."

I knew right then there was no doubt he intended to kill us. He had a car at his disposal parked wherever it was he wanted us to take him. If the concierge was dedicated to his employers, he hadn't told the police that fact unless he was asked. Maybe no one asked. We'd dock and Sean would shoot us and take off. There could be no other plan. He would be able to carry out the plan—to kill us—even if he hadn't killed Kathleen Sullivan, even if he'd accidentally pushed her the way Jean Connealy said she had pushed the Irish girl. But it hadn't been an accident. He'd cut her hair off first, probably felt he could still extricate himself from that sand trap. Until now. It was Willie asking after the children that made it clear to Sean he was not going to manage a light sentence based on some debilitating psychosis.

I said to him, "Kathleen didn't try to blackmail you, did she? She wanted something else."

He looked into my eyes.

"What did she want?"

No answer.

"You must have met her twice, isn't that right? The first time she asked to meet with you. What did she ask for?"

One corner of his mouth turned up. He'd found what I said amusing. "She told me to resign from the bench or she'd expose me."

What Kathleen Sullivan wanted was retribution.

"I just laughed at her. I walked away. Then she left me a message in chambers; she said she'd get Nora to back her up. Nora is a weakling but Kathleen was determined. I couldn't let that happen—let her get to Nora—could I?"

"You met a second time. Only you invited her. Where?"

He didn't say.

"At a place where you could drug her. A bar?"

The other corner of his mouth went up. "She liked the drug. Made her feel happy."

"Then you took her with you. Where?"

"An old deserted pier at the end of Boston Harbor."

"You couldn't find time to rent a private plane like you did a few days ago, could you? To be rid of her permanently."

He didn't respond. Not finding the time was a big mistake, and he knew it.

"You cut her hair off before you pushed her in. That was really stupid."

His lips grew tight. He raised his gun so it was pointed at my face.

I said, "And you weren't very good at tying a rope around her either."

"Shut up."

In a tiny piece of my peripheral vision, I could see Willie taking everything in. Please be calculating, Willie, I thought. Please be deliberate even if you are a kid.

Willie's hands remained wrapped around the wheel except for his right index finger, which was now pointing toward the port side of the boat. As soon as he confirmed I'd noticed his finger he'd go into action. What I wanted him to do was to distract Sean long enough for me to disable him. The distracter would shoulder the heavier risk, but there was nothing I could do about that. He should have waited, though, until we were moving again. He didn't because the expertise that is derived from experience had barely begun its development.

He dashed for the port side of the boat and leaped. As I threw myself at Sean, threw myself into what felt like a telephone pole, Sean's gun discharged. We went down, both of us, before I could get my own gun out of the holster. Lying on the deck, my body crushed under the weight of his, he freed my gun from my belt and threw it over the side. And then the muzzle of his own gun was pressed against my temple.

We were both aware of the two splashes, first the big one, the cop, and then the small one, my gun. Sean stood, dragging me up with him, the gun now pushing so hard into my temple I thought it would break through my skull. Willie's body bobbed a few times before it went under. Such a small hole in the side of his neck but his life had already slipped out of it.

I said to Sean, knowing I was about to die, "You piece of shit."

But he couldn't kill me yet. He needed me to answer the dispatcher if he called in again before we got to the dock. I had a quarter of a mile, about five or six minutes, and only a hope of luck to prevent his escape and, at the same time, remain alive. I could have done something risky, right then, like the cop. But seeing Willie dead not one minute after he'd been standing next to me kept me rational.

Sean put his face in front of mine. "Drive."

He meant pilot the boat. Joe has a boat. He'd had me charging all around the waters of Block Island such a short time ago. Ten years ago, though, is when it seemed like. I revved up the engine.

Sean said, "Don't do that. Keep it just above an idle. I want you to pull up to that dock nice and easy. If the radio comes on, you tell them you're going to search a couple more boats and then come in."

The pressure of the gun had eased the slightest little bit. I said to him, "Then you'll kill me, disable the radio, and have a window of a very few minutes to escape, except that there are cops and agents barricading every road out of here."

"So what? I've got a lot of bullets."

The dispatcher's voice came on. "You still at it, Willie?"

Sean raised his gun. I radioed back. "This is Agent Rice. We're heading northeast to check out a boat tied up to a dock at a private home."

"Got to be the last of them."

"We'll come in after we've finished."

The whole time, I was begging God to have the dispatcher ask to speak to Willie. But God was busy elsewhere.

I steered the boat and kept Sean in my peripheral vision.

"Speed up."

"We'll attract attention."

"Go, damn it."

In the instant before I pressed down on the accelerator, both of us suddenly became alert to the noise of a second engine, not ours. We turned to look. Another boat was heading right toward us.

"Call it off."

"That's not a police boat."

"Call it off anyway."

It was a small dinghy with a motor stuck on the back, and it was traveling full throttle.

"He hasn't got a radio. The net must have missed him. It's a big lake."

Sean took hold of my wrist. The gun went hard into my temple again. "Some fucking rubbernecker." Sean was experiencing a brand of road rage. Good. He'd need a drink all the more. He said, "I'm going to duck down under the window. Get rid of whoever it is."

He squatted down. "My gun is aimed at your crotch. Don't leave the pilothouse. Talk to him though the open window. Identify your-self and tell him to return to the town dock."

I watched the boat come closer. It was rigged with a chair behind the wheel so the fisherman could be lazy and enjoy his hobby of sit-ting and doing nothing even more. My brain was whirling. How could I take advantage of this without getting the nosy boater killed? He was standing up straight, peering at me, holding the boat steady with one hand.

It was Tom Connealy.

I had to say something before he did, before he recognized me. I shouted at him—barked, actually. "Police! Back off! You are to return to the town dock. You are interfering in an investigation. You—"

But I couldn't prevent him from seeing what I didn't want him to see. The night was too clear with starlight. He shouted right back. "Poppy Rice! It's Tom Connealy. Sean Scanlon is *gone*. He—"

Sean stood up and pointed his gun at the priest. I flipped on the radio and then ran over to the side of the boat, hoping Sean wouldn't be such a good shot the second time around. I leaped. I heard the gunshot and then another one immediately after. He'd fired at both of us, me and the priest.

Underwater, I knew I was alive but I didn't register if I'd been wounded or not because something heavy slammed into me. I fig-ured I'd collided with the boat itself. I opened my eyes as I rose out of the water. Sean came up with me. He'd fallen off the boat or else he'd jumped, too, and landed right on top of me. I looked into his eyes yet again, wide open now, and then he started to roll away from me. The back of his skull was gone. His brain was pale blue. He went down.

He hadn't fired two shots, he'd fired one—at me—and missed. The other shot, the one that killed him, had to have been fired by the priest.

Tom's boat came near. He was still standing at his motor and his gun was still pointed. I shouted his name. He saw me, dropped the gun, and hurried to the side of the boat. He wasn't used to guns. The thing could have gone off again.

I sank. A sweatshirt will do that to you. I remembered what Nuala O'Neill had learned as a child on the isle of Inishmore. I pulled at the sweatshirt, got it off over my head, then went to my sneakers, pulled at them. I was still going down. My belt was loaded with clips. I got out of it. I yanked at my clothes and when I surfaced Tom was in the water diving for me. I grabbed at him. And then he grabbed me.

He said, "Thank God."

What else would he have said? He was a priest. "You're all right?"

"Yes."

We both swam for the Chris-Craft's ladder. Tom's boat was chugging off, unmanned, into the night; he'd never turned off the outboard. I told the priest to climb aboard and answer the dispatcher, who I could hear shouting questions. "Then, Tom, look for a blanket or something, hold it up for me, and avert your eyes."

He did, but I climbed out in full view of three boats racing toward us and a helicopter hovering above with huge spots aimed downward. All Tom could find to hold out was a shirt—Willie's shirt, the one he'd pulled off because he was hot.

Tom turned his back to me while I put it on and he said, "If I could have killed him a second sooner, you wouldn't have gone over."

I was losing the calm of finding myself alive when I expected to be dead. And I was feeling the warmth of a dead cop's shirt. Young cop. Good cop. The responsibility expected of me at this moment held me together. As the police boats came toward us I picked up the gun Tom had used and dropped it overboard.

I said to him, "I shot Sean Scanlon, not you."

And he knew enough to say nothing in return.

I told the Tahoe officers converging all around me that I'd lost Willie. I led them to where he went down.

A dozen cops went in. The royal blue water was darker now, navy in the lateness of the night, but still so clear they only needed their flashlights to find him. They brought him into the boat. Monsignor Connealy prayed over his body, did the thing Catholic priests do. I looked away—all those cops crying their hearts out. I had to sit down.

And then Tom Connealy turned to me. Not to offer comfort, though, to seek it.

He said, "She told me what had happened to her. She didn't say who, only that he was a member of the family. I didn't even know who the family was. I encouraged her to see him. To confront him. To find out for herself if he had come to realize what a terrible thing he'd done to her. Exactly *how* terrible. But I had no idea. I never grasped . . . not until I read in the *Globe* that—"

"Stop," I said to him.

He could seek comfort elsewhere.

# 16

The next day, I caught up with Rocky, who winced at the sight of my two black eyes. Willie's prediction had been accurate. Rocky had a hard time paying attention to the blow-by-blow until I reminded him that a black eye always looked worse than it felt.

He said, "The bruises are painful to me, personally."

Empathy to a Hindu degree.

Rocky said he would not go back to Boston until he repaid me in some small way for all I'd done for the Boston Police Department and, mostly, for his guilt at not getting to the monsignor in time, not shooting Sean himself. I told him it wasn't necessary. But he insisted— it would be a special treat for me, which I was so deserving of.

"No buts," he said.

I needed a treat. Every time I passed a mirror I knew I needed a treat. And besides, Rocky was riven with guilt. I'd let him do something for me, treat me.

He drove up the mountains toward Reno and then got on a gravel track. The track led into a deep valley. It was early evening, not quite dark. Below us the valley spread out, as emerald green as Lake Tahoe. I said, "It's beautiful, Rocky. Makes you want to meditate, I'll bet." He turned to me and smiled that smile. Not sweet. Sturdy and magnificent.

The treat was still to come.

As we descended, I could make out white dots covering the green expanse, not unlike the stars that reflected on the lake in the black of night, except it was early dusk.

The white dots were sheep. Hundreds and hundreds of sheep. Thousands of sheep.

He said, "This land is a piece of the Basque."

The little town at the base of the valley had a store, a post office, and two lines of houses on either side of the road. Fewer than a dozen: the homes of a third generation of immigrant Basque sheep-herders. One house had a sign in the front window that read RESTAU-RANT.

We went in. There was a large family inside having dinner, and they made a place for Rocky and me. Some of them didn't speak English. They spoke a language that didn't sound anything like Span-ish either. Rocky said, "The newest immigrants. They haven't learned English yet."

A man came out of the kitchen with a bottle of wine, unmarked and uncorked. It tasted like especially sour grapes. Dry was not the word, sour was. Really sour. Just what the doctor ordered.

Rocky gestured to the glass in one of the children's hands. Juice. A woman took up a pitcher and poured juice into a cup for him, passed it down. Then she scolded the children for staring at me. She said to me, "Forgive them. They are worried about what happened to you."

So I told the children how dumb it was to run around in the dark. They smiled knowingly, loved and protected children that they were.

The man came back with one wide flat bowl of consommé and a platter holding a huge round bread. They seemed to know Rocky would be eating mostly the bread. Too bad for him. Lamb broth is divine.

My appetizer came next—barbecued spare ribs. Lamb spare ribs. Rocky got a little dish of figs.

Next, a thick slab from a part of the lamb, which part I wasn't sure. I managed a smile. I didn't say to Rocky, I don't like lamb *this* much.

With it, boiled potatoes and some sort of beans, which Rocky and I divided up, most going his way.

The meat was quite wonderful—juicy, tender, delicious. When I'd finished my meal, I felt as though I had a twenty-pound boulder in my stomach. Rocky had sensed I needed to feel heavy. I needed to feel my body, not my mind. There are alternate forms of meditation that only Gujarati Hindus seem to know about.

Dessert arrived, a thick, creamy, golden-brown mound, surrounded by a syrupy puddle: a Basque flan. It was not flavored with lamb stock. But it was made with ewe milk. Milk condensed and sweetened and cooked until the water in it was evaporated. Rocky loved it. He said, "I like milk products." I could barely get it past my teeth, it was so thick and sticky.

My second dinner with Rocky. I wished his wife could be with us. It wasn't the same.

∿

Late that night, we said our goodbyes at McCarran airport in front of a gigantic Elvis Presley slot machine.

"I told you so," I said to Rocky.

Elvis ate my three quarters and Rocky's five. Then Elvis sang "Hound Dog." The person behind us, about to take her turn, said, "You win, you get 'All Shook Up.' "

When it was time to go through the gate, Rocky didn't hug me.

He took my shoulders, pulled me down gently to him, and pressed his forehead gently to mine, sending me something—comfort. Comfort from him, Jesus and Shiva, together.

~~~

Back at the office in DC, Delby was leaning against my doorjamb.

"Guess who's planning to camp out on the sidewalk till you come out?"

"Danny O'Neill."

"Yes. And he said, barring that, he'll be at Kinkead's at five."

Delby turned to leave, turned back. "I bought a bunch of Rolling Stones CDs, boss."

I had to laugh.

"They were really good, weren't they? I mean, they were the vanguard of a lot of stuff."

"Yes, I'd say so."

"I loved the show."

"Me too."

Before I left, I saw a square envelope on my desk, linen vellum. From Nora Sullivan. Letting me know she was working on her jobs, all of them. Also, that she and her husband had been invited to dinner that night at Lucy's restaurant. They were looking forward to seeing Rocky, and she hoped one day our own paths would cross again too.

Nice.

Danny's mother wasn't with him. I'd left my shirt on and hadn't exchanged gold loops for diamonds. I was lugging my briefcase. A lot of work to do at home after meeting with Danny. The investigation into the disappearance of prostitutes in train stations would begin the next day. I was wearing sunglasses.

First thing he said, after a smile and a smooch, was, "When my mum told you what you must do after falling overboard into the sea, she left out one detail."

"Which?"

"You don't strip off *all* your clothes. You leave the underwear on."

I laughed, which made me forget about the blackened, now greenish state of my eyes, and took off my sunglasses. He said, fairly loudly, "Holy Mary, Mother of God!"

I put them back on for the sake of the rest of Kinkead's clientele and waitstaff.

"Poppy, can't you try to be more careful?"

"No, I can't."

He smiled. "Fine. So do you still want my mum's connection to all this?"

"Why not?"

First, two stouts appeared. "Danny, I've gained five pounds since I saw you here last. How many calories are there in these things?"

He didn't answer the question. He said, "I wondered why you looked even more splendid than ever. Five more pounds of splendor even with two black eyes."

I dipped my lip under the foam. Ah, blarney.

"Our drowned Maeve Doyle's mother was an American."

"That you already told me."

"But the American woman's father was an Irish immigrant. He would talk all the time about a united Ireland. This was in the fifties. She's a teenager, all romantic about the cause, so she goes off to Ireland to join the Sinn Féin. She went alone—not with him—because her dad didn't intend to put his money where his mouth was. So she leads a bohemian life, goes through a string of lovers, has two children, and then she's one of the civilians killed on Bloody Sunday.

"My mum knew of her. Knew of the American who wouldn't go home, who felt her home was in Ireland. This was around the time of my father's death. My mum wanted to find out who in the gardai had had her husband killed. But she'd bided her time, her and the other women, until they could find out who the dead Irishwoman was they buried by the sea wall in Inishmore. It was not until the possibility of DNA testing that my mother began to hope.

"She knew Jean Connealy had been having an affair with a garda around the time my father died. The man followed orders; he was one who went out of his way to harass members of Sinn Féin. Because of the likes of him, curfews and blockades were put into effect, among other things. Getting to work, getting to school, buying food became difficult. But Jean, consorting with her garda, was left alone, because her brother was studying for the priesthood. Consorting with the enemy but out of bounds for retaliation.

"Jean would lose her protection if her brother left the seminary. It was her garda boyfriend who helped her throw Maeve's body into the sea. He dumped it from a police boat."

"How do you know that?"

"I spoke to him and he told me."

"Just told you."

"Sort of. A plea bargain. He will never be held accountable in my father's death."

"Because he has information about who was responsible?"

"Yes. And he's revealed that information, as well. But—"

"I know. From my standpoint, it's for you to see to, not me. This time, I would agree."

He smiled. "I was hoping for a little acquiescence there, Poppy. But what *will* interest you is that the garda told me Maeve Doyle never spoke a word at all to Jean Connealy, or Jean to her. Maeve arrived at the pier in the sailor dress, just as Jean said. She carried a bag, the strap around her neck, across her chest. As Jean approached her, Maeve put her arms out in the way of Christ crucified, closed her eyes, and fell back into the water. She had a cement block in the bag."

Only rarely do I find myself speechless. Maybe it was the Irish dramatics.

"Almost the Victorian solution you scoffed at, Poppy. The girl chose to die at sea as her brother had."

When I could speak, I said, "Poor thing."

"No one knows any of this except for the garda and Jean. Jean wanted to take credit for pushing her, but she hadn't. The garda asked me not to tell anyone. Because as a suicide, depressed over the loss of her brother—and her in a hopeless situation—Maeve would have to be exhumed yet again from the consecrated ground they've moved her to."

Me—speechless, twice in less than a few minutes.

Danny said, "And I won't tell either, just as he asked, and the reason is not so much the misery of moving Maeve Doyle's body yet again. I just don't want Tom Connealy to have to hear it. Let him think it was an accident. What's the difference?"

"But Danny, why didn't Jean just say she saw Maeve kill herself?"

"Because that wouldn't have diverted the police far enough away from Tom. And she was still protecting the garda who helped her dispose of the body."

All right. Let the priest think it was an accident. Monsignor Connealy would have some comfort from me after all. I'd say I owed him that. He did save my life, after all.

Tom and Jean, Sean and Rosemary, Nora and Kieran. Brothers and sisters, all so out of whack.

"The garda is at present under arrest, though. For helping to dispose of a body illegally. Because of our private plea bargain, he will never be under arrest for any role he might have played in my father's death himself. But when he gets out of jail—his reputation in the gutter—he will not receive his pension. And the gardai know my mum knows. She is content with that. Let them squirm now, she says to me. When my mum told you that the women of Inishmore had been betrayed, she was the one guilty of doing the betraying. She set a trap and now she knows the truth of my dad's dying. He was murdered, no doubt about it. That is enough for her. She says all she ever wanted was for the truth to come out, and she'll leave the rest to me."

His mother was a grand manipulator. I didn't point that out. Instead I said, "When are you going back to Ireland?"

"Soon as my leave is official."

"I wish you well then, Danny."

He drained his Guinness. "It's been a long time. I will try to be optimistic and hope those responsible are still alive so they can answer for their crime."

"And Jean Connealy? She had to answer to her brother. At least there's that."

"At least."

He wiped the foamy mustache off with the back of his sleeve. Then he said, "What are your plans now, Poppy?"

"Complicated. There's someone out there disappearing prostitutes. Only he—"

"I meant personal plans. For tonight, for example."

Oh.

"I have a little date." I looked at my watch. "At six-thirty. I'm late."

"He does have a grip on your heart, then."

Maybe. Joe Barnow was certainly more than a fling. I knew that.

◂◂◂

Joe was waiting for me on a bench across the Tidal Basin from the Jefferson Memorial. One of our favorite spots. He was wearing sneakers, no socks. Seeing him was like coming upon a favorite sweater you'd thought was lost. I wasn't so sure I'd get to my briefcase full of work after all. I sat down next to him, my shoulder nudging up against his arm, which rested across the back of the bench.

We didn't talk, not yet anyway. Instead, we just watched the monument as we had many times before, as it was slowly illuminated by spotlights as night fell. The white marble took on a shade of rosy pink, the spotlights competing with the reflecting glow of the setting sun. There were lightning bugs in the thick grass at our feet, merrily mating, the males flickering their phosphorescent backsides at the girls.

Joe referred to them as fireflies. That's what they call them in California where he's from and where they don't even have lightning bugs.

I turned to him. I took off my sunglasses.

# ABOUT THE AUTHOR

MARY-ANN TIRONE SMITH is the author of seven novels including two other Poppy Rice mysteries, *Love Her Madly* and *She's Not There*. She has lived all her life in Connecticut, except for the two years she served as a Peace Corps volunteer in Cameroon.